Put Out The Lights and Cry

A Diner Noir

Anthology

Curated by

Craig Clevenger

Outcast Press

Fiction From the Fringes

Table of Contents

Foreword

By Nevada McPherson , author of *Poser*, A Eucalyptus Lane Novel

In the film *Casablanca*, Rick's Café Américain is the meeting place for an exotic array of characters: straight, shady, and downright dark, including fascists, resistors, collaborators, lovers, and haters. Internationally, the café as gathering spot, is a place to regroup, plot, plan, eat, drink, and listen to piano music.

In America and parts of Great Britain, the diner serves as a setting for disparate elements to converge for the same purpose, only—instead of the smoky, nocturnal activities that take place in bars and cafés—the diner is usually a well-lit way station for comfort food, the familiar fare of breakfast, burgers, and pie served with bottomless cups of coffee, and—whether it's day or night—a place to regain some form of clarity, to get the story straight.

The stories featured in this book include the usual suspects of transgressive fiction: the liminal, criminal, and clueless, such paths occasionally intersecting with the addicted and the insane. Here, the diner is a last connection to what passes for normality before all Hell breaks loose from beneath its shiny, bland, or greasy confines.

Even the cheeriest diners have their dull patinas: the crud under the seats, the sloppy mop bucket by the back door, the sticky tiles on the way to the bathroom, past the ominous vault of a walk-in freezer. For some, diners are a place of soul-searching or soul-baring, and if such spiritual excavations result in dark discoveries over a thick mug of black coffee, the diner becomes a vortex to the terror behind all that seems ordinary in our modern world.

Along open highways or tucked within towns and cities, the neon sign of a diner beckons with friendliness and promises sustenance, a respite from the journey or streets, but, in the noir universe where these characters reside, promises are broken, needs go unmet, and familiarity breeds contempt.

Somewhere in popular imagination, between Rick's Café Américain, "Hotel California," and "The Nighthawks," is the brick-and-mortar edifice housing hope and broken dreams, where the usual—and unusual—suspects still gather, and innocence goes to die. The rules, fundamental or otherwise, don't always apply, 'cept one: Don't forget to tip the waitress. And in some cases, the ferryman.

"Get in, loser. We're going to Waffle House!"

**By Manny Torres , author of _Cabrones Perros_,
part of the Dead Dogs Trilogy**

We've all dipped our hungry faces into the trough, trying to rescue ourselves from a hangover. Settled for greasy fries and cold buns over questionable meat patties, mud coffee, and the remains of last week's apple pie. We've spent several lifetimes in places like Denny's, IHOP, Village Inn, and Waffle House. Places where batcavers, bohemians, alcoholics, nighthawks, insomniacs, convicts, and the brokenhearted find solace over a coffee urn. Late-night pit stops where wounded posers pay their last respects to the one who they won't see or ever speak to again, the one they had to let go, the one they owe money to, the one they want to murder; where bad poetry was written or at least conceived, but mostly where diners came to decompress. In some of these places, anything goes.

So, what you're holding in your hands is a collection of stories from a group of up-and-coming and established writers, and they've all gathered in the most beloved of eateries: the diner. Why a diner? Why diner noir? Because open-late restaurants and lowkey eateries often invite experiences and stories of solemn degeneracy.

Most of the dates I went on in high school and the years immediately after took place at the Denny's by the Tampa International Airport (when they still had a liquor bar in the back), the Village Inn on South Dale Mabry (now a Ruby Tuesday?), or the tiny Denny's inside La Quinta Inn near the Rock-It Club, where Marilyn Manson would play shows when he was an unknown Spooky Kid.

It was where the hippies I ran with hashed out dreams and prophecies of our future selves. Where strangers rendezvoused, and nightcrawlers lounged in self-importance or misery, sweating, and crying over their eggs, sausage, toast, and coffee. There, exists a friction and nudge towards felonious contemplation.

After all, if it's your first night working a shift at Waffle House, you're probably going to fight—something not on the application but seen in a meme.

When I was a teenager, my girlfriend Billie and I would frequent the graveyard shift at Denny's, drinking coffee, floating on a nicotine cloud, shooting the shit. Everything else was closed, we couldn't afford high-end places, we were too young to hang out at clubs (her fake ID was confiscated), and too chaste to do anything else since we still lived with our parents. Decades later, I'm sure our shadows are still burned into that carpet.

Years later, coming home from a night out at King Richard's bar in Ybor City after the radio show I hosted, I'd stop in at a Denny's in Valrico, Florida, where Mary, the octogenarian waitress, patiently and exquisitely served an entire dining room crowded with drunks all by herself. Sometimes, the food was good. Sometimes, there were brawls in the dining room, but mostly the parking lot. Like dinner theater but with angry rednecks and foul language. It was a prerequisite to the dining experience, disappointing if you didn't witness it.

That's where we begin with these stories, these tales of loneliness, remembrance, unpaid tabs, random gunshots, and pie.

Why a diner? The sight of gravel parking lots piled with trucks, tour vans, and cars with steamed-up windows are always where you can turn and step into. Terminals of solace when there is nowhere else to go. Sanctuary for somnambulants, freaks, and beatniks all strolling and passing each other in the night. Nothing beats recovering from a night of heavy drinking like a greasy spoon, conveniently located at the outer limits of every city and off-ramp. Wasted, and waiting for your tired soul to perambulate before a haggard hostess biding her time.

A diner is a throughway to the drunks and degenerates of the night. You're seated and given a plastic menu that smells of all-purpose cleaner. You order breakfast or the late-night special. You hope the coffee is strong enough to slap your stupid face. And while you eat, you talk, you recover. Will you truly take over the world as you planned? Will you actually show up to rehearsal for the new band you formed? Will you finally break up with the person you once called a soul mate, and never see them again?

Well, at least you have your handshake drugs and club sandwiches. Milkshakes and burgers.

The food's never perfect. Sometimes, it's great (a grilled cheese with tomatoes washed down with black coffee at 3AM is a blessing from the gods). Sometimes, the dining is cold, indifferent, and tasteless. Like your date. Like the plans you are trying to manifest that are forgotten once you exit those fogged glass doors.

Anthony Bourdain once said, "The perfect meal, or the best meals, occur in a context that frequently has very little to do with the food itself."

It's that place, that person, that time, where you didn't matter, where you escaped. Getting over someone, getting under someone, or getting into something. Binging on food that soaks up the alcohol in your belly.

You were there to bask in its steamy ambience when no other place welcomed you. Sometimes, it was a place where kids OD'd in the bathroom, customers spontaneously boxed, or crossdressers threw their food back at the service staff. These are sacred locations where any and all illicit activities occur freely, where anything is possible, as if cruising over international waters.

This table of contents rounds up some of the most transgressive writers working today. In spirit, this book is its own gathering of sleepwalkers, rejects, and eccentrics all passing through the nocturnal hours.

Watch out for those nighthawks; you never know what they have stewing in front of them.

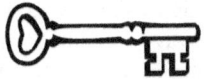

Moths

By LG Thomson

There's a place like Gerry's adjacent to every bus station in every city in the country. A down-at-heels greasy spoon, the kind of joint where they keep the toilets locked. **For customers only**, the sign reads, key on request. Keeping the junkies at bay, the winos and homeless out. Even a place like Gerry's gets to be snooty about some things.

Though it sits there plain as day, most people don't notice the café on the corner with the yellow, peeling paint. You won't find it written up on Tripadvisor. It's not the kind of place people admit to frequenting—never mind recommending. There's no category asking, "How embarrassing was your experience of requesting the key for the Ladies'?" and no way of being discrete about your needs when the counter assistant hands you a wooden key fob long and weighty enough to pass for a blunt instrument. They do that so you don't pocket the key by mistake, which makes you figure that, at some point in the past, they must have had a heap of keys stolen.

Hefting the fob with the key dangling at the end earns you the side-eye from every one of your fellow diners, but no-one says a word. If it wasn't for the sizzling and hissing and clattering and banging and under-breath swearing from behind the counter, the place would've been so swollen with silence, you could choke on it.

The toilets are in the basement. Using the facilities means descending a flight of stairs: steep, narrow. Moth husks are silhouetted in the opaque glass lightshades. The shades are flush to the wall, making you wonder how the moths got in there, but there they are, all the same.

Though the light is dim at the bottom of the steps, it's still bright enough to illuminate the entirety of the confined space. The sensation of unseen things scuttling in dark corners is all in your mind, but the smell is real. Dank threaded through with the whiff of drains.

Gerry's has been here since forever. As part and fabric of this part of the city as much as the bus station pigeons fluttering through diesel fumes, alighting to peck at spilled chips and a puddle of something that looks like vomit, but you don't want to know about that any more than you want to know about what passes for life behind the café's steamed up windows.

The passers-by, the city commuters, the shoppers, the shoplifters, and shop workers are blind to Gerry's, the same way they're blind to the woman across the street, sitting in a fire exit doorway, the lower half of her body wrapped in a manky blanket as she begs for change in a foreign accent. They don't see her, and they don't see here. That's what makes it so good.

It wasn't always invisible. Check out the framed photographs on the back wall. Yellowing black-and-white in cheap frames, glass coated in layers of grease and dust. The grubby patina flattens the images but if you look beyond the grime, you'll find youthful faces smiling for the camera, dressed hip to the times, dancing to songs long forgotten and played on a jukebox long gone. Those were the days before Gerry's became an elephant's graveyard for old waitresses with dodgy knees and sagging skin and zero tolerance for taking shit. Back when there was still a guy called Gerry running the grill and calling the shots.

Look at it now, inhabited by ghosts who don't know they're not yet dead. A barely-clinging-to-life clientele well-suited to a place overlooked by most. The thin woman at the corner table is a regular, more coat than person, her trembling hand making ripples on her tea. The narrow man with the oversize, heavy-framed glasses and greasy hair, his skin the same pallor as the gray filling in the mutton pie he's just taken a bite from, is another. He checks the racing section in his newspaper while he chews, brushing away the crumbs that fall from his mouth, grease rendering spots in the paper translucent. Pay attention and you'll realize he's younger than you first thought. He was born old, looking 55 since the day he turned 15. Beyond him, the couple who come in three times a week for the old folks' special. They sit across from each other, eating in silence, jackets still on and done up to the neck, no conversation, no shared looks, nor hint of warmth. Makes you wonder what keeps them hanging on to each other, to life.

You hate it here with the has-beens and never-beens and the coffee that comes in two varieties, black or white, poured from a jug that's been stewing since before you had your first sip of macchiato. It's the kind of place you'd never notice and—even if you did happen to catch sight of—you wouldn't normally be seen dead in and that's why we're meeting here. You couldn't say no, not after what you did. Guilt can be a useful tool.

This place is an affront to you. There's a sneer quivering around your nose and mouth that you can't quite control, a look of disdain in your eye that you don't even try to disguise. You want it to be known that you don't belong here. That you're nothing like the girl sitting alone at the window table, picking at a donut, a cold sore festering on her lip, and even less like the man who's around your age, sitting at the table to your left. He's hunched over a bowl of soup. His jeans are stained, the bounce in his trainers worn flat, and there are frayed edges on the cuffs of his hoodie. These are not your people, this is not your tribe, but here you are, all the same.

You don't want to order, don't want to eat or drink here, but when the waitress comes with her pad, there's an obligation. You order coffee, wince when you take the first bitter sip then add an uncustomary half-spoon of sugar to take the edge off, scraping away the crust at the top of the stainless steel bowl, mining the virgin granules below.

Ignoring the hush on this side of the counter divide, you attempt to bridge the gap across the table. You seek understanding, forgiveness, redemption. Not because you care but because you cannot abide mess, loose ends, blots on your immaculate landscape. You don't like ugly. That is the essence of you. Also, there is that tiny niggle of guilt. The feeling that you went too far.

Though the greasy spoon becomes your stage, the customers in Gerry's your unwitting audience, you—as ever—are the only star in your firmament and you cannot abide the thought of your brightness being tarnished. You are here to justify your actions. To explain the pain away so that you may shine on.

You lay it all out in clearly enunciated words. It was an error of judgement. You never meant to hurt but there is no going back, no undoing of deeds already done. Consent was given, mistakes made on both sides, but your sly accompanying smile lets it be known where you think the weight of blame lies.

Vowels and consonants stream from your lips, swirling through the café, filling it to the brim with your presence. That moths are drawn to your light is your burden to bear for you are only interested in butterflies. You don't like ugly.

The waitress returns to the table. She is carrying a jug of coffee, one-third full. She offers you a refill. Tells you it's free. You look at her, bathe her in your light even as your eyes drink in the white, undyed roots of her hair, the make-up she applied in poor light at 6AM, the roughness of her hands, and you thank her and say, "Yes, please."

She slops the muddy liquid into your cup and slopes off.

You said yes. Not because you want more coffee, nor out of politeness, but because you are only warming up. Now that you have explained your guilt away to nothing, you can focus on your favourite game of wrapping up insults in clever words, your honey-coated razor-blade quips carrying to every table.

Sipping at your second cup of sugared coffee, you do not care that the sizzling and hissing and clattering and banging and under-breath swearing from behind the counter has ceased. That the waitress and the cook and the assistant have paused their mundanity to pay attention to your clever oration, to your manipulation, your bending of facts.

Caught up in the charm of your own performance, you fail to pick up the seismic change in mood that your words and manner are causing. "Seismic" may seem too strong a word but think about it—What's happening here is a deep vibration, an almost imperceptible shifting of tectonic plates.

Coat Woman places her cup in its saucer. The narrow man sets the remainder of his mutton pie on the plate. The couple raise their gazes and look into each other's eyes. The girl sitting alone at the window table pushes her donut aside, wipes the sugar from her fingers with a napkin. Soup Man's spoon pauses mid-flight between bowl and mouth and, behind the counter, the waitress with the white roots nudges the cook and the assistant.

"Seismic" is small. It's the repercussions you need to watch out for. The tsunamis, the aftershocks, the volcanic eruptions that follow. But you are not watching. You, who prides yourself on your sensitivity, on your aesthetic values, your knowledge of poetry, are absorbed by yourself.

You claim to have no control over who falls in love with you. To be desired is also your burden to bear, but you must be true to yourself. You can only have things of beauty in your life.

Mirroring the smile before you, you assume forgiveness and acceptance. You think you are still adored, still coveted. Satisfaction gleams in your eye as you take a sip of coffee before moving the conversation on to the silk socks you are planning to buy in a more salubrious part of town, a treat from you to yourself.

All this talk has been thirsty work, you are two coffees down and, before you depart, you must use the facilities. You look around, grimacing when you spot the sign, **key on request**. Walking up to the counter earns you the side-eye from every table. You scoff when handed the heavy, wooden fob marked **Gents'** but necessity compels and off you head to the door that leads to the stairs: steep, narrow.

By the time the door has swung to behind you, the waitress with the white roots has handed over the heavy, wooden fob marked **Ladies'**. On hearing the door open behind you, above you, you glance over your shoulder, surprise displayed on the visible sliver of your face, but it's already too late. Your body responds in a pleasing way to the hard push. Your tricksy dance as your feet teeter and slip is balletic. Your flailing arms are poetry in motion. For the length of a gasp, you sway on the cusp. A deft kick helps you on your way, tumbly-wumbly, head-over-heels, all the way to the bottom.

There is nothing balletic about your descent. You are transformed into a mess of limbs, squelching thuds, hard cracks. At the bottom, you lie in a tangled mass, breathing in the dankness, the whiff of drains so strong, you can taste it. Your legs are akimbo, pale flesh exposed between sock line and trouser hem. You would hate that—if you knew. Perhaps you do know but there is nothing your broken body can do to remedy the situation.

You groan and make a pitiful mewl for help. Footsteps sound on the stairs. The cavalry arrives and relief washes over your face—only to drain away when you understand who delivered the push and the kick. You track the raising of the hefty, wooden key fob, comprehension blooming in your eyes. The key fob is no longer a key fob but a blunt instrument, similar in weight and length to a baseball bat.

And now there is no talk of consent. There is only fear and pain and darkness.

Upstairs in Gerry's, the waitress with the white roots takes the baseball bat and drops it into a deep sink filled with hot, soapy water. Coat woman has a fresh cup of tea before her, along with a slice of lemon drizzle cake. The narrow man has finished his pie and is folding up his paper. The couple chat quietly while rounding off their meal with apple pie and ice cream. The girl at the window table is joined by a friend. Soup Man has emptied his bowl and is scrolling through his phone.

A generous tip taken from the kind of leather wallet that might be owned by the kind of man who treats himself to silk socks is left on the counter. Outside, the road is crossed, and the remainder of the notes are taken from the wallet and handed to the woman sitting in a fire exit doorway, the lower half of her body wrapped in a manky blanket.

Tears fill her eyes. A nearby pigeon coos.

The wallet makes a satisfying *splosh* when dropped into a drain. There is a bus at the second bay in the station, engine rumbling, door open, destination out of town.

You were right. There is no going back, no undoing of deeds already done.

Author Bio

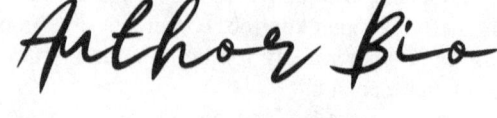

@LGThomson1   @L.G.Thomson

Scottish novelist LG Thomson lives in Ullapool, a fishing village in the Highlands on the same latitude as Lost Cove, Alaska. Her noir thrillers include the titles *Boyle's Law* and *Boiling Point.* Her latest book, *Modernist Dreams, Brutalist Nightmares* (Outcast Press, 2022), is a searingly honest & brutally funny memoir about the first generation to grow up in Cumbernauld, an experimental post-WWII New Town, known for its wild architecture and supposedly progressive ideals.

More From Our Authors

Poser, the first novel in the Eucalyptus Lane series, offers a class-conscious, peeping tom gaze into Silicon Valley's bedrooms and back-alleys, where dreams come true and unlikely, life-altering connections are made—for better or worse. Ambrose, a failed Bay Area drug dealer, has run afoul of his wicked connection too many times. He hides out in Palo Alto by posing as a Stanford grad student.

Pluto's Place

By Stephen J. Golds

Frank eyeballed the front doors of the diner, hitched his sleeve, and checked his wristwatch. A single droplet of blood stained the white linen cuff. Crimson gone a rusty brown. He tapped at the crystal. Fucking thing had stopped again. He impatiently shifted his weight in the booth. The oxblood vinyl and chrome seating groaned. Frank growled underneath his breath and waved the waitress over. A blue-eyed, petite blonde with a heart-shaped face caked in make-up. He had the nagging notion that he knew her from somewhere, but couldn't place where.

"What can I do for you, handsome?" she sing-sang. A Texas belle chewing bubblegum. Her perfume smelled good.

"Yeah, what time is it, sweetheart?"

She frowned. Dark lines flaked the foundation on her forehead. She placed the coffeepot on Frank's table and her hands on her hips. "Well, I can't rightly say." She grabbed at her naked left wrist and massaged it as though it were painful. "Must've forgotten to put on my Elgin this morning when I got out the shower. Do know I should've been home a long, long time ago. Folks'll be wondering where I got to." She giggled nervously.

"Where's home?" Frank asked.

"A long, long way away from here now. How about you?"

"Me? Oh, you know, here and there." He winked.

"Heard 'Here and There' is pretty nice this time of year." She returned the wink and turned to leave.

Frank took hold of her arm. Squeezed. Her flesh was ice-cold. "Where you been hiding? The freezer out back?"

"Maybe, I just run cold."

"And here I am, sweating buckets. Weren't you a coat-check girl at The Stork Club? Couple months back?"

The waitress popped pink gum, contemplating. "Nope, can't say I was, hon. Why's that?"

"It don't matter. Just thought I recognized you, is all."

"Got one of those faces perhaps." She shrugged. "You want a refill on that coffee or not?"

Frank glanced down at the empty cup in front of him, eyebrows flashing. "Didn't even realize I'd finished this one. Must be too tired to think straight."

The waitress chewed her bottom lip, glancing around the empty diner. "Sure is one of those nights, hon. This place is deader than the Lindy Hop. Stormy out too." She nodded at the rain trickling rivulets down the darkened windows and their wraith-like reflections.

Frank thought their faces looked like death masks. In the distance, the faint wailing of police sirens faded to nothing. He looked away from the rain-spattered windowpane, lighting a Lucky with a match from a red and black book with a pig's cartoon face on it. The matchbook read: **PLUTO'S PLACE**. He tossed the matches on the sticky tabletop and blew smoke rings at a pair of black-and-white framed headshots of starlets on the wall.

He recognized the broads in the pictures from newspapers years ago. The Black Dahlia and Jean Spangler. Two B-movie actress who turned up dead or didn't turn up at all. The photographs gave Frank the heebie-jeebies. What kind of freak would hang these up in an eating establishment? He reached for the girl's arm again, changed his mind then picked up the coffee cup instead. "Who's Pluto and where's he at tonight?"

"He's the fella behind the grill," the waitress whispered. She nodded over her shoulder at the fat, sweating mass of meat schlepping back-and-forth in the kitchen.

"He a Greek?" Frank asked.

"He's been called that, sure. How'd you know?"

"I don't know." Frank frowned.

The man draped in a dirty white apron peeked his large, pink head out of the kitchen's swinging doors, as though sensing talk about him. Dark eyes shone dully in the dim diner lighting. He grinned yellow teeth and waved. "Hey, Frankie Boy."

Frank's guts tightened and he popped a cold sweat. "He know me?" he asked the girl.

"Pluto? He just about knows most folks 'round here, it being his place and all."

Frank loosened his silk necktie, pulled his collar, and wiped sweat from his brow with a paper napkin. "Maybe someone should tell him to turn down the heat, huh? You may run cold but it's hotter than Hell in this place."

"A/C's always on the fritz. I'll bring you over some ice water if we got some in a New York minute." She poured his coffee, halfheartedly smiled, and went to check on a couple old-timers schmoozing in a booth by the shitter. Frank watched her go. Focusing on her peachy ass swaying side-to-side as she went. Afraid to glance over towards the kitchen again. If the Greek was still grinning at him with a face like a stiletto blade, Frank didn't know what he'd do. He'd have to do something about that later maybe. Couldn't have the guy dropping his name if somebody came sniffing around. How the hell did he know Frank?

Frank didn't know. He didn't like it. He snubbed out his cigarette in an overflowing ashtray and slid his hand into the side pocket of his camel hair sport coat. Running his fingertips over the cool, smooth, pearl-handled grip of the .38 revolver. Letting go of a coppery breath he didn't know he'd been holding in.

Someone must've slid a dime in the juke because an Otis Redding song started drowning out the heavy rain on the desolate blacktop outside. Frank tapped at the crystal on his wristwatch again and looked at the front doors. Who or what he was waiting for, he couldn't remember. He massaged his temples with calloused knuckles. An awful feeling of emptiness in his guts. He seemed to have lost track of things. Heartbeat like a jackrabbit in a snare.

Frank was contemplating getting up and getting out of the place when the shrill wail of the payphone at the far end of the counter startled him. Porcelain rattled. The record skipped. The jukebox cut out. Coffee splashed and pooled on the table. He quickly peered around the diner, making sure no one had witnessed. The old couple were still yammering away with the waitress. Other patrons—a thin kid dressed in a scarlet bellhop uniform, and a dark-haired woman in a white blouse—were staring heads-down into their coffee cups at the counter. Poor schmucks must've just finished the nightshift or something, Frank thought and snorted. Working schmoes.

The waitress held the telephone to her ear, nodding her blonde head, then she waved the receiver through the air. "Hey, handsome, it's for you."

Frank glanced over his shoulder. The booths behind him were empty. He straightened his burgundy necktie, fingering the pearl-and-silver tie clip. "Who? Me?"

"Yeah, you."

He shook his sweaty hands in front of his chest. "It ain't for me, sweetheart. Nobody even knows I'm here."

"You Frank?" She blew another bubble of pink. It popped.

"Yeah."

"Then it's for you, hon."

"I said it ain't for me, sweetheart. Can't be." He pushed himself deeper into the booth.

Pluto leaned through the kitchen's swinging doors. "You're the guy, ain't ya?"

Frank slowly turned to Pluto, swallowed, and stuttered, "I don't know what you mean."

Pluto impatiently wiped his large hands on the apron front, made a pistol with his thumb and forefinger and brandished it towards Frank. "You're the guy. Take the fucking call."

Frank got up slow, walked down the length of the diner slower. The sound of his scuffed Oxfords on the black-and-white tile echoed too loud. Every face watching. Frank could feel their glassy eyes on him like the barrels of shotguns. He gently pulled the telephone receiver from the waitress's grip, catching a breath of her perfume again. No, not perfume. He wrinkled his nose, cringed, and stepped away from her as she smiled and moved past him.

The girl smelled as though she'd shit her panties. The stink caught at the back of his throat. Frank coughed into his left fist and gagged. Held the telephone up to his ear. The Bakelite plastic fever-hot and damp against his ear. "Yeah?" he murmured after getting his breathing back steady.

Nothing. A dead silence and then a clicking down the line. *Click... Click... Click...*

Frank wondered if the Feds had the fucking thing bugged.

"You really fucked up this time, boychic."

He swallowed a lump in his throat the size and texture of a penny.

Sounded as though a party was happening in the background of the call. Muffled jazz music, women's laughter, the tinkering of glasses and mumbled small talk.

"Who is this?" Frank asked.

The voice gurgled laughter, "Fucking Howie Unruh over there."

"How's that? Howie who?"

"We put you on a one-man job and you turn a hotel into a fucking bloodbath. Fucking Howie Unruh over there... Things are fucking hot right now... Look it, we're sending a couple of the guys over to pick you up and get you outta town..." The line crackled and hissed.

"Sal? That you?"

"There's a diner over on the corner of Seventh and Circle Avenue. Take a booth at the back. Be there waiting."

"I did what I was asked to do, Sal. Tell the old guys. I did my best."

"You really fucked up this time, boychic."

"It wasn't my fault, Sal. This farkakte situation. It was supposed to be just him in the suite. No one said there'd be a broad up there. And the others saw my face. What the fuck was I supposed to do?"

The slurred voice at the end of the line repeated itself. "Fucking Howie Unruh over there. Things are fucking hot right now... Look it, we're sending a couple of the guys over to pick you up and get you outta town. There's a diner over on the corner of Seventh and Circle Avenue. Take a booth at the back. Be there waiting."

"Sal, I really need your help. Sal?"

Click... Click... Click...

"Please hold while we connect you..."

"Hello? Hello? Sal?"

"Betaking themselves to prayers, they besought him, that the sin which had been committed might be forgotten... the most valiant Judas exhorted the people to keep themselves from sin... they saw before their eyes what had happened... the sins of those who were slain..."

"Hello? Who is this?!"

"Through me, you pass into the city of woe."

"Please hold while we connect you..."

"A boy has never wept... nor dashed a thousand kin."

"Hello? Operator? I think the lines are being crossed over."

"I don't know yet, because I haven't counted them yet...but it looks like a pretty good score..."

"Who the fuck is this? Sal? Sal? You there?"

The line clicked and cracked and went dead.

Frankie stared at the receiver in his fist, bug-eyed for a moment. He wiped the burning moisture from his face with the crook of his elbow, swallowed, and placed it back on the hook with a trembling hand.

"You okay, hon?" the waitress asked from behind.

Frank turned around. "Yeah, yeah, it's no—"

She was standing directly behind him. Her destroyed face inches away from his. Ruptured, splintered bone piercing jagged from split and shredded flesh. The stench of blood and shit and gunfire raping his senses.

Frank forced a fist into his mouth. Bit down on the knuckles. Stumbled backwards into the elderly couple's booth. The table painfully colliding with the backs of his thighs. The old-timers lay slumped, gaping and vacant-eyed. Blood splashed the table's surface.

"What can I do for you, handsome?" the waitress asked, her feet slowly dragging over the tiling towards him. Hands reaching out for him.

Frank staggered and fell towards his booth. A gurgle of a scream escaped his stubbled and scarred mouth. Someone sat in his place. In the booth at the back. A camel hair sport coat, burgundy tie. Nervously fingering a silver-and-pearl tie clip.

Frank was staring at himself.

He pulled the .38 from his side pocket but left it hanging at his side. Unable to lift it.

"What the fuck is going on here? I-I don't understand what's happening," he croaked.

The bell of an elevator chimed behind him. Frank looked over his shoulder. No longer in the diner but standing in a hotel suite. An ebony door swung wide. Brass number plate: **643**. Green and purple peacock-patterned carpeting. Cream wallpaper. Oxblood leather Chesterfields. The scent of gunfire stinging his eyes. An Otis Redding song on the record player.

He staggered over the body of the waitress sprawled at his feet. Only she wasn't a waitress no more. She was dressed in an emerald silk and lace slip. Her heart-shaped face blood-splattered and ruined. Fragments of skull pushing up through the left side of her scalp like broken glass from a picture frame. She wheezed. Blew a bubble of blood from her lips. One blue eye dreamily gazing up at a small, crystal chandelier above Frank's shoulder. She blew another bubble of blood. It popped. She sucked in a last shaky breath and voided her bowels.

Frank gagged. Clumsily stepping over her and making his way deeper into the suite. He spotted The Greek, a bath towel wrapped around his thick waist, as he laid face-down in a doorway leading to a lime green and porcelain bathroom—a dark brown stain haloing his pale, flabby flesh.

The elevator bell chimed again.

Frank slowly backed out of the room, into the corridor.

The elevator chimed again.

A lanky bellhop slouched against the wall, little hat askew, head draped. Ditto, a Mexican maid on the opposite side. Spatters of crimson dripping down the ivory wallpaper like heavy rain on a windowpane.

The elevator chimed, chimed, chimed.

Frank pawed sweat from his itchy eyes with the back of his blood-drained fist tightened around the revolver. Shuffling down the corridor towards the elevator. He peered into the bronze cage, at the white-haired couple in eveningwear collapsed in a heap, gape-mouthed. Blood pooled on the flooring around them. Soaked into the hallway carpet.

Frank breathing heavy. Gasping. Spluttering. Fucking asthma attack. Hit the fire door at the end of the corridor, running and slipped across checkered flooring. He lost his footing and landed on his back.

Staring up at a flickering bulb on the ceiling. He was back in the fucking diner. He slowly got to his feet, swaying like a drunkard. The place was much hotter now but empty. No one was there. Nobody except for a man in a camel hair sport coat anxiously smoothing down a burgundy necktie and smoking a cigarette in a booth at the back.

The bell above the diner's front doors rang.

Two guys in dark overcoats, dark hats, brims pulled low and scarves covering their lower faces, strolled into the establishment.

Frank stood with his arms outstretched to embrace them. Smiling, relieved.

"Hey, Frankie Boy," one of the men cheerfully called as he passed through Frank like a ghost.

The man in the sport coat in the back smiled, snuffed out his cigarette in an overflowing ashtray and started to slide out of the booth.

Frank and the man screamed identical when the shotguns were pulled from the dark coats and the gun blasts ripped the evening apart for the second time that night.

Frank eyeballed the front doors of the diner, hitched his sleeve, and checked his wristwatch. A single droplet of blood stained the white linen cuff. Crimson gone a rusty brown. He tapped at the crystal. Fucking thing had stopped again. He impatiently shifted his weight in the booth. The oxblood vinyl and chrome seating groaned. Frank growled underneath his breath and waved the waitress over. A blue-eyed, petite, blonde with a heart-shaped face caked in make-up. He had the nagging notion that he knew her from somewhere, couldn't place where.

"What can I do for you, handsome?" she sing-sang.

Author Bio

@SteveGone58

Stephen J. Golds was born in England but has lived most of his life in Japan. Editor of *Punk Noir Magazine*, Golds writes everything from transgressive poetry to hardboiled noir. *Half-Empty Doorways and Other Injuries* is his illustrated collection of 30+ poems, while *Shadows Slow Dancing in Derelict Rooms* is his latest novella about a Londoner reliving his lethal romance through psych-ward cocktail-induced dreams. His and Craig Clevenger's short stories appear in the subversive anthology *In Filth It Shall Be Found.*

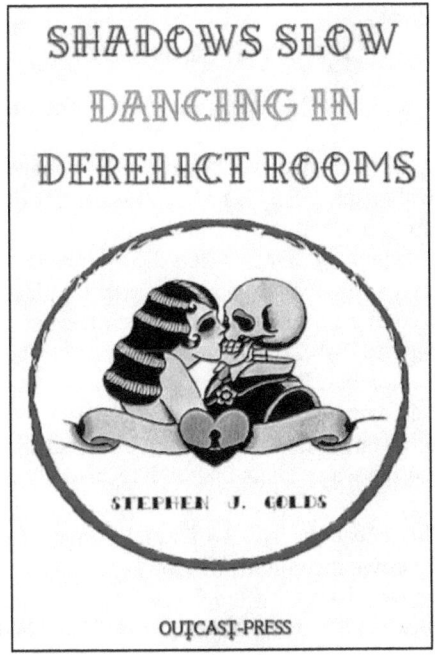

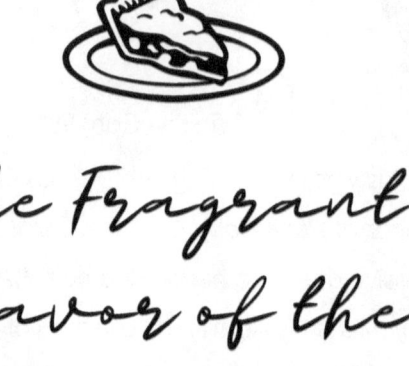

The Fragrant Flavor of the Strawberry Rhubarb Pie

By Jhon Sanchez

~For the New York Mills Cultural Center and Eagle's Cafe

I had hoped that once Liz tasted the strawberry rhubarb pie she would agree to the abortion. That was why I was driving her to this diner. I'd brought her to New York Mills, a tiny town in Minnesota partially named after the big city in which we lived. When she asked why I chose New York Mills, I gave her a sly smile that hinted at my surprise plan: I wanted to show her a site for the wedding I promised we'd have after her due date.

That was more than 20 years ago, early on a Thursday morning in the beginning of September. Beyond our windshield was an endless horizon with golden brushes over the still green of the hay, cornfields, and—from time to time—the bluestem that dotted the bottom of the sky. There were almost no trees, and the water tanks looked like spaceships ready to take off over the prairie.

Liz would repeat the lyrics of radio songs to help improve her English. She turned down the volume on Bob Dylan's "Positively 4th Street," and said, "I could never live in this loneliness. And walking in winter would be like trudging between a heavy blanket of clouds and bedsheets of snow."

It was a warning that I'd better not even consider trying to move us here, which wasn't an issue, because we already had our brownstone in Brooklyn.

What I loved most about Liz, besides the taste of her lips, were the moments of silence she would let hang comfortably in the air. From time to time during the car ride, she'd try to make me say something by asking things like, "Minnesotans? Minnesotonians? Minnesotanese?"

I never responded because I knew that, for her, love was a poker game of guessing the cards in the other's hand. For me, love was the taste of her lips, for which I still drool, even now, 20 years later.

"New York Mills probably has a tiny Central Park, and maybe even a Broadway!" was another of her attempts to get me to explain—I don't remember how many times—that it was not just a diminutive replica of New York City as she wished to imagine it, with a scarecrow in a cornfield as the Statue of Liberty.

What I wanted then was for her to taste the strawberry rhubarb pie so she could become more a part of me, or at least understand why I loved to kiss her, the only woman I have ever loved to kiss. Our first kiss at the office Christmas party baited me. I couldn't imagine that an 18-year-old in her first job would have brushed her lips against mine, saying only, "You're my favorite engineer in the company." The kiss was cool, visceral, and very red. She'd proposed marriage to me one afternoon in early summer while I stared at the Bank of America building from my office window. "I'm afraid, and all alone in this country," she'd said. "I don't know when my parents can come here. I don't want to be alone with your baby in me." She honeyed her speech with kisses on each corner of my mouth and then yanked my tongue with a bite. I had never bitten hers. If I had, I probably never would have stopped.

I was a well-paid engineer, 10 years her senior. I guessed that what she wanted was a sense of security. Her parents would never have approved of pregnancy before marriage, and, for that reason, they never knew about me. But neither my job nor our house could save us from my desire.

As we pulled into that diner in Minnesota, we saw a giant plaster eagle perched on top of a neon sign that said **EAGLE'S**. I joked to Liz that eventually all neon signs were bound to disappear, to be replaced with holograms. "Probably with an eagle flying down at its human prey," I said as we got out of the car.

Inside, we sat at a booth by a window, facing the small library across the street.

The waitress looked me straight in the eye, so different from New York City waitresses, who were looking for their next customers while handing you the menu. "Where've you been?" she asked, treating me like an old friend.

"He's been back home," Liz said, with a sort of jealousy that I couldn't understand, because even though the waitress was beautiful, with perfect cheekbones and adorable dimples, nobody had the same flavor as Liz.

"My fiancée," I said.

"He came here every day for an entire month," the waitress said, "and had our pie every morning at 8 o'clock. Nothing else. Not even coffee..." Then, perhaps noticing Liz's annoyance, the waitress added, "The woman who makes the pies is so ancient, we all call her Old Betsy." The waitress pointed to the wall above the counter, on which hung a painting of a woman wearing a green turban with black polka dots.

At that exact moment, Old Betsy appeared at the counter. I'd guess she's over a hundred now, but, back then, she'd come in every day to make the pies from scratch.

I knew that I had to explain my pie obsession to Liz, since I didn't like the taste of anything other than her sugary lips. Ever since I was small, all food tasted bland, yet my grandmother and my aunts who raised me still forced me to eat. Ice cream tasted the same to me as grass. Grilled ribs were like rusted metal, and clam chowder was tar. It seemed that my taste buds were only activated by two flavors: Liz's lips, and strawberry rhubarb pie.

I asked for a double order of the pie. Liz looked at me, her dark eyes like lagoons in a dense forest, and ordered milk, saying, "For the baby."

My heart turned into a furious bull that rammed the cage of my chest at the mere mention of the unborn.

The pie arrived.

When Liz finished the first piece with a red drop of filling left on her lips, I couldn't resist, and leaned in for a kiss. Even though our mouths didn't zip tight, it was the perfect kiss, slightly bitter and yet sweet. I noticed the guys sitting at the long counter, staring at us.

"We haven't had so much fun since Miss America visited this town 10 years ago in 2004, right, folks?" one of them yelled, standing as he rolled up a checkered shirt sleeve.

"You like this pie?" Liz asked me, drying her lips with a napkin.

"It's about my dad," I whispered.

"What about your dad?"

"My biological father was from here," I said.

"We're about to marry, and you didn't trust me enough to tell me this before?"

An obsessive drive to know where my spunky hair, a nose shaped like the tip of a knife, and dark-toned skin—almost rust-colored along the jawline—had come from had been so disappointing that I'd considered giving up. But these indigenous features kept me searching. Ever since I saw my mother—with her flat nose and dark brown face—in her coffin; since I felt my aunts' lips—round and wet like seals—on my cheeks; since my aunts first smiled at me with their long marble teeth; since I first asked Grandma—with hair like cauliflower florets—whether there really was a Santa Claus, I had wanted to know who my father was.

Liz frowned and pouted her lips, pretending to be angry, but I knew she was eager to hear the whole story. She alone knew about the times I would sleepwalk, moving my hand as if to catch a white fog that streamed from my nose, which, in those night visions, represented my soul. She alone heard the words that I repeated during those dreams: *"Mi alma, mi alma."* She alone had seen my drawings of the strange faces that appeared in my dreams. Two faces were the most frequent and vivid: a one-eared man with long hair, and a woman wearing a green polka-dot turban.

Liz had started on her omelet, having lost interest in the second half of the pie and its mountain of whipped cream. I knew that I needed to get to the point quickly, and so I told her, in a somewhat dramatic fashion, that a few months earlier I had hired a private investigator, and he had discovered the true name of my biological father. "Alejandro Charleston." The investigator had added, "It is unlikely that he had ever met you or your mother." He had died in a motorcycle accident in his twenties, shortly after my conception.

"I was an embryo or, should I say, I am one of three that my mom rescued from experimentation," I explained to Liz. "My mother won those fertilized eggs in a legal battle. I am the only one who survived."

Liz blinked, as she did when nervous, probably guessing that there was something more serious coming. She avoided any more questions and squeezed my hand.

When I explained that I was a product of research, it felt as if I had confessed to being some sort of mutant. Liz was so in tune with me, however, that I was sure that once I explained it all, she would connect the dots between the taste of the pie and the abortion I wanted her to have.

I told her more of the story that the investigator revealed to me. A group of scientists wanted to explore whether genetic information could transmit trauma from one generation to another. They believed that they could isolate the genes governing a person's disposition to depression or other emotional problems. They recorded the thoughts and memories that arose in men and women at the peak of orgasm to eventually look for their biological imprint in the afterwards-fertilized egg. Immediately after fertilization, while the embryo consisted of just a few cells, they applied a substance that marked the genetic information tied to memory. Unexpectedly, this caused a preservation and amplification of those memories in the fetus.

"Does that mean they can now read the thoughts of babies? Can they do that with our baby?"

"No, no." I covered my eyes with my hands. I couldn't tell her that the problem was that the experiment resulted in enhancing the embryo's memory capabilities. It made me more attuned to memories that were not my own, memories that seemed like an endlessly repeating tape at times. They came to mind spontaneously, and had become more frequent, and somewhat obsessive. And so, what I said then was, "I shouldn't even have been born in the first place."

"Your father never wanted you? At least this won't be the case with our baby. Are you sure your father never knew about you?"

"Certainly, he died without knowing of my existence, or apparently even caring about it. I guess this experiment was just easy money for him, good money for a college student."

Liz began biting her nails, a habit that disgusted me.

"The research was shut down after a journalist broke the scandal of doctors selling fertilized eggs to cosmetic companies. My investigator had been able to find notes and tape recordings of my father's mental images during eleven ejaculation sessions: a diner counter, a gust of wind, gloves, a sweet red bite, a woman with a green turban, and the letters E-A-G-L-E-S." A sweet red bite, indeed, he thought.

I told Liz that my father had been selected for the research because he suffered starvation as well as other kinds of trauma as a child. In fact, a Dr. Charleston and his wife, who were on a rescue mission at the time, had found him wandering the streets of Medellín, Colombia, when he was seven years old. They adopted him and brought him to their home in New York Mills.

"So, you came here to find your adoptive grandparents?"

Even though I said, "Yes," I'd known that the doctor and his wife were already long dead. At that time, my only surviving family member was a paternal aunt who showed me a picture of my father. Dr. Charleston, my grandfather, was in the photo too, his arm around my father's shoulder. My aunt told me that her brother Alejandro had a very strange way of eating: He mixed everything together in a single dish—coffee, soup, and even dessert, which was often a slice of pie from EAGLE'S. In the photo, my father appeared as a small child, and something that looked like whipped cream was smeared around his nose and mouth. Before giving me the photo, she said, "Alejandro was obsessed with strawberry rhubarb pie. He always said that Old Betsy's pie reminded him of the first time he came to New York Mills."

After reading the private investigator's report, I'd gone to New York Mills in the hope of finding some information about the images from my father's memories. I'd been driving around aimlessly when I suddenly saw the neon sign for the diner—**EAGLE'S**—shining through a distant fog. I went in and asked for coffee, but my waitress—the same one who later served Liz and me—came back with a piece of strawberry rhubarb pie and said, "It's free." She pointed to the end of the counter, where an old woman with the same sleepy eyes as those in the painting above the pass-through window behind the counter sat, blankly staring. "Old Betsy says you remind her of someone who died long ago. This slice is on her." Old Betsy's staring, and the waitress waiting for me to stab the pie, reminded me of my grandmother and aunts holding open my mouth to shovel in food. I closed my eyes and tried the pie, hoping to drive those women from my memories. As soon as I took a bite, I thought of Liz's lips: the tenderness, the natural red color, and the taste of the celery water she liked to drink.

Now, with Liz by my side, I placed a folder on the table containing two drawings I had created when I was 12, as well as a photograph of Dr. Charleston taken during his Army days. One of my drawings showed a man in a uniform with an indentation where his left ear should have been. "Don't they look alike?"

Liz stared at them for a moment and cautiously nodded.

"Look at this other drawing, and then look at that," I said, pointing to the painting of Old Betsy above the counter.

"A green turban with black polka dots," she said, holding my second drawing and examining it. "You made this when you were a kid?"

"There is something else. Dr. Charleston lost an ear during the Korean War." I was so happy to have gotten this far into the story that I ordered a second piece of pie.

The waitress smiled. "Old Betsy says that you always have seconds, just like 'her Alejandro.'" As she made the air quotes, I felt a stabbing sensation in my abdomen, fearing the memories that my father had given me.

"I really don't like cherry pie, and you love this strawberry stuff," said Liz. "Maybe our baby will like pumpkin."

I released a frustrated puff of air. Then I calmed down and told Liz what had happened when I ate the pie for the first time. "Do you remember those nightmares when I'd yell, '*Mi alma, mi alma?*'" Liz slightly opened her lips as I said, "I wasn't dreaming about myself. The dreams were always about my father, Alejandro."

"You were dreaming about your father..."

"Not really. It was Alejandro's memory playing back in the dream. I suppose it was the very first time he came to New York Mills." I paused and took another bite of pie, closing my eyes to live that memory again as if it were mine. "I'm Alejandro as a small boy, standing in the parking lot, right out there." I continued as I rubbed my hands. "I can feel the cold, the winter cold of that day." The movie started again, moment by moment. "I saw the world through Alejandro's eyes. I was frozen by the cold, by the fear of this strange place. As the man took off his woolen hat, I saw a crater instead of an ear on his left side. You know, Liz, I wanted to run away. I wanted to but, at the same time, I felt paralyzed. I took a deep breath and, when I exhaled, I saw a cloud coming out of my nostrils. I tried to catch it with my hands, saying, "*Mi alma, mi alma.*"

"That's funny. You thought the fog coming out of your nose was your soul leaving you." She chuckled.

"You don't understand. I know it's not true, but I felt anguish, as if I were dying. But I calmed down when the man without an ear whispered to me, 'Just breathe, my boy.' Then he blew out a white wafting cloud, which morphed into the letters E-A-G-L-E-S. He grabbed my hand and took me inside the diner, where I saw Betsy's portrait, her green turban and intense red lips. Old Betsy then appeared before me with a pie in her hands and said, 'This is for you.' She bent down and kissed me on the lips. A hot sensation arose inside me and became an overwhelming desire to nibble on Old Betsy's lips. Liz, I actually wanted to bite into Betsy's lips. I wanted to eat them, but I sat down and ate my piece of pie instead." I stopped talking to drink some water.

It seemed as if Liz was only half listening when she said, "This is all so very sad. But I wonder what kind of lipstick Betsy had on."

"That's not the problem. Your lips taste like the strawberry rhubarb pie in the dream. If you hadn't kissed me at that Christmas party... I would have never..." I hesitated. "You know, I never liked kissing... Only you.... I have these urges..." I couldn't tell her that I wanted to eat her lips, that this would be the only thing that could quench my desire.

Liz reached for my hand. "Thanks for telling me this," she said. "My mom always said that if I wanted to know my husband, I should examine my father-in-law. Now, I know you better, the future father of my child."

I wanted to yell that this wasn't the point of my telling her the story. She couldn't comprehend that, since I possessed these obsessive memories because of the experiment, I would pass them on to our child. I took a napkin and rubbed it in my hand, shredding it into tiny white pieces. "Think about the risks of having a child. The physical burden. The liability, so to speak."

Liz blew the white shreds out of my hand.

"I am talking seriously. What if he has all these memories that aren't his? How is he going to live with that?"

"The doctor said our baby is perfectly healthy." She tightened her blouse over her belly button, which was the size of a cherry. "And no matter what, it will be our child. I love you. Every time that I feed our baby, I'll remember that he has a taste for me, just like his daddy."

I stabbed at the remnants of Liz's pie with my fork until it became only crumbs.

Later, while driving to our lodgings, I asked, "Aren't you concerned that I have all these crazy dreams? You've seen my drawings."

She crossed her arms and looked through the window at the town's water tower, which looked like a huge egg with four legs. "It doesn't matter. I've always wanted this baby. I want the baby to have your eyes."

It was only when we arrived at our room that I finally revealed, "I don't want the baby."

She was in her robe, standing in the bathroom with her hands on her hips. "What the hell? You might not be ready, but I am. Why did you buy that brownstone? You got cold feet now, just before we move in together? Coward!"

"It's the pie!" I tried to explain, knowing how crazy I sounded.

She began to yell at me and call me terrible names, and threw a container of liquid soap, the hair dryer, and three bottles of water at me. Then she stopped, fixed her eyes on the mirror, and panted, "Is it another woman?"

"No." I knelt at her feet. "We just can't have this baby."

She gently pushed my head between her legs and replied, "It's my baby, too, with my memories: the times you made me laugh, the sensation of your kisses."

I never told Liz that my mother had also given me her memories. She had participated in the research to pay for surgery on her cleft lip. Every time I masturbated, I saw my mother making up her plump lips, always trying to cover the scar on the left side. She kept trying to apply her lipstick even when it was below the tube's rim, which made her lips bleed. Oh God, how could I give that terrible memory to another human being? If Liz loved me, why did she refuse to listen? Why didn't she understand?

"Overeating all that pie made you sick," she said, crying as she got into the bed.

I followed her, and she soon fell deeply asleep. I turned toward her, intending to taste her lips, but stopped. Instead, I took a pillow and held it over her face. After that, my mind went blank. I heard a train whistle in the distance.

The following morning, I placed her body in the car's passenger seat and covered it with a blanket. She looked asleep, and I kissed her for the last time. Her lips had no taste. I was relieved that there was no flavor, no aroma left, or else I would have nipped, kissed, and relished her lips as if I were devouring Old Betsy's pie.

Death had taken it all away and ended my hunger. Killing Liz was the right decision. Our baby, that poor creature, was destined to live with desires much worse than mine.

I drove around for hours until I found a spot near the bank of a lake.

Now, 20 years later, I often visit the place where Liz's body is buried. During the summer, I can even smell strawberries in the bushes nearby, although that could be my imagination. I quit my job and left New York City. It had been easy to convince my coworkers that Liz and I had decided to move to Colombia, the country where her parents lived.

I was drawn back to the New York Mills area and settled in nearby Fargo. I'm no longer the clean-cut engineer that I once was. I let my hair grow, and rarely shave. I survive. Every Friday, I drive about two hours west to relive the taste of that pie at Eagle's. I relive what my father must have felt when he came to this country: a sense of the security of family. I come here to calm my urges and to taste Liz's lips again.

Sometimes I imagine myself holding a little boy. In my dream, he is an eight-year-old boy, nibbling a lower lip that is as plump as my African grandmother's. This gesture reminds me of the many times I kissed—or should I say, *tasted*—Liz.

For several weeks at the diner, I've been told a woman has been asking for me. One day, the waitress gave me a slip of paper containing a name and phone number: Liz's sister.

I don't want to see her, or even to smell her. I imagine that, if she tastes like Liz, my urges will turn me into a bison in stampede. Liz never understood; her sister would never understand; nobody understands. Perhaps the only one who might have understood was that unborn creature, my son, who would now be 20 years old. He would have had to live with his grandfather's compulsion for that pie, and with my obsession with Liz's lips.

I could never handle hearing a news story that one, two, three, or more other women's bodies had been found with their lips missing. I didn't want to imagine the other horrible desires this being could have had because he was born from me.

Originally published in *New Found Magazine,* 2017

Author Bio

&@Jhon_Author /WriterJhon

Colombian-born Jhon Sánchez arrived in NYC to seek political asylum, where he is now a lawyer. His most recent publications include "A Weekly Call" (*Everybody Press Review*), "United Tombs of America," (*Midway Journal*) "Handy," (*Teleport Magazine*) & "The DeDramafi," (*The Write Launch*). He was awarded the Horned Dorset Colony for 2018 and the Byrdcliffe Artist Residence Program in 2019. In 2023, his story "Tigui" appeared in the *I Used to be an Animal Lover* anthology and his own collection debuts, entitled, *Enjoy a Pleasurable Death and Other Stories that Will Kill You* (New Lit Salon Press).

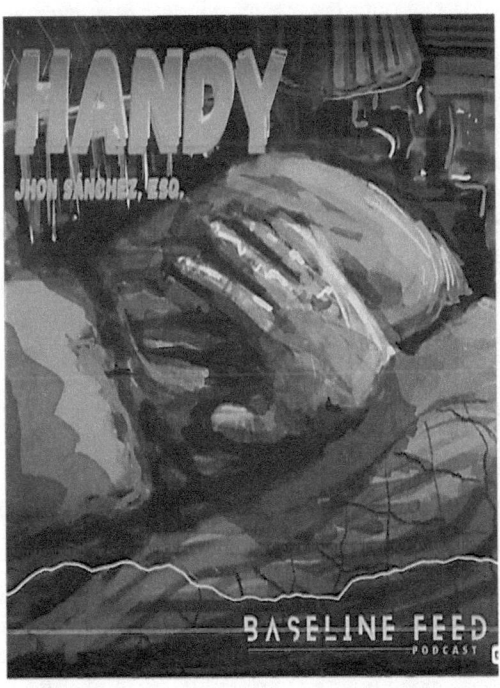

Honey Oil

By Paige Johnson

I used to roofie myself just to see if I could conquer an altered state of consciousness, or to get through a boring date with a long-time mistake. Now, I use them to make a living. My girlfriend says we're like chemsex Thelma and Louise, seducing bad men to steal good money, but I rather be sober, financially stable, and make it out alive like a smarter, quieter Cardi B.

So, whether I'm drugging myself to "train" like a cop who takes a face full of mace to get into the enemy mindset or doing it to incriminate a sleazebag with a hush fund, I'm dosing at least three times a week. Usually, it's inside the Denny's my girlfriend works, conveniently connected to the motel where we live and where I lure guys on fake dates.

Okay, okay, so there's some recreational fun to be had with the drug more formally known as GHB. It's like booze with a better buzz, hornier euphoria, and no hangover. It's sweetly discreet, dissolving into water or soda with no more look or taste than a pinch of salt. If anybody knows that, it's my girl, Cassie. Sure as shit, she's dipping into my stash right now. While I've been cutting back and only drugging my male marks, she's been picking up my slack.

"Again?" I ask as she stumbles out of our bathroom, feigning like she didn't just smack her funny bone against the door.

"What? Huh? No. I'm straight." She rubs her elbow and tightens the apron on her waitress' uniform. "I just tripped and skidded on a puddle." There's too much song in her speech to spell sobriety.

It's hard to be mad when she's wearing that stupid, toasted-yellow, red-collared dress. She looks too much like a puff pastry not to crack a smile: She's stacked and steamy as a plate of strawberry pancakes. Still, I crinkle my nose. "Why was there a puddle if you didn't shower?" I ask as evenly as I can, sure her pits are just the gasoline whiff of half-inoffensive I like to nap-nuzzle into. Too bad her shift starts in a minute. "I just toweled off the tile," I complain. "Unless you pulled a quickie with my toothbrush and squirted all

over, I don't see why the floor'd be wet the five seconds you were in there."
I make a jerk-off motion like throwing a Yahtzee cup.

She sticks out her tongue, the ball piercing waving *fuck off* in place
of a wrist flick. "If anyone's gonna rag on someone for cleanliness, it should
be me on you." She rests her weight on one leg and leans against the wall.
Shoddy balance *surely* unrelated to tapping into my dissociatives. Her neon
nails gesture towards my "crime pile" of creamed panties, holed socks, and
stretched shirts in the corner. "Get rid of that stink museum, Lace. Don't you
know the best part of living in a motel is the maid service? Duh."

I roll my eyes. "I need those." Maybe it's paranoia, but the way I
see it, my mini "mountain of evidence" is a good safeguard if any guy ever
comes creeping back with a lawyer. I'll have what passes as DNA proof,
circumstantial or not. "*You* need those, Cas," I clarify. "Serving senile
boomers pie isn't gonna get us to Malibu. You forget they tip literal pennies
on the dollar?"

Her emerald eyes circle the sallow room. "You need 20 ripped Ts
clogging the small hall, really? As what, like a speed bump when your guys
have to primp before the big nothing, then wake up covered in drool?" She
says this like it wasn't her idea to cut up the Good Will finds to appear
assault-distressed. "You're wasting what li'l space we have with junk!" she
accuses.

I shoot her a side-eye and swivel my laptop towards her on the
wobbly coffee table.

Her eyes narrow at the homepage heading. "All Things Worn," she
reads. "What's that? God, don't tell me you're buying more clothes."

"Of course not." I swallow a curse. "The site is what it sounds like.
Selling all the shit we wear." The jackets the marks leave behind, the bras I
jerk comatose "johns" off onto, the boyshorts Cassie can't fit into during the
diner's cheesecake season. So, if a guy comes to and doesn't cough up
enough moola after I present "proof" of our shady hookup, I can still make
money off online perverts. Sure, most dudes don't mind tossing their wallet
at a girl to get her to stop slinging around the word rape, but that's only one
revenue stream. "Listen, Cas, motherfuckers on this site will buy anything.
Sweats a cute girl wore on a hike, smelly shoes, bikini bottoms a guy or girl
sexed in. I bet, even if I told these people I stage rapes in these clothes, they'd
eat from my palm like little piggies."

"Hmmm," Cas murmurs, trying not to sound impressed.

"Admit it, honey bun." I flick the ponytail off her nape as she leans
over my computer. I smile, hoping to reignite hers. It's been missing too
many months, since she fell heavy into G. For better or worse, "I'm the queen
of contraband."

"All hail Princess Pervert," she monotones.

"That's right." I lean forward on the couch. "But I can only be that
if I have a supply to pull from... Cas, be straight with me." I hook her chin to

face me, slowly say, "Did you go into the bathroom and get high on top of what I already gave you?"

"Of course not," she says as quick as hard. "What're you, crazy? I have work." She bites her teeth and glances at the clock on the TV stand. "Like, starting two minutes ago. I'm late." She strides toward the door—a little too breezy. Catwalk fast.

"It's not that you use," I sigh. "It's that I wish you—"

"I *didn't.*"

"—could just ask me before—"

"I would. I always do."

"—you dose. I don't even—"

"I said, I didn't!" She shoulders her purse and widens her gaze in a *Shut it* stare. "Besides, Jeff is coming after my shift to re-up you. Christ, fucking chill. " Swiveling, she throws open the door as fluidly as she slams it.

"I'm chill," I murmur to the stock photographs clacking against the wall. "*Sooooo chill,*" I say to the dust bunnies and date rape laundry I shuffle through on my way to the closet. I yank out a dress and purse, throw them onto the bathroom counter. Flicking on the light, I see what I figured: a flat Pepsi Mini beside the sink with a few clear droplets on the rim too syrupy to be water.

Of-fucking-course she didn't even trash the evidence, 'cause you know how many soft beverages the Average Jean enjoys on the shitter. *Uck, right.* I crouch under the sink to inspect my makeup pouch. Def turned a different direction than I left it. Even if I'm paranoid, the GHB vial within *does* look a tad lower. So, she took some for later, atop what I gave her to slip into my date's drinks. *Just righteous.*

Swiping through my dating app messages, I think, I should pretend to fuck this mark for real to make her mad. He's a real nerd: blond pencil neck with Harry Potter glasses, ironed polos, and *ding-ding-ding* real estate job. Hinge has the homeowning boys on lock, less poor and aggressive than Tinder bros, for sure. Not too stuffy to meet at Denny's either.

Calmed, washed, and eyeshadowed, I stand in the air-conditioned foyer of the diner, trying to shake a bug-eyed dragon from the crane machine. Even though I'm pissed at Cas for lying, I'd like to see her clutch the plush during make-up sex or the flutter-eyed after-snuggle. The red velvet of the dragon would clash nice against her baby-pale skin, her lips sucked of tinted gloss.

Three dollars later and I'm the proud mama of the crinkle-winged beast.

"Right on," a squeaky voice cheers behind me, but it ain't a kid. My dinner date raises a small fist. "If you would have waited a minute, I could have won it for you." He's all smiles and zero muscles, though he flexes a boney bicep like there's a correlation between joysticks and arm strength.

"Ha-ha, you can get me one next time. I also like unicorns—so long as they've got a flaming mane. Like that Pokémon, you know?" I hold up the stuffed animal and squeeze, hoping I'm playing into the "video game vixen" his profile said he's seeking.

"I believe you mean the Fire Pegasus," Glasses points out with a wry smile.

It's gonna be a long night but I'm up for the challenge. Won't mind fooling this one.

We get in a booth to order soup and smoothies like we've had our tonsils taken out but want our mouths to experience summer and winter. As Glasses stacks the table creamers into a pyramid, I look behind me into the kitchen window. My dealer Jeff, pink-faced and steam-shrouded, squints over the griddle. The sounds of girlish giggles, gristle scrapes, and sausage sizzle-flips float out the little porthole. I can barely make out Cassie's black bangs, she's so short, but she must be preparing our drinks. Jeff might be aiding the process. You can always count on a line cook to carry an array of uppers, downers, and a little side-to-side stuff.

Cas hasn't told him why we need so much G, but even if she garnishes a drink a little close to him, he's good at looking the other way. Or he assumes she's giving me—not my many male friends—a special cocktail on request. Hell, I don't care if he thinks I'm a prostitute who needs a pick-me-up/toss-me-down to get through the deed. Dude's been to prison, undoubtedly fucked more guys than me.

"…and that's how my guild got ranked to such a high tier before the Arena championship."

"Huh? Oh, yeah. That's awesome. I could never," I say like waking from a dream.

Glasses retracts his hands from his pile of shredded straw wrappings. "Maybe I shouldn't boast so much. Let me hear about you. You seem so down-to-earth for a model. Can't believe I'm sitting here with you!"

"Oh, naw, it's just freelance internet things. I just mention it in my profile so guys don't think I'm fatfishing them." It also implies that I'm feeble but with a following when they wake up and I drop the word rape like a bomb. The R-shell, I call it.

Cassie laughs a little too hard while delivering our drinks: strawberry for me, peach for him. Not sure if her chuckles are leftovers from Jeff's comedy routine or directed at the geek I'm playing.

"I love these little umbrellas," I say, twirling the tropical toothpick.

"Oh, yeah. *Totally* like being on the Cali shore," Cassie teases, tossing Glasses more straws to strip.

"Malibu," I whisper, imagining white sands instead of vinyl chairs with fork puncture wounds that scratch the back of my thighs. Mocktails at a pool bar instead of juice from concentrate inside a mold-brown diner. Maybe Cas rehabbed in a polka dot 'kini, splashing me with an uncorked nosecco... Girl can dream, one dime at a time.

"Oh, have you been? To California, I mean," Glasses asks, eyes brightened by the conversation-starter.

Cas walks away, shaking her head so all her curls sway-dance like Hollywood starlets.

"Naw, the closest I've been is the island logo on rum bottles. But one day, I'll be there," I assure. "I'll live on the beach, any beach warm and sunny, even if it means I have to plop down a tent and catch fish to survive."

"Ambitious."

"Or maybe the opposite." I shrug, watching Cas bring a vacant table's tray of buttery plates to the back. Enough food waste to feed a few battered mothers—or at least the stray weenie dog I saw sniffing the cigarette bin outside.

"Well, the West Coast sure sounds fairytale compared to our rainy flyover state."

"Anything would," I admit. "This forever overcast, I can't stand it. It either puts people on edge or makes them shut down. I guess because of all they can't do or experience. Everything is traffic in the rain, indoor work or canceled dates, delayed flights. You know how many people I hear bitch about vitamin deficiencies and depression? I see why the suicide rate jumped—er, okay, maybe not the best choice of words, given how close we are to 'Heaven's Gates' bridge, but you know what I mean." I clear my throat and sip away the smidge of embarrassment. "Don't mean to ramble or be a downer, just something I've noticed."

"No, I understand you. It is no wonder about the opioid crisis when the world here really is colored as gray as the news makes it sound," he says. "Saw a guy nodding out on the way over here. During a drive with my nephew last month, not knowing any better, he called them sleepyheads."

"That's cute in a morbid sort of way." My laugh is light, head heavy from the brain freeze.

"You're kind of cute in a morbid way." He points out my sparkly gothic makeup.

I roll my eyes. "*Smooth.*"

"*-ie,*" he adds, clinking his smoothie against mine.

"Thanks. I love cheeseballs." They're more naïve.

I endure more quirk as Cas lags on the entrées. Maybe she's making me suffer on purpose or too caught in Jeff's web. I hear him holding court with her and the teenage bussers, reciting stale memes and street jokes he oversaw on his smoke break. Cas is usually a tough laugh, having grown up on Comedy Central and Showtime specials, but she's lapping up Jeff's one-liners like me with this berry-banana blend. It fills the pauses between fun facts and anecdotes well.

Not sure if it's because Glasses hinted at how well he's doing selling property in the post-pandemic housing boom, but his latest story genuinely tickles me.

"...and then the duck fell out of her bag!"

"Ohmigod, that's *in*-sane." I give him a playful shove and he pushes back my hand with a wink. "Oh, a fighter?" I purr, watching Cas pinch Jeff's hip as he hands her a coffee pot behind the cake counter. Weirdly flirty. I thought they only tolerated each other (I mean, the dude goosed the last high school waitress into quitting and Cas's resting bitch face lays clear her demeanor). Two can play at that.

When she comes to top up our waters, I stroke Glasses' wrist. He smiles, choking a bit on his orange slush.

"Just a few more minutes on the loaded potato soup, guys. It's a fresh batch," she says even though I coulda sworn it was microwave slop.

"Take your time," I assure, scrunching my fingers over Glasses' wrist in a sort of cat knead, a testing of claws. "We're having a great one."

Forehead creasing for only a second, Cas nods along. "Bet... See, I'll havta add in an extra dollop of love to your bowl, sugar."

"Thought it only came with sour cream," Glasses quips to a space sucked cold of laughter.

"Certain you will sprinkle in some of that downcountry love, so double up on the crackers, please." I toss her the triple-laminated menu. "And I prefer strips, not bits of bacon, if you can. Steve here was just saying I could use some meat on these bones." I wink but I'm not sure he sees it as he further smudges up his specs with brown paper napkins.

"At your service." Cassie salutes, off to prepare the order and probably a hefty sigh.

Her reaction isn't much, just a twist of the lips, but it keeps me beaming. Maybe this guy isn't so bad. I don't feel the full-body cringe I do on most of these meetings. His jokes don't all turn into dirty double-entendres and we're loosening up.

"So...any crazy exes I should know about?" he asks after discussing our mutual love of *Scott Pilgrim vs. the World*. "Less than seven to fend off, I hope."

"Ah, no. Nothing like that... There was this brunette I used to go with who looked a bit like Romana Flowers." *Totally not the alt-girl ladling us liquid potato as we speak.* "We're still mostly cool, but..."

"But...?"

I lower my voice. "She's not...the most honest or even-tempered person. Not that I'm the perfect peach or whatever, but... We started besties and we'll probably die that way, but the middle ground we're in gets shaky, you know?"

"Was your breakup spurred on by infidelity?"

"Nothing like that. Well, okay, maybe worse. Everybody has their vices, right? Well, she likes to party. Maybe too hard and solo to call safe." The words slip out like a sneeze: a disgusting outburst. I slump forward, guilt weighty in my tummy. "It's not like she's one of those street sleepers who'll wind up in a box, letting strangers film her doing TikTok jigs for money. Nowhere near, but I worry. I didn't ever wanna leave her but it's like my best friend faded into the mist over the course of a few months and hasn't been able to re-materialize. She's got a hair-trigger rage. I get it but it doesn't mean I'm not sick of it or always act right." My voice cracks a fraction. I slurp up smoothie but still feel a scrape at the back of my throat. "I didn't leave her," I clarify.

He nods, sympathetic. "She left on her own accord, some fucked terms."

I nod, squinting, unsure I got it right even in some multiverse scenario. I sit on my cold hands, shiver from the fruit concoction, but admit the venting takes a bit of my edge off. "Whatever. She'll get better once she realizes how different she's become, then we can resume our friendship." Maybe it'll take the magic of Malibu, its seagull songs, sugar sand, and tranquil waves to reset her mind, but it'll be worth it. We're almost there, our safe crammed full of dollar wads, gift cards, and the odd ID that could lead to vacations one sunset at a time. The dream grows one guy at a time. Nothing personal, Glasses.

"Right on." Glasses stares into his smoothie, evening out a frown. "All you can truly help is yourself in this world."

"I heard that." We clink drinks even though they're near-empty. I estimate 10 minutes before the wonkiness works him over. I already see some distance in those pupils, a hunch developing.

Cassie slips steaming bowls of cheese and meat hunks onto our table with a clatter. There's hardly a splatter but she wears an ironic smile to match the ones she drew in our soup: whole bacon slices to make mouths, cheddar clumps for eyes. "Special treat for your first date," she says.

"Aw, nice. How could you tell?" Glasses asks, grabbing his second water.

"Oh, please. You could hear the laughter from next-door. Also, you look a li'l nervous." She nods in my direction, seemingly pinpointing my sweat-through jacket.

Flushing, I press my pits closer to my body and squeeze shut my purse so she can't see the dragon plush peeking out. "Just a pinch." I make eye contact, drinking up her canopy-green eyes and pinned pupils. "Thank you. This's cute. Looks too good to be true. Wish you could join us."

She laughs me off, throws a rag over her shoulder that nearly misses. "Trust me, I'm having plenty fun of my own." She returns to it, hooting beside the grill with Wigger J in no time.

We chow down and I pretend not to hear Jeff over-flatter Cassie on the pin collection she's accumulated on her collar. I know he doesn't really give a shit about the *Aqua Teen Hunger Force* enamel set I bought for her birthday, it's just a ploy to peek at her chest, but I don't know which bothers me more.

"You alright?" Glasses asks. "Eye's twitching a bit."

"All good. Just got some chowder in my eye. Stuff's hot and didn't skimp on the salt." I don't expect to devour the bowl, but here I am, belly full, body sweltering and a bit sluggish. After he balls his napkin over the shallow lake he left in his plate, I ask, "Hey, um, do you wanna go back to my room to see that fantasy series I mentioned? Sounds a lot like the Marvel movie you brought up. You can borrow the first book I just finished." I told him I'm staying at the motel around the corner while my apartment gets renovated.

"Sure!" You'd think I asked if he wanted to star in a superhero franchise with all that cheer.

"Great, let me just—" I go to stand up but a headrush sits me back down. Jeez, how much MSG is legal at an American diner? Can only imagine a metric ton. "Uh, let me just get myself together." I'll wash up in my room, wipe the Denny's dinge off my skin, and brush good. Fuck, I might even have to purge this meal. It is not sitting right, my temples clammy. Maybe it's for the best. I'll have to dab on a few Visine tears anyway for the big reveal.

After he pays, leaving a showy tip (*go, Cas!*), I take his arm. I'm surprised how much my body craves him, my lean magnetic. He's not my type (uh, a penis is strike one), but his smile is infectious, warming my cheeks and fluttering my stomach as we walk. A bit like being starstruck or love drunk, or maybe that's just how fed up I feel with Cassie.

At my place, I trip over the metal threshold bump, falling into the bed and laughing like an idiot. It's only half a ploy. "Stupid heels," I excuse to fling them off.

While I massage some sensation back into my toes, Glasses peruses the room, trying not to look offput.

"Sorry, it's madness here. The demo-reno is taking longer than the landlord said. Who'dda thunk, right? Besides, I didn't expect to have company after a first date. First time deal, you know?"

He grins. Boys always like hearing that.

I shrug, eyeing all the laundry lumps sprouting from the threadbare carpet. "This is just a temporary stay, so I guess I've been treating it bad that way." Suddenly, Cassie's demands for order don't seem so outlandish. "Been party time longer than I realized." I sigh, counting 12 mismatched socks and 10 wrinkled bralettes. The scent of stale perfume and deodorant-streaked band Ts is making me nauseous. "I'll clean up before you leave," I promise. Leave two good surprises for Cassie: the dragon on a spotless coffee table and a walkable living space. Get all the garb listed on that site, sorted away in bags and drawers. Then maybe we'll have a calm night like old times. Play some Tegan and Sara, pop on an indie flick, and fall asleep in a cuddle puddle without the aid of GHB. It's about six hours before she gets off though, so gotta get down to business. Invest in the bigger dream, one nail at a time.

"Don't worry about it," Glasses says. "A cluttered room points to an artistic mind."

"Talk about putting a positive spin on it." I guffaw.

"Speaking of spinning, I think that soup gave me an insulin spike. I'm Thanksgiving-groggy. Cholesterol must be off the charts. Tryptophan, something." Politely sitting at the farthest edge of the bed, he removes his glasses to rub his temples.

Glad I'm not the only one. I was starting to worry Cas confused our drinks. Shoulda had faith, she knows our mini umbrella system and I'd never touch anything citrus. "'Round these parts, they call grease flavor."

"Well, next time, I'll take you to a real place and you'll see how a little spice and clean cooking can go a long way."

"Denny's ain't real enough for you, tiger?" I toss a pillow at him. Leaning against the headboard, the earth seems a little stiller. "That's Americana, bud. Crust and all."

"What I'm trying to say is, I hope to take you out again." He crawls up the bed, fumbling an elbow or two.

"That so?" Dropping my face into my palms, where I could blow a kiss, I bestow my best bedroom face. One best for Instagram or OnlyFans if I didn't require the safety of physical tender. A face I practice after every mouthwash rinse: pouted lips, laser gaze, butterfly lashes.

If only this sleepiness wasn't teetering my lids too close together or sinking my arms to the side. Before I know it, his lips mush against mine, slick, and sliding down my chin.

Fuck, why is it getting so dark?

It's like my bones are shaking in their sockets, food poisoning flu-ish anxiety. But my skin is way too comfy making contact with the cool, puffy sheets or his feverish forehead as it moves to rest in my lap.

What the hell?

Did I get too much G on my skin while checking up on Cassie's bathroom binge before I left?

At the restaurant, I made sure to grab the bowl on Cassie's right. Why would Glasses AND I be drowsy? We didn't share any—

The door bursts open with such a jolt, I think it's gotta be the authorities.

But it's Cas.

"What're you," I start but it comes out like underwater bubbles: Wuuutorrrryuu… I fall on my side, the stitching of the comforter downright seductive.

Glasses is already taken undertow, softly snoring by my pelvic bone.

Shadows tentacle around the walls. Got me feeling like a Rolling Stone; I just want to paint it all black, crash in the murky recesses of a trashed rented room.

Yyyuuuuuacudentliiii d-doooseded. I don't even know if anything comes out, if these developing visuals are open- or closed-eye.

Cassie smiles, wider than I've seen in sober days. "How'd your last date go?" There's a saccharine quality to her voice. Is it because she's so high, or am I?

Baaaaad, the date went baaaad, I wanna bleat like a lamb, voice trapped inside my teeth, my lungs, crevices around the room.

It's not until she's fluffing my hair that I think she might be teasing because she tucks in Glasses like a little boy.

Looking into her face is like beholding your sleep paralysis demon: living dead as a functional addict, cables of hair with fried flyaways, bruise-violet bags under tired eyes, chapped lips picked apart as a nervous tic.

I can't tell if her defects are exaggerated by the drug or revealing what I ignored. Indirectly caused.

I can stomach no more dread when Jeff moseys in, shooting up a peace sign punctuated by a casual, "Hey, Lacey."

Cassie props me on a side.

My head lolls over the bed so I can splatter the waste basket and avoid death by vomit once the convulsions roll through like thunder.

Jeff kneels at the safe, lightning-typing the code without consulting Cassie. She shoves my makeup bag, my most resale-worthy dresses, and my purse into an oversize canvas tote I've never seen before.

I've become as inert as how the sealant of my fate smells: rubber cement. Can't connect the dots. Assume these must be shadow people, HD deviations of the Hatman you see when delirium comes for you.

When did this...? Why did this...? A long-time con or a prank concocted during a ciggie break? With the dealer I pushed her into befriending before her addiction grew legs, no less?

No way.

Three years and a recent rough patch between us?

Fuck that. This can't be. We were class-dodging buddies, a cast-iron dropout pact with no relatives to run to. All love and adrenaline. All the nights belting ride-or-die lyrics, campfire secrets, on-the-run road trips. This won't compute.

I see our silhouettes on that Californian shoreline that parts and ripples "Welcome!" just to us. The blinding rising sun. Ivory tower lighthouses illuminating our path to sandbar paradise. So goddamn close.

I'm having a night terror, a bad trip unrelated to this reality.

Has to be.

Must've taken ketamine or a laced molly pill and gone into panic mode. That explains away my uninhibited talk with Glasses, my sputtery memory, chest compression. The sense of a warm rain pelting me, heating and cushioning me from the inside out into sedation.

Right?

The purpling bruise on Cassie's elbow taunts me as she pockets the few belongings I have: slim watches and wedding bands I've taken off men, palm tree water globes from landlocked giftshops, the camera she gave me last summer before the skies bunched up into volcanic cries and never seemed to clear, never seemed worth photographing.

Hypnotized, I stare into her bruise like it's a monsoon eye, the dot on the map safe from the tornado points meeting between my head and heart.

Funny, that was the injury I was gonna caress and kiss if we ever got to steady ground tonight. Funnier that the stupid little dragon I won is gonna pop out of the ashes of this when she's tallying all the other prizes that I racked up for her. I see that, too.

Her flicker of remorse when she's alone in a new hotel tonight. When Wigger J comes knocking to collect his cut in both flesh and greenbacks. Then, as her black marble eyes reflect in the dragon's, will she be sorry?

If I could cackle crazy like an asylum patient, I would.

This is how the dream sours. 86ed by the girl I was saving for?

I'd rather she sucker-punch the teeth out of me—not just because you can't feel a Brazilian wax on G. But because this shit scorpion-stings.

And that's just now.

When I wake up in an hour, left with nothing but pre-guillotine silence, I'll be crying for a coffin. I know I will.

I'll keep clawing for something that never comes.

Always have been.

Author Bio

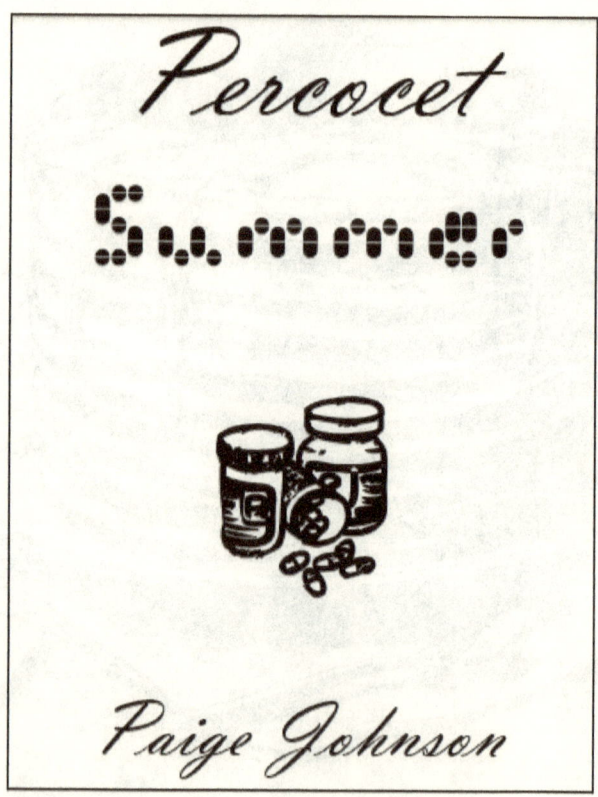

🐦 @OutcastPress1   Ⓕ /OutcastPress1

Floridian **Paige Johnson** authored her first poetry collection, *Percocet Summer,* part of the seasonal series Poetry for Distancing Dates and Doses. One of the upcoming sequels is called *Aurora Shards of Winter.* It most extensively explores her ketamine therapy sessions and bisexuality with the backdrop of cold romance and candlelit delusions.

Percocet Summer

Paige Johnson

What's Left of the Sun

By Michael J. Riser

I can't help but think that dying in a pile of garbage behind a Chinese restaurant was better than being alive in this fucking dump. It's the kind of place that makes Waffle House seem tolerable, where the only thing edible enough to chew is the coffee. I won't go so far as to say this is a fate I don't deserve, or that it's all because of Marie that I woke up in the wrong life after dying in the right one. I was asking to get shot. Because I wanted everything, and everything I wanted was wrong.

I finish my coffee and leave most of the soggy hash browns, and I'm back at the clinic again in the space of 10 minutes, sweating from the summer heat reflected by endless Texas pavement. I'd kill for a cigarette, but they tell me I don't smoke. They say I don't drink either, that I never took a header from a balcony after getting plugged in the back of the head. These people sit across the desk from me, one after the other, asking me questions, informing me of who I am as if they know better than I do.

The woman across from me is brown, sometimes. Brown skin, brown eyes, hair like dark mud. Then sometimes she's a man, ghost-pale like he's forgotten the sun, trapped inside the white halls. Sometimes he's a smaller man, yellowed, balding head in the shape of a lightbulb. Every iteration of this person wears glasses, dragging a clipboard as if to be caught without it, would strip them of all their authority. They ask how I'm doing and write my answers down in the indecipherable chicken scratch all doctors write in. The facts never change, but I know they'll keep asking until they get the answers they want.

There's a group of friends and associates who come and go, looking in on me at the clinic to see how I'm doing or taking me to the shitty diner because somehow, it's the only thing within walking distance. They smile and nod and talk to me about things, some of which I can almost recall, some of which sound like elaborate fabrications.

I recognize most of the faces, if not always the people. They come in new and old aspects, each in some way different from the images in my mind. A few faces feel like they've been stolen, like you'd see usurpers hiding underneath, unknown people burrowed into familiar skins. One of these, called Margaret, is particularly painful to look at.

"Feeling okay today?" She's sitting in the other chair in the clinic lounge. Her eyes are on the man I'm not. "Feeling…present?"

"In such and such a time, such and such a place."

"I've been trying to understand." She stares out the window at the courtyard with me for a few minutes. "It hasn't been easy, but I'm trying."

"Yeah? How's that working out?"

"A little better than it was." She reaches down to pick her purse from between her feet, and I can't even look at the momentary glimpse of her cleavage without the knife in my guts resuming its sawing motions. Her fingers come up with a pack of cigarettes between them. "I got you these," she says.

"What's the catch?"

"I'm just trying to understand, James." She sees me twitch at being called the wrong name and wilts into a grim smile. "Sorry, I can't quite bring myself to call you anything else."

"Forget it. Got a light?"

"You're not supposed to smoke in here."

"According to them, I'm not supposed to be addicted to nicotine, either."

"Fair enough." She holds out a book of matches but stalls on passing them to me. "Look, I'm trying to meet you halfway."

"I know." I pluck the matches from her fingers, flip the book open, light up.

"Can't you at least try to do that for me too?"

I stand and take a long drag.

"Please, Jim."

"Thanks for the smokes." I don't want to be an asshole, I don't. It's just…what else can I say? Sorry, Margaret. You're a problem for me.

Her eyes choke me all the way back to my room.

It's been long enough now that they let me out sometimes, but I'm no less trapped outdoors, and there's nothing to do anyway. I go to the diner on the corner and order whatever slop on the menu seems the least repellent. The coffee's the best thing but still bad, which is an easy excuse to make it Irish. It becomes a ritual, something that marks off the days before it all starts to smear together. I've simply built myself a more comfortable prison out of my own haunted bricks, mortared together with a paste of pancakes and corned beef hash.

Sonny stops by later to join me for coffee, and he doesn't seem so different. He brings me cookies his mom baked, and they taste so warm and reliable, I almost want to believe this is real. God bless Italian mothers from the old country.

"Back home, you have a mustache," I tell him.

"Gotta be kidding me."

"Not at all. Ladies love it too. You should consider it."

He cracks something close to his usual grin. "Don't suppose it would hurt to try."

We each eat another cookie. There's something beautiful and hideous in the chocolate chips still soft from the summer heat, the same thing that's lurking in the streets outside these walls, bittersweet and strange. Slipped into a pocket like a dream inked on aging newsprint. We walk back to the clinic in silence. I still can't believe he doesn't smoke.

"Maggie come by again?" he asks, leaning back into the uncomfortable chair in my room.

I nod from the bed. My eyes shrivel at the mention of her.

"She really does love you, you know."

"I know. That's the problem."

"It never used to be."

"That's because it was before—" I stop, because there's no point. "Well, it was before."

He knows, and I don't know how to talk about it, besides. Every time I do, it feels like the urn of my own ashes crashes into the back of my skull. Because this life isn't the first, that's just what they keep telling me. The life I lived before was real, real as concrete. I can't get cloudy about that if I want to hold onto my sanity. I repeat it like a mantra.

Marie walks toward me somewhere in my memory as the fractured explanations of the doctors' piece themselves together again, their tale about why I'm here, why I'm now. It comes back to me while I'm talking to Sonny, but messy, like reassembling a broken egg.

"What you call your first life, Mr. Collingwood, was just an interruption of your real one." That's the way the lightbulb put it. The pretty brown one said, "You fell asleep. You dreamed. You invented the man you're describing to us." I don't remember what the pale one said because he mumbled into his collar, making eyes at the clipboard.

"I go back and forth on who's got it right," I say, looking through the window into the sunset. I wait for it to burn my eyes out, leave me alone with the better view in my head, but it's already too far below the horizon. "What's really so wrong with an invented man?" I mutter this under my breath, but apparently New Sonny has a set of ears on him, because he responds like it was part of the conversation.

"I mean we're all inventions, aren't we?" he says. "We invent who we are by the things we choose."

"But that's just it. I didn't choose any of this."

He stares, like he's finally figured out I'm never looking for an actual answer. We sit in uncomfortable silence, staring at the cookies on the table.

I mumble an apology and light a cigarette, speaking just so something will be said. "Do I even own a camera?"

He raises an eyebrow. "Like a video camera?"

"No, for pictures."

"I'm sure you've got one somewhere, why?"

"Never mind." The thought only just occurred to me, as nobody's told me what I do on this side of the divide to keep myself in sandwich bread and rolling papers. It's just another thing I'm afraid to find out.

"Still so weird to see you smoking," Sonny says, breaking a long silence.

"So they keep telling me. And apparently, I didn't like overpriced bourbon and cheap gin."

This, at least, makes him chuckle.

I snort smoke through my nose and cough, squirming with the weird, too-clean feeling all over my lungs. What I want to be is a dragon, big and pissed off and exhaling fire. Things would make sense if I was living over a pile of private riches in a cave that all the townspeople were afraid of but too fascinated by to leave alone. Then maybe something would feel like it was slotting into place. Instead, I feel small and squishy and pink, and I don't understand how so many people are so concerned.

"That's the problem," I say, in response to my own thoughts. "I smoke but I don't have the lungs of a smoker. I'm a photojournalist who doesn't own a camera. I'm none of the things I think I am, and there's plenty of evidence to prove it, but the more I get to know the new me, the more I hate this piece of shit."

Sonny makes a sour face.

"What?"

"You just...didn't used to swear so much."

"For fuck's sake. Was I also 12?" As far as I remember, we always swore like sailors.

"You were a churchgoing man."

"Of course I was." My eyes roll until they hurt. "Look, believe me or don't, but I drink, I swear, I smoke like a peat fire. I used to hit Sunday mass once every other month out of some misplaced sense of obligation to my dead Irish father. And I know you don't care, that I could say I pissed in the holy water and it wouldn't make any difference to you, but—"

Sonny holds up his hands. "Look, Jim—"

"Cal."

"Fine. Cal." His chair gets shoved back by his legs as he stands up. "You didn't do those things. You've just convinced yourself you found a way to be someone you never were."

"Who are you to say what I did or didn't do?"

"Because I was there. I watched you. You were my best friend."

I say nothing, because arguing about this is pointless and I just want it to be over.

Sonny shakes his head. "That guy is standing right in front of me in the same stupid green coat he always wore, the same stupid blue jeans."

"It's what was in the fucking drawer, man. Come on. Clothes only make the man if you're interviewing at a law firm or working for the mob."

"The same face, too."

Now I'm standing. "Okay, do I still love you and hate my brother?" Do I still have a relationship with my sister? Is my dad still dead? The same heart, do I have that?"

His arms cross, making his muscles look bigger than we both know they are. "Maggie thinks so."

"Don't tell me that."

"She loves you, Jim."

"Stop it." You asshole.

"We all do."

Something cracks in me like frozen glass, and I have a half second to remember this is what it's like to snap, clenching my fists into little balls of vitriol, teeth clamped behind the butt of the cigarette and making a grinding noise that drags through my skull. I grab Sonny by the shirt, loose tobacco falling out and dotting it with ash.

"We all love you, Jim."

"Will you fucking listen to me?" The old violence kicks up, motor oil and turpentine in my mouth, and I go down before I've even gotten started. New Sonny's right cross distinctly resembles Old Sonny's. The laminate is cool and calm under my back.

Well. At least these two things are familiar.

Just as I'm ready to get up and lose it completely, I hear Margaret saying this isn't me, this sad and angry thing.

I don't believe it, but everything drops out of me anyway, leaving me hollow and sad.

"Maybe you're right." His eyes stare down at me through defeat. "I'm sorry. I'm pushing too hard."

I rub my jaw and check that we didn't attract the attention of an orderly.

"And maybe I need to listen better," he says and offers a hand, helping me up. "Maybe you really aren't the same guy I knew."

I throw out the rest of the cookies after he leaves.

My apartment is the definition of miserable. At long last, I'm deemed no threat to myself or others, a psychiatric diagnosis that proclaims I'm essentially just a grumpy, delusional asshole who's allowed to live at home again. It's not a shock that I have an apartment, but the one they direct me to is too clean, even with the layer of dust it's collected, the edge of every cabinet and corner razor-sharp. Even the bookshelves and chairs are all knife-point angles unobstructed by debris. I remind myself not to trip, to hit something on the way down and bleed out, my body waiting for a neighbor to notice the smell.

The walls are worse than the furniture. Pictures hang on each, but the frames are spaced too far apart between gulfs of off-white nothing, the art itself just dementia-looking vomits of color without shape or form. This guy's apartment may be too tidy, but his art's too much of a fucking mess.

My place, the walls are heavy with pictures I took. I never thought of myself as much of an artist. Most of my photography jobs are for pay, either for newspapers, capturing culture or local life, or for private individuals—all varying levels of unsavory. These latter always need snaps of spouses dirtying roach motel sheets with someone they shouldn't be or need leverage on. It's all blackmail, but what do I care? While I don't frame any of those pictures, some of them are my favorites, real in a way nothing else can be. And even the other stuff, still life shots or portraits of interesting people, studies of the urban skyline, has been rendered more notable for its absence in this godforsaken wasteland of an apartment. Maybe I'm more of an artist than I gave myself credit for.

The answering machine is full of messages—67 of them, if the blinking number is to be believed. I push the button out of morbid curiosity, thumbing through doctors' appointments, dental checkups, and a host of hang-ups. The rest are mostly well-wishes from a pack of strangers, insultingly religious, and I'm simultaneously annoyed and bored. Once I can't take anymore, I press down the **delete** button and hold it for two seconds to put these out of my misery.

"Cal, it's me, are you—"

Marie's voice.

What the blue Christ?

I'm quick as lightning taking my finger off the button, but it's too late. The message, and all the ones I hadn't listened to, are gone.

"No no no no," I say out loud, to God, to the Devil, to the screaming void, but none of them are listening.

I spend 20 minutes trying to find an undo button, and another 20 pacing the too-clean floor. I move between desks that should be cluttered with papers, a shelf that should be loaded with camera film, corners that should be piled high with newspapers and manila envelopes stuffed with pictures of naked people fucking each other, asking myself if what I heard was real.

I remember the pictures of Marie's loser boyfriend and his side piece. He was just some off-brand mob fuck and I thought she'd leave him for me, but she got pissed instead, told me I was being possessive, that it was over. Now I think it might have just been to put distance between us, to try to save me from what was coming, but I was wrecked. Drunk every night, paying no attention, and it turns out even a low-end goon can work up the wherewithal to kick in a door and put a bullet in one of his girlfriend's ill-advised dalliances.

Did I ever matter? Was she somehow trying to get through to me from wherever she was now? Did I fuck up the only chance I'd had for answers so far? Was it just Margaret leaving some desperate message, a voice that just happened to have the same tone as Marie, the same lilt?

I smash the answering machine against one of the most hideous paintings on my way out of the apartment. I don't bother to lock the door.

There's no day I don't dream of that city that isn't a dream, but even aside from Marie, the food is what I miss the most. The food in this town is shit, and nowhere more so than our corner diner. I'm staring at a chicken-fried steak with a side of fries, but what I really want is Joe Cheng's chow mein, Hong Kong-style with the kitchen sink in it, the craving gnawing at my insides.

But there is no Joe Cheng, at least not here. I looked in three phone books, called a dozen operators, went to the library and researched. No such animal as Joe Cheng's New China Restaurant anywhere on the eastern seaboard. "New China better than Old China," he always joked, and he laughed, that man who never was.

I can feel someone watching me poke at my slab of gravy-laden meat, soggy and dead on the plate. I know who it is without looking. "Margaret, please. Why won't you leave me alone?"

She sits down. "I just want to talk."

"It won't change anything."

"I don't know that, and you don't either. Ever hear of a self-fulfilling prophecy?"

I stick a bite of food in my mouth, rolling it around, teeth reluctant to chew.

"I'll listen if you just want to tell me about it," she says. "About where you were, I mean. Your such-and-such-a-time, such-and-such-a-place."

My jaw limps around a mountain of gristle.

"Maybe if you just tell someone," she says, "really talk."

"You won't like it if I do."

"Fine, then I won't."

I push my plate back and signal the waitress for another beer with a raised hand, two fingers held together, thumb out. I do this unconsciously, but I wonder which version of me originated it. I already know which one appropriated its use as a flare gun, firing it nightly into stormy skies, waiting for waitresses and bar girls to throw me a lifeline. "You look like her," I say. "I mean mostly."

"The other woman?"

You're the other woman. "Marie."

The waitress sets down my beer and Margaret orders a coffee.

"You talk like her too," I tell her. "Say some of the same things, have some of the same little mannerisms."

"Did it ever occur to you that you might have been dreaming about me?"

Every possibility has occurred to me, but they all fail under the weight of what I know is real. If it's like the docs said and I was asleep in the cocoon of a long coma, then God got it wrong. Woke up the dream, not the dreamer. "Similarities aside, it wasn't you." I light up and drain half my glass. "You're a doppelgänger at best."

Her eyes soak into the counter, spongy with grief, and this is how I know she's different. She's gentle and sensitive. I can make sense of her. She's everything that's unexciting about a woman, all the things that make her worth pursuing but leave you with no desire for the pursuit.

"I'm sorry, I didn't mean it like that."

"I'm afraid you did," she says, getting up to leave.

"Wait." I grab her elbow. "Look, I really am sorry. If you think it would make you feel better to listen, then I'll tell you."

We tried this before. In the hospital, I tried with everybody, and they stopped listening, one by one, as soon as it got too big. When I didn't just believe it too much but could remember more than I should have been able to, could tell them about the smell of the pavement, the sleep at the bottom of the bottle, the tastes of food and women they tell me I never tasted... They want to divorce me from my life. They want to keep me here so I can't go back, but if I'm ever going to escape this booth, this shitty diner, this city, I need an ally. You and me at least have that in common, Cal, I think. We're both too pathetic to do it alone.

"We can try again," I tell her.

From the hurt on her face, I know it is the wrong choice of words, but she sits, pulls out and lights a cigarette.

"Your mother wouldn't like that."

She blinks. "You remember my mother?"

Shit. The wrong thing again. "No, sorry, I didn't mean—"

She shakes her head. "It's all right."

"I mean I might remember. If I saw her. I do recall things, almost like déjà vu, but it's like they're trying to fly to me on paper airplanes in a rainstorm."

"Ever the poet." She smiles.

I was never a fucking poet. "I thought you didn't smoke, anyway?" I ask.

"Been putting off starting."

Just what Marie would have said; which is of course exactly what this girl's after, why she's trying to be something she isn't. She'd probably put on fishnets and pay for a cheap room if I wanted, would probably do anything I asked her. But there's nothing to ask for. Marie did it all for me already, tea candles and incense at midnight rendezvouses in strange rooms, never the same one twice. I don't want any of that on this empty half of the divide.

Marget waits for me, trying not to cough from the smoke and give away who she isn't. Fine, then.

I talk her out of this backwater Texas dream, into the big streets and narrow skies of my real life. I tell her about all my old haunts: bars, brothels, billiard rooms, the beautiful, inspired awfulness of the city's human heart. I tell her about why that life was objectively so much worse than the one I woke into, and how the better things in this one all turn to flies in my mouth. I tell her about Marie, how we met, fell in, fell apart. How I died in the drink, laughing through vomit, heart gone to a dead stop in a pile of back-alley garbage, which is the last thing I remember after getting shot and falling off my own balcony. I tell her how I woke up in the hospital on her end of things, where everyone wants me to believe my life was a lie born from delayed airbag deployment. They'd even shown me the remains of the car.

"Maybe you're psychic." She's three beers in and slurring. Her cigarettes are starting to look more comfortable in her mouth, between her fingers. "Maybe what you saw was the future, not a different person. Maybe it was me and we finally got out of here like we always said we would. Maybe we grew up."

"Maybe. But that woman still left me, remember."

"So maybe I'm a second chance."

Looking at her parted lips, it's a tempting thought. "Margaret, it's not—"

"Call me Maggie, like you used to."

"Maggie, then. But you're not her, okay?"

"Fuck you. Why can't I be?"

"Because she was someone else and I don't love you."

"You did, once."

"I loved Marie."

"Who looked like me." She takes my hand in hers. My other is on her knee. "Can't you just— I don't know, wait for me to catch up to her?"

"If you wait for the past, you'll be waiting forever, because it never shows up."

She gets up and sits next to me, the booth cushion rudely squeaking, making the motion comical. She's nearly on my lap but doesn't hear the whole bottle of pills I swiped from the clinic rattle in my jacket pocket, doesn't hear the darkness in my voice that seeps in from what I'm thinking of doing with them. She puts her palm on my cheek.

"Do you think I'm crazy?" I ask. Maybe that's all I want, the reassurance that someone thinks it's possible I am who I think I am.

"No, Cal, I don't." She leans in close, her breath sour with hops and smoke. Her lips envelope mine, just as warm and soft as I remember. Maybe it's just cheap diner beer in quantity, but the moment feels charged, arcane, tapped into a conduit that moves beyond us. A pathway I could step onto, pulling Maggie with me.

I finger the pills in my pocket, wondering if the switch could work both ways. If death could take us somewhere else from here, too. "Did you call my apartment?" I ask. "Leave a message?"

"When?"

"I don't know. Before I moved back in, I guess."

She shakes her head. "Not since the accident. Why?"

"No reason."

She kisses me again, and my hands are on her thighs, against my better judgment. The feeling of energy grows, a blue fire stretching between this world and the next. She brushes her hands against my pants and pulls away from what she finds, a look of mock surprise beneath the extra makeup she's put on. Her eyes shine through it like exploding stars.

We get up and she takes my hand, pulling me toward the bathroom. My other hand is still in my jacket pocket, wrapped around the orange prescription bottle, its white top like a snowcapped mountain over a sunset. I feel the pull of relentless gravity from below the horizon, a darkening view like the one beyond my window into the clinic courtyard, and I wonder how much I can salvage of what's left of the sun.

See, I have this idea about what's right, a kind of perfect clarity of contrary vision. But not a vision, because you can't breathe one the way I did, walk in it as if underwater, drowning every time you open your mouth. It never leaves you because it's who you are; in such and any time, such and any place. So, you keep your eyes locked to that burning on the horizon. You sit and wonder if any of the wrong things—wrong girl, wrong space, wrong guy with the wrong intentions—will ever become the right ones.

"Come here," she says, pulling me through the door. "I'm going to show you things you won't believe."

I grip the bottle in my pocket, and—for the first time since waking up—I'm starting to think I might be able to return the favor.

Author Bio

 @MichaelJRiser

Cali editor Michael J. Riser has fiction and poetry that have appeared in *Despumation* and *Sheepshead Review*, as well as the print anthologies of *Pantheon Magazine* and *Solarcide*. Recently, his flash piece, "Observance," was picked up by *Coffin Bell*, about two men shooting the shit about what life is and isn't outside a haunted house, the least of their problems. More from Riser can be found at Bookruptcy.com.

Ramblers, L.B.C.

By Nolan Knight

The suitcase slid out Jesse Brinkley's grip and slapped concrete—heatwave forcing her to unbutton a burgundy flannel, exposing breasts bound by tape under a heather-gray beater. Couldn't remember from her youth the last time Long Beach was under such a magnifying glass. Should've paid the five-spot and caught that airport shuttle. Hell, when Stan said he'd pick her up, didn't realize it'd require a map. She'd been walking a good mile now, sweat bombing her brow. She swiped some with a palm and ran it through her auburn flattop, spraying salty mist about the shoulders.

Few more blocks, and she saw Stan's Chrysler New Yorker idling curbside, its bone exterior now ailed with osteoporosis. The driver's door creaked, and Stan launched out, pounding the roof with a fist. She knew he wasn't going to come take her bag. Big brothers were like that. He looked frailer than usual, nearly 40, six-foot, slicked caramel hair—a walking crayon since kindergarten. By the way his head held steady, she could tell he was straight these days.

"How's it going, Jess?"

"I'm back here, ain't I?"

"Thought that's 'cause you missed me. They run outta pussy in Austin, or somethin'?"

She scoffed, tossing her bag onto the back seat—the beast's vinyl interior slick as a killer whale. "Thanks for swooping me up, dickhead."

"Yeah, yeah—don't act surprised. You know I hate airports. Cops. Dogs. People."

"Would've hailed a cab."

"Saved you some cash then. You're welcome. Get in. Late for a hot date."

Here we go, she thought, sliding inside. Could use a coffee and bear claw from Bartha's right now...

Before her door could shut, Stan tore down Cherry Ave., engine louder than airplanes dropping out of the sky.

Jesse leered upon Signal Hill oil derricks put up a hundred years ago, each perfectly humping the Earth: an old whore gone numb. The New Yorker hit the crest of the hill, windshield beaming a coastline peppered with steel cargo ships. Early morning fog trapped Catalina Island. She opened the glovebox in search of smokes.

"I quit—a ways back."

"For shame, Stanley. Nobody likes a quitter."

"I can make a stop—but I wasn't kidding about being late."

"Where we headed?"

"Alamitos Beach."

Jesse thought of the last time she smelled the Pacific, wiggled fingers in hot sand. "I can wait. Cut back myself. Why'd you stop?"

"Doctor said it wasn't helping Johnny's COPD—me filling the apartment with secondhand smoke."

Uncle Johnny was the real reason Jesse had returned, although she didn't want Stan to know. A girlfriend of hers had run into Johnny at a bus stop and e-mailed her of his health woes. Had a hunch he was in decline, but the extent of which she hadn't a clue. From what she'd heard, he didn't have much time. If she'd called Stan and told him she was coming home to help, he would've denied everything. A Big Man, thinking he was in control of the chaos around him. To Stan, the world was only as cruel as you allowed it.

"How's Johnny doing?"

"Has his spells. One doctor said dementia. Johnny says, 'Senior moments.' But every doc so far has their own diagnosis—they're running businesses, after all. I'm trying my best to support him. Times are tough, but nothin' I can't handle. Don't leave him alone anymore either. This neighbor helps keep an eye on him when I'm at work. Checks in throughout the day."

"What are you doing for work these days?"

"Work?" Stan grinned as he pulled into the beach's parking lot, cruising into a slot apart from other vehicles. He reached into the center console and removed a pair of binoculars. "I'm on shift right now actually. Here." He handed her the scope. "Follow me."

Sunrays blasting through holes in his bedroom curtains weren't to blame for Johnny's startled awakening: The wild parrots were back amongst dead palm trees, fighting and fucking—reminding him of youthful summer nights. 70+ years in this city, and he couldn't remember the first time he'd heard or seen the devils; one day, like some burning bush, they'd just miraculously appeared. Today, their riotous squawks had him enraged, putting the kibosh to a dream where he was drowning in a harem of beauties. He sprung from bed and slid into corduroy slippers—his precisely-combed hair like liberty spikes on a punk. Muttering expletives, he threw on a sweater and headed outside.

As always, the moment his front door creaked, soon did the neighbor's, directly across. Cliff Bengston was a retired civil stooge whose only contribution to any conversation they'd ever had consisted of sports or the weather. Johnny's grimace didn't deter his stout neighbor, often shirtless in boxers, his rubbery nipples warmed by a novelty mug that steamed with green tea.

"Mornin', Johnny. Grabbing breakfast?"

Johnny's eyes rolled. "*Yeah*, in my slippers an' PJs. Get real, man."

"Any big plans today, then? We're both on the back nine—can't be wasting any more sunsets, am I right?"

"Wrong. Didn't you hear?"

"What's that?"

"I'm gonna live forever, motherfucker."

Cliff smiled.

"Anyway, I'll see ya. Gotta get a move on, man. Need a fresh cut today. Been too long."

Cliff took a slurp, admiring what little hair Johnny had left. "Which barbershop you headed—"

The parrots ignited in frenzy. They both peered into the trees.

Johnny belted, "Jesus fucking Christ."

"Can't shoot 'em, John. There's laws."

"What about poison?"

"They're annoying, I agree. But, they are majestic."

Johnny's stare bounced back to Cliff, his neighbor still admiring those green cocksuckers. "Fancy yourself one-in-the-same, Cliffy?"

Cliff choked tea.

"Come on, man. Help me gather some rocks to pluck these bastards."

Jesse gazed through lenses at a glittery sea, devoid of waves and seagulls. A pair of paddleboarders pushed themselves up the coast, laughing at each other, soaking in sunrays before heading back to normal lives. "So, what am I looking for again?"

"Just make sure those jerks stay in the water." Stan fiddled a plastic wedge into the top doorjamb of a vehicle, some import—the only car in the lot with a board rack atop. He slid a long, thin antenna down through the wedge's crease to press the electronic lock button. In seconds, the door was open, and he was rifling through the interior's guts. On the backseat, he found 32 bucks in a wallet and a three-quarter wetsuit. "How we doin'?" He exited, slamming the door, removing leather gloves.

"They're still out there."

He walked back to the Chrysler and opened its trunk.

Jesse caught wind and followed. The trunk harbored a slew of tools and stolen merch. Stan neatly folded the wetsuit in a corner, then began sifting through a bin filled with cellphone parts and DVDs.

"Who the hell buys DVDs anymore, Stan?"

"Those aren't stolen, alright? They're mine. Fingerprints Music gives me store credit for 'em—keeps me in good tunes."

"Used cell parts?"

"I got a guy, sells at the Harbor College Swap Meet—he kicks me a few bucks for 'em." He pulled out a ream of stickers, all reading **KOOKS, GO HOME!** "Here we go." He caught her odd stare. "Some shitheads in Huntington started putting these on cars to keep inlanders from poaching their break. Can buy 'em at any surf shop."

"What do you need them for?"

"Scapegoats." He peeled one off, slapped it on the windshield, then flicked open a pocketknife to slash all four tires. Jesse waited inside the car. Stan cranked the ignition, smile washing from his face once his eyes met hers. "Don't give me that look."

"Couldn't just rob the bastards—had to pull some bullshit."

"Honey, that wasn't for nothin'. Where's the closest tire store 'round here?"

"Andy's."

"That's right. Fucker throws me a sawbuck for each tire he sells out this lot. You've been gone way too long, missy. I'm hustling on levels you never dreamed." He recounted the bills from the wallet score. "Now...can I buy you breakfast?"

"Bartha's?"

"No donuts, Jess. Somethin' with sustenance."

"Long as they have coffee."

"A'course."

The Potholder Café sat at the corner of Broadway and Euclid. On weekends, it had a line down the block, but weekdays like today were spotted by locals. Pictures filled the walls with folks holding **Eat at The Potholder** signs all over the world. As kids, it was their favorite breakfast spot. Johnny used to take them twice a week. They entered and sat at the counter. Sounds of crisp newspapers and percolating coffee stirred the brain. A dead-eyed waitress approached with two mugs. The moment she slid both before them, the sight of Jesse brightened her day.

"Jesse Brinkley?"

"In the flesh."

"My gosh, how long has it—"

"Six years."

"Is that all? Feels like a decade."

Stan: "Hey, Donna. Lemme get that Chorizo Scramble—"

"Hold on. I'm catching up with your sister. So, where you been this whole time?"

"All over, really. Brooklyn. Denver. Austin."

"I hear Austin is killer."

"It can be." Jesse thought of the reason she'd gone there: a girl, naturally. That's what initially brought her out of Long Beach—sent her reeling across America. Six long years, zero lessons learned—new love intoxication, a terrible drug. "How are the kids?"

"Well, me and Bo divorced, but you prolly knew that. Yeah, I'm seeing his brother now, Mikey—we get the kids during the week. They're in middle school—can you believe it?"

Jesse smiled, stomach grumbling. "I'ma take the Barroom Eggs, please…with sourdough."

Donna pulled a pad and pen out her apron, expelling a sigh once their conversation terminated.

Stan placed his order and took a pull off his coffee, marveling at Donna's curly hair—like shit-brown bubble wrap cascading out a scrunchie.

The waitress tacked their ticket to the order wheel.

Stan eyed the girl's poutiness. "Didn't you steal Donna's boyfriend sophomore year?"

"I didn't steal him. They were on hiatus. I was just…finding myself." Still searching.

"Better make sure she doesn't spit in your eggs."

"You kidding? She knows I'd break her fucking jaw."

"Ain't childhood grand? That's the perk about living in one place your whole damn life."

"What's that?"

"Never have to grow up."

Jesse smirked, eyeing Donna, feeling sorry for the girl. She was glad to have left for a spell. Only way to truly see one's hometown—its lousy, brittle bones…

A busser topped their fourth and fifth mugs of coffee as they dug into slices of apple pie (topped with cheddar) for dessert. Before the young man could return to dish-gathering, Stan questioned him through a mouthful.

"Hey, bud. You guys got a lost an' found? Friend a mine left some sunglasses at a booth here, other day."

The kid nodded, retrieving a cardboard box from beneath the counter. He placed it before him and returned to work. Jesse watched as Stan licked his fingers before rifling through the treasure chest, pocketing two pairs of Ray-Bans and a lone skull earring.

"You done, Jess? I'm tappin' out."

She nodded, swiping a pack of Camels from the box.

Stan stabbed the skull into an empty slot on his left lobe. "Might have someone that could use that wetsuit—just up the block."

"Could you swing me by the apartment first? Wanna see Johnny, say hi."

"After. The old man sleeps in late these days. Don't worry. It'll only take a minute."

They both rose from their stools.

Stan dropped cash between their plates, then closely eyed the tip before taking back two dollars.

Spero's slaphouse casino was located on the second floor of a strip center off Willow. The average passerby would look upon its street windows to see gaudy neon featuring tarot cards and an ominous palm. Past/Present/Future. Body/Mind/Spirit. Spero was a huckster, and she sang the part. No one streetside would ever guess that a psychic center fronted a back room with card tables, craps, and a sportsbook. A low-key outfit for lowbrow clientele—and patronage was on an invite-only basis. Johnny being Johnny, he was always welcome. The entombed stairwell pulsed in purple as Johnny climbed through the glow to a door, reading **Madam Spero** in chrome filigree.

Four locks unlatched before the door opened, expelling sharp chamomile incense.

Johnny smirked.

The woman on the other side of the door was young and slender with a light-skinned complexion. Fake eyelashes fluttered under a tight afro and vibrant headband. "I've been expecting you, Johnny."

"I know you were," he said. "Cappy dealing tonight?"

Spero returned to her table with tarot cards splayed before a large crystal. "You know he is, dear. That's why you're here."

"He's my rabbit's foot, baby. And today's the day I make good in this life."

"Whatever you say, old man." She hit a buzzer under the table, unlatching a far metal door.

Baddeley's Pourhouse was a neighborhood bar on Broadway, just west of Redondo. Hell, the whole damn block was flocked with dives, this one just happened to open at 9AM, not 6 like the others. Jesse sucked down a Camel, pumping nicotine into her system. Gave a cringe once she realized where they were headed, adjusting a pair of Stan's new Ray-Bans on the bridge of her nose. Used to love the place—back when her ex, Shekita, tended bar. Many a night were spent at the pool table, pounding free booze and popcorn while screaming at the Lakers. Jesse hadn't been back since Shekita broke it off (seven years and change). They were together for nine months, the longest relationship she'd ever had. The gal was gorgeous, too— smooth, dark features under tiny, pink dreadlocks. She missed hanging with her—those overnights at Bartha's, binging donuts and talking about how bright their future was...

Stan barged in as if he owned the joint, wetsuit over a shoulder, heading to a far table occupied by an obese Samoan. Jesse eyed the guy, wondering if he was stuck in his chair. She left Stan to his business and approached the empty bar with trepidation, not quite sure who had the Friday morning shift. It'd be awkward as hell if Shekita walked out, but Jesse almost willed it so. Where was she in a life without her Jesse?

The sight of a curvy bottle-blonde plastered with tattoos cut the tension. "Howdy, stranger."

Jesse gave a warm grin. "How's life, Maegan?"

"Been good, I guess. Searchin' for a man among a sea of boys. You're the last face I planned on seeing this morning."

"Just flew in."

"Where from?"

"Austin."

The blonde paused to write a note on her own palm. "What you drinkin'?"

"Screwdriver'd be nice."

"Vodka?"

"Well...or whatever."

"You back in here's a special occasion, momma. How's Grey Goose?"

"Perfect." Jesse turned to see Stan showing off the suit's various features. Couldn't imagine how this guy would ever get it around one of his legs. Had to be for his kid. She admired the broken juke, thinking about all the dance parties they'd had here. A note clung to it, reading, **I HAVE ISSUES.** Her drink thumped the bar, its hue downright clear. "How much?"

"This one's on me, sister."

Jesse raised her glass in cheers.

Maegan poured herself a tumbler of Dickel Bourbon and kicked it back. Before their glasses re-touched wood, Maegan said, "You know Shekita quit, right? Not long after you took off."

"No, I—that's not why I came in here."

"Yeah, she got her master's and took a new gig—one of those people that goes to bars and implements a business model to save the place. Could use her in here but we can't afford her." She pulled her phone from her back pocket. "Got her number though."

"Not a big deal. I just came in with my brother."

Maegan's eyes darted to the corner. "Thought I smelled something."

Stan approached with both arms up in surrender. "Maegan, my dear. I'll only be a second. Is it possible to buy my pal over there another vino?"

"Sure, but you gotta go—pronto. My boss comes in here and sees you, he's gonna shit."

Jesse turned to Stan. "What ya do this time?"

Maegan: "Wasn't what he did, more what he tried to pull on—well, you know her—Terry. They call her P-Hound."

"Yeah, I know her."

Maegan pointed to Stan. "This dunce walks in here, places a good...how many was it, dozen drinks on her tab?"

"It was like six—and she totally bought me the first round, Maeg, you know that."

"Anyway, your brother got caught with his hand in the cookie jar. Terry takes him out front and cleans his clock. Fucker collapsed in front of the door, creating a whole scene—most the randoms inside fled because of it. Ruined a perfectly good Saturday night."

Jesse nearly spit vodka. "That true, Stan? P-Hound laid you out?"

He gave a shrug. "Ah, come on. You know me, Jess... I ain't one to hit a lady."

Grins washed about their faces.

Maegan composed herself, cracking an airplane Sutter Home and pouring its "merlot" into a glass. "So, your brother's 86ed. This all happened last weekend." She handed the wine to Stan. "Finish up and get out. I'm telling you this as a friend."

He put a palm over his heart and headed back.

Maegan turned to her phone. "Here it is. You want her number?"

"Nah. I'd feel too weird. You still talk to her?"

"Every so often."

"Does she ever say anything…?"

"About you? No. Might be single though. She's well off too."

Jesse nodded into the dregs of her glass.

"You still on the far side of the law—with Stanley there?"

"Sometimes." Most the time. "Not as much, I guess."

"Heard about Johnny. I'm sorry."

"It's a shit situation. What can you do, right?"

"My grandpa had liver cancer too. Wasn't pretty."

Jesse paused, trying not to look perplexed.

Stan whistled in the distance, hoisting cash received for the wetsuit. "Ready, Jess?"

She stood and tossed a tip on the bar.

"Wait." Maegan came around, arms out for a hug. "Stay strong, sister. You know this city's got your back."

"Great catching up, Maeg. 'Til next time." She slid on her new shades.

Stan pounced back through the door. "Maegan, you guys got a lost an' found. My friend—"

"Get the fuck out!"

Jesse smirked, pushing her bro onto Broadway.

"Liver cancer? She said that?"

"Yeah."

"Well, the town will talk. I know one doctor mentioned something about jaundice. Maybe someone saw him a bit yellow and assumed. I mean, the whole city loves him—he was a regular at Joe Jost's for 50 fuckin' years. It's only natural they'd gossip."

"So, he doesn't have cancer?"

"No. Like I said, dementia, maybe. They're running tests as we speak. Who knows? Shit, ask him in a minute. I'm sure he'll tell you he's ship-shape." Stan parked the car before a tattered Beaux Arts box on Anaheim, one that housed tenants above fledgling retail. Rusted neon clung to its side, stating the place was a hotel in a past life. Jesse had never been here before, her departure prompting Stan and Johnny to downsize their living space. The beaten state of the brick structure sparked guilt. Their old home at least had charm, a '20s-built Spanish quadruplex in Belmont

Heights. To go from beachside to the Eastside was an aftershock Jesse would have to own.

They climbed the stairwell, careful not to kick a snoring vagrant. Stan jiggled a key into Unit D, and, with just the right touch, the door popped.

"Put some pants on, Johnny—you got company!" Stan fished through mail splashed about the dining room table.

Jesse surveyed the living room. It was much cleaner than she'd anticipated, the only real clutter being prescription vials strewn atop a wood-framed television. "You finally learned to clean up after yourself."

Stan eyed the room. "Nah, nah...I know a guy with one of those topless maid services, he lost a bet and *voilà*, now we have bare titties come vacuum every month." Without any sound resonating in the apartment, he went into the hallway, looking in Johnny's bedroom then smacking the bathroom door. "Come out, Johnny. Your niece misses you?" He wiggled the handle and found it unlocked, so he opened it.

Jesse caught the look on her brother's face. "What's the matter?"

Stan darted into his bedroom, then back to Johnny's. He stormed past Jesse and into the kitchen, before turning back to her. "He's not fuckin' here."

"Seven, winner!"

Johnny slapped his palms together, reeling in a well-deserved hot streak—the only player at the craps table. He'd come for blackjack, but the tables felt cold. He made an adjustment, attacking the dice with a measly 40 bucks, knowing damn well Stan would miss anything more from out his wallet. The kid owed him anyway; not like the money was clean either. What, just because he was ancient meant he had to stay cooped up 'til the reaper? Actually, he knew better: Stan's long con involved his ailing health, so he couldn't be on the streets with rosy cheeks. But he was done with all that, only hadn't told Stan yet that he was out the grift. And these winnings would soothe that wound, when he came home strapped with cash to the gills. Hell, this streak was so hot, they might just be rich forever.

A stout Filipino in a Nike tracksuit shot dice back Johnny's way with a rake.

Johnny picked them up with soft hands, as if cradling hardboiled eggs. "Cappy, I ever tell you about the time I wrestled Gene LeBell in the back room of Joe Jost's?"

"About a million times, Johnny."

Johnny blew on the dice. "Turns out you shit your own teeth when you swallow them, Cappy. Bet you didn't know that." He chucked the rocks and closed his eyes.

"11! Winner."

Johnny's fists punched the ceiling.

Cliff was in Unit E, directly across. Stan knocked twice before kicking the door. "Come on, Cliff! It's Stan. I can hear you in there." Two more kicks and the door swung, revealing a sausage-like man with black wisps about his skull.

"The hell, Stan? Was takin' a nap."

"Where's Johnny?"

"What? He ain't in there?"

"No, so where the fuck is he?"

"I dunno. I mean…he was there earlier."

"How much earlier? An hour? 15 minutes?"

"Couple hours."

"And he didn't say shit about goin' anywhere?"

"Listen, he prolly just went to grab a bite or something. It's lunchtime. Relax." His eyes went around Stan, focusing on the young gentleman with the flattop.

"That's my sister, Jesse. Jess—Cliff."

Cliff's eyes said, *Sister? Oh…*

Jesse: "Cliff, you sure my uncle didn't say anything peculiar earlier?"

"No, ma'am, just bullshitted. We chucked rocks at the parrots. Did mention he wanted a fresh cut though. Maybe he's at the barber?"

Stan: "What barber? He's got 50 hairs on his dome."

"How the hell should I know? Maybe he's gettin' a shave."

Before Cliff could shut the door, Stan and Jesse were halfway to the Chrysler.

Hours passed. They'd worked in concentric circles from the apartment, scoping for spinning barber poles, street to street. **Fades/Razorbacks/Syndicate**. Flashy names just to lop off hair. When Stan or Jesse went in, everyone knew Johnny—just hadn't seen him in ages. As dinnertime approached, they felt defeated, gazing out at bus stops and donut shops for any sign of their uncle. Stan circled through Retro Row, thinking there used to be a barber nearby but was mistaken. He parked in a metered slot across from the Art Theatre.

"We gotta eat. I'm fading, Jess."

She nodded, lighting another smoke off a cherried butt. Had to find Johnny before it got dark. Couldn't imagine him cold and hungry on the streets without his faculties. As Stan walked toward a Vietnamese restaurant, Jesse gazed out at the movie house, a team of revelers anxious to enter and catch some new flick. Ma used to take her and Stan there when they were kids—never went inside but dropped them off with a snack bag and enough coin to gain entry. They'd spend summer days at matinees while Ma went out copping free drinks at the V Room or downtown. They always asked her where she went but never got a direct answer. Jesse had learned most about life from fictional worlds: *Edward Scissorhands, Fried Green Tomatoes.* Could see Ma's stern face now, towering over her, holding Stan accountable for "her baby's safety" while she went on her jag. Stan creaking open the door startled her; he plopped inside, tossing a bánh mì sandwich on her lap.

"These are huge, so we're splittin' one."

The scent of lemongrass steak and jalapeños perked her up. She watched as Stan tore into his half, wiping his mouth with the back of a hand—same way he did with PB&Js when they were just two lost kids huddled inside that theater. Had they ever been anything else? "Thinking about Ma a bunch lately."

"Yeah. It is June."

She hadn't even thought of that, the anniversary of her death approaching 22 years. "Just wish she were around, you know?"

"She never would've made it."

"You don't know that."

"I'm positive. If it didn't happen to her then...she would've met up with some other jerk, then another... Eventually, one of 'em would've beat the life outta her. I say that with love too. She was who she was. Doesn't mean I love her any less."

"I wish things were different, is all."

"Who doesn't? Say she was still here, you want her to see what we've become? A hustler and a nomad. Gimme a fuckin' break. You play the shit hand you're dealt—make some bluffs—hope for the best."

Jesse took a small bite of bread, marinating in the cold reality of their world.

Beef shot from Stan's mouth. "Shit!"

The Chrysler roared to life.

"What is it, Stan?"

"Johnny wasn't going to get a haircut. He went to play cards."

"A fresh cut?"

"Of the deck."

"Where?"

"Spero's. I bet 20 bucks he's there. Son of a bitch. Hold yer ass."

The car swung a sharp U-turn from its parking spot, sparking car horns and middle fingers before it hauled up 4th.

"Seven! Out."

Johnny's gnarled fingers washed about his face, pretending this run was all a dream, from high to low in a matter of hours. He gazed at his remaining cash, a meager sum considering the amount he was up, well over a grand. Two of the twenties on the pile went back into his pocket, the original 40 he could slip back into Stan's wallet when the kid was asleep. Cappy tapped the rake before him, signaling that a bet must be made. Johnny nodded as the dealer swiped his last 60 dollars and shoved over dice. Johnny blew the rocks, closing his eyes and praying to a god he never once believed in.

"If I lose this, Cappy. You know what I'll be doing."

"Shitting teeth."

"You said it, man."

The dice bounced to an all too familiar crash, rumbling to a halt, snake eyes leering back at him.

Dusk kissed the treetops golden, turning their limbs into blackened bones. Stan pulled the New Yorker into an empty lot at Spero's rear—same one he'd wept in after losing three-grand on the Stanley Cup Finals, barely a year ago. Jesse surveyed the upstairs unit before following her brother inside. The entombed stairwell pulsed in purple hues, leading to a door reading **Madam Spero** in chrome filigree. Stan motioned for her to stay back on the stairs and let him do the talking. His knuckles hit the door in a cryptic rhythm.

Four locks unlatched before the door opened, expelling sharp chamomile incense.

Jesse tried to see who was inside but only heard a raspy voice.

"I've been…expecting you."

"Cut the shit, Spero." Stan stepped inside, whistling for Jesse to tag along.

The woman was younger than Jesse had imagined, reminded her of Prince—if he were a woman. She was seated at a table, tarot cards splayed about a large crystal. Propped to the stone was an iPad, spouting the nightly news.

"World's gone to shit, Stanley. I'm guessin' dat's why you here. Come to make another run?"

"Came for my uncle. Where is he?"

Her eyelashes pointed to a far door. "Was here earlier. Might've left. I dunno—just finished with a client. Go an' see for yourself. Cappy's back there. He'd know for sure. You know the rules doh: Dis new gal's gotta stay put."

Stan nodded to Jesse. "Be right back, 'kay?"

Spero pressed a button beneath her table, buzzing the door open.

Stan pounced through, a lazy clamor omitting until the door shut.

Jesse approached a chair beside the woman.

"Siddown, girl." Spero sparked a blunt. "What's yer name?"

"Jesse."

"Well, Jesse. What ya think? The world gone to shit?"

"You're the psychic, you tell me."

She inhaled in reflection. "No...it hasn't. Least not yet. All signs point to things getting much worse." She extended the blunt to her new friend. "This'll help us forget."

Jesse politely refused, eyeing that far door every few seconds.

Spero puffed away, the fingers on her right-hand strumming cards. She picked one up, blew smoke across it, then tossed it back onto the pile. "You're a rambler, huh?"

Jesse broke her trance on the door. "What?"

"You always moving?"

"I've been around."

"Searching for something, I suppose." Her eyes shrunk to slits. "But for what, is the question." She pinched another card, put it before her face, then tossed it away. She picked up another, stoking the blunt, rolling her eyes.

Jesse tried to ignore the woman, watching news footage of a car accident on the Hollywood Freeway. There were no fatalities, but traffic was at a standstill throughout Los Angeles: an entire city, trapped in time. She pulled out a Camel. "'Kay if I smoke?"

Spero shrugged, sliding her ashtray between them.

Jesse lit up, seething plumes out her nostrils.

"Can never leave this place, you know?"

"What place? Earth? No shit."

"Your hometown. No matter where you go in life...you always take yourself with you. That's the rub."

"Alright. I'm done talking. Please, let me just sit and wait for my brother. This whole situation is starting to freak me the fuck out—"

"*Shhhh.*" Spero took another card, flipping it for Jesse to see.

Wheel of Fortune.

"The wheel keeps on rolling—no matter what. A progression of ups and downs that could free us from the shackles of our past. Don't be scared, girl. Recognize the fantastical. Trust your instincts. You might just make it."

Jesse cashed her smoke and picked up the card, admiring odd symbols and imagery. Was hard to believe in such nonsense. Then again, comfort came with such trivial things. "Can I keep this?"

"For sure." Spero smiled. "Twenny dollars and it's yours."

As the card hit the table, Stan pounced through the far door, flanked by the legend himself.

The whole cruise home, Jesse was giddy, repeatedly hugging Johnny's shoulders from the back seat—smooching his saggy cheek. He looked the same as the day she left, thin hair slicked back into a silver helmet. Clean shaven, he smelled of Murray's Pomade. Clothes were clean and ironed. No labored speech or trouble concentrating. He seemed high in spirits, too, happy to see his girl. The opposite could be said for Stan, eyes like knives in the rearview, shaking his head.

Jesse accompanied Johnny upstairs to the apartment while Stan strolled the block to Tommy's Burgers. She turned on the lights as Johnny eased into the worn sofa like it was a hot bath. She filled two glasses with tap water and brought one over.

"Did you win anything?"

"You know me, honey. Always breaking even. What are you doing back here? Thought you were chopping cars out in Texas?"

"That didn't pan out. It's okay though, I'm here with you now."

A smile split his face. "Plan on staying this time?"

"For a stretch. Listen, you should've called Stan, or left a note where you were headed. Had us worried sick."

He looked like he wanted to say something but, "Didn't mean to startle you, hun," came out instead.

She sidled beside him on the couch, powering the TV. Searching channels, she noticed him gazing upon her. "What is it? I got something in my teeth?"

"Your face."

"Yeah."

"You finally grew into it." He placed a hand on her cheek, remembering her as a child.

She grabbed it, closing her eyes, holding it there.

Felt good to be home.

They were glued to an old episode of *Airwolf* when Stan came back, tossing the greasy bag onto the coffee table before charging into his bedroom without saying a word.

"Don't worry about him, Johnny. He's tired. We had a long day."

Johnny just grumbled, reaching for his supper that felt downright cold.

She talked into the night, catching him up on all that she'd seen the past six years. How she used to drink at Sophie's—his favorite spot in the Lower East Side—back when she and Rachel were a thing. Rachel was a sweetheart but too focused on becoming some great chef. So that ran its course when she met Ana at this punk show at Saint Vitus. Girl was a gnarly singer; Jesse toured part of the states as the band's merch gal, 'til the van broke down and the band broke up. She and Ana settled in Denver. But Ana was never able to hold a job, forcing Jesse into double shifts, bartending. She told Johnny about the morning their heat got turned off—first time she stared down at her sleeping lover and didn't see a great musician—but a world-class mooch. Then a girl she knew back in Brooklyn, Carly, hit her up from Austin. She didn't even leave Ana a note, just a stack of bills she would no longer pay. And Carly was cool, too. Least 'til she got drunk. Reminded her of Ma. After landing in the tank from a domestic dispute, Jesse knew she'd met another dead end. Never told Johnny of that e-mail she got about him. But he didn't need to know everything.

She replayed the entire conversation in her brain, feeling at ease with being home, nearly asleep on the couch. Hadn't felt such tranquility since counting stars, camping along the Colorado. Soon as she was set to dream, muffles down the hall startled her awake. The light was on in Johnny's room. Could hear Stan talking in high whispers. She approached with caution, eavesdropping their conversation.

"I'm saying it doesn't look right, Johnny. If we're gonna pull this off, you gotta play the damn part. Out hitting Spero's for the day—I mean, come on. Who's gonna believe that you're sick? And liver cancer?"

"Who said that?"

"It's out on the street, man. People are talkin'."

"What am I supposed to say when someone asks me then?"

"Be vague. I've been skirting around it, sayin' tests are being done, *blah, blah*. We're just starting to buzz the block. Next week, I'll set-up the GoFundMe page, and we'll figure out an ailment, okay?"

"I had it, Stan. I fuckin' had it all, man."

"Had what?"

"The score, kid. The whole enchilada, right there in front of me on the craps table."

"Who cares? We got a long con going—"

"Yeah, but it's too damn long for this old dog. Just too dang long. I'm tired—"

"Christ, you gotta be kiddin' me—you want out now? We're in too deep, Johnny."

"I'm out, kid. I had it all tonight on a small roll, and I can do it again. Just need to pony up somehow—"

Jesse pushed into the room, anger stewing in her eyes.

Johnny slumped on the bed.

Stan went into damage control. "Shit. Alright, Jess, hear us out."

"Just another bit, huh?" She focused on Johnny. "And you're in on it too? Friends 'round here have always been off-limits."

Stan sighed. "Don't start getting righteous on us now, Jess."

Johnny remained silent.

"Shame on both you. And fuck you, Stan!"

"Fuck me? You been slicing stolen cars since you were 17. We're both in the small-time, honey. Get it straight."

"That's different than this?"

"How so? Crime ain't crime?"

"Insurance pays out. People get another car. And I don't steal from locals, bilk friends of what they got. I know we're pieces of shit to this world, but all we have is what this city provides. You want to toss it all for what, some lousy bit?"

"I know how it looks, but this is a major score, Jess. Think of it as Johnny's retirement fund. He's been a staple in this city his whole damn life. We bank on him dying, ask for help with medical bills, take the city's loot and bail to Reno or Vegas. Rent us a nice pad, call it a day. No more petty hustles. Johnny can relax into old age. We can both have new lives. This is it. With or without you, Jess, this is the move."

"I want nothing to do with it."

Johnny: "Neither do I, hun."

Stan: "Where you gonna run to, Jess? You need us—you're one of us. That's why you're back in town."

"I came home because of what everyone told me about Johnny! I was scared, man! Another mark, I guess—"

Stan scoffed. "Please. You came back here 'cause you had nowhere else to run. All them bridges...burned."

"Maybe so. And now I ain't even got this pace no more." She darted into the living room for her boots and suitcase. "I might have nothin' now, but I prolly never had anythin' to begin with."

Stan's whiny plea for her to stay fell on deaf ears. She bolted, nerves sparking with each stair to the street before darkness swallowed her at the gutter.

That beachy breeze now had bite as Jesse lumbered up sidewalks, suitcase in hand, avoiding tweakers and creatures of the night. Police sirens added a soundtrack. She climbed aboard the first bus she saw, gazing out its window, contemplating the past 24-hours—the fantastic incidents she'd experienced.

Life: A wheel of fortune that scraped you to the bone.

The world was beginning to wake. She watched folks scurrying across front lawns and into cars, scrambling to office jobs, ready to grind, rotting through another shift. Everything became clear. Stan and she were still those kids in the Theatre—only difference was that Stan owned up to it, while she'd spent this whole time running from a life she was born to live. She ran from conflicts of identity, romance—family. After all, she was who she was: her mother's daughter.

Destiny was set. She could see that now, and it hit like a brick.

She took one final look at the neighborhood, zooming past Bartha's Donuts, imagining a better life—one she wouldn't know if it punched her in the goddamn mouth.

You always take yourself with you.

The bus careened into a new day—another cog in a wheel that just kept rolling, rolling, grinding her to the bone. Who gave a damn about tomorrows anyway?

Author Bio

@Nolan_Knight_

Californian **Nolan Knight** is a fourth generation Angeleno whose fiction has been featured in *Akashic Books, Thuglit, Crimespree Magazine, Shotgun Honey, Tough,* and *Needle.* He is a former staff writer for Los Angeles' biggest music publication, the *L.A. Record,* and resides in Long Beach. His novel, *The Neon Lights Are Veins,* "is a dope-fueled, gutter-punk odyssey through a gaudy nightmare version of L.A. With echoes of James Ellroy and Nathanael West," reviews Richard Lange, author of *Rovers, Dead Boys, Angel Baby,* and *The Smack.* Knight's first collection of short stories from 2008 to 2022 is *Beneath the Black Palms.*

Vonyetta Mosley's Marzipan Palace

By David Simmons

"These kids are all serial killers." Yuri closed the folder and placed it on the table. "So what? What would I want with that?"

"Spree killers," Eddie hissed. "Not serial killers. And technically not anything-killers. Not on paper."

"Fine. Spree killers. This benefits me how? Get me there. Lay it out for me in a way where I should feel whole."

Eddie squeezed his eyes shut, left hand shaking. It was fine. Everything was fine. He could explain it again. No big deal. "So, these two rival sets, they both have rappers that rep their shit and—"

"Sets? What is this 'sets'?"

Eddie could feel his blood pressure rising. "Gangs. Well, not gangs per se, but factions. Rival factions under the same umbrella, but enemies. It's hard to explain. They call each other their opps."

"Opps?" Yuri poured two fingers of Casamigos into a crystal glass. "What is this 'opps'?"

"Opps. As in opposition."

"Go on."

"These two factions have been killing each other since the '90s. I mean, their daddies and their daddies' daddies been killing each other. But now, the kids kill each other and make songs about it, dissing each other and making music videos where they say they're smoking on their dead homies. It's very disrespectful, Yuri."

Yuri killed the Casamigos. "This tastes like shit, you know? This disrespect, you say. I should care, why?"

"Because these diss videos get millions of views." Eddie let his selling point hang in the air. "Hundreds of millions of views. And they make new videos every week. The overhead is nothing. They're all just heavily FX-layered Final Cut bullshit, 9 or 10 of them with their shirts off in a one-bedroom apartment, waving around guns with hundred-round drums and infrared beams. They cost nothing to make, and these kids are making thousands off the monetized views. Hundreds of thousands. You need to get in on this, Yuri."

The two men sat in a corner booth in Vonyetta Mosley's Marzipan Palace, a frilly, antique-furnished joint inside a historic Tudor home in Downtown Silver Spring. It had a quaint, country inn atmosphere. Good brunch. A stone-and-brick wine cellar in the basement.

"The play," said Yuri. "Get to the play."

"Well," said Eddie, "the more they kill each other, the more views their videos get. You sign them under big 360 deals when their videos only have views in the hundred-thousands. So, you own all their shit. All their monetized YouTube views and subs. Give them a good advance to make it sweet. $80,000, $100,000, who cares?"

"I care," Yuri growled.

"Okay, but hear me out. You take out life insurance policies on these kids. You can do this. Put it in the contracts. For fuck's sake, Yuri, they know they're not gonna live past 21, they say it in their songs. It's not crazy. It's not far-fetched to have them sign papers for that. And you get a big payout when they die, sure, but you're still making money off their views after they die. That shit is forever, Yuri. Endless passive income. And it's all legal."

Yuri clipped the end of a Davidoff. "It's nefarious, no?"

"Fuck nefarious," said Eddie, slamming his fist on the table. "It's called key person insurance and companies take policies out on their big players all the time. Some will finance their nonqualified deferred compensation plans with COLI because of the preferential tax shit. All the Fortune 500 companies do this. It's completely legal and they're already killing each other anyway. We're just getting paid."

"Eddie, my boy, settle down, you piece of shit." Yuri put flame to the end of a cigar. "Did you know that the house this restaurant is located in was built in 1930?"

Eddie sighed. "Okay."

Yuri motioned to the waitress. "You don't appreciate history, Eddie."

The waitress, tall with jet-black hair pulled up in a messy bun, walked up to the booth and smiled with her mouth closed.

"Darling. The heart of palm. I want it. The heart of palm, get it for me."

"Like, what we put in the salads?"

"Yes, yes!" Yuri reached into his jacket and came back with a stack of blue hundreds, waving them around and slapping them on the table. "Just slice up as much heart of palm as you have and bring it to the table. I don't care about price. No number is too high for Yuri."

The waitress frowned. "Sure, I mean, it wouldn't even be that expensive. I can definitely do that."

Yuri flared his nostrils at her. "Then go."

"So back to this money," said Eddie. "The thing is, we've already lost the opportunity on a few good ones. This one kid, Ogun37thStreet, he's got like 150 million views on each of his videos."

Yuri sneered and held his hand out, palm up. "How much?"

"150 million views is $97,000. That's nearly $100K per video."

"No," said Yuri. "It's $97,000."

The waitress came back with a plate of heart of palm. The off-white ringlets looked like squid.

"So, this Ogun37thStreet, he is looking for financial backing?" Yuri unfolded a napkin and placed it neatly on his lap.

"No," Eddie said, shaking his head and craving nicotine. "Ogun37thStreet is dead. Ogun37thStreet was killed two weeks ago. Now LosWorld TY is dissing him. He's going at the whole 37th Street set. He's got a music video with over 100 million views right now called *Smokin' On Ogun*. The video has only been up for a couple days. 100 million, Yuri. The streets are saying that LosWorld Ooski is the one that killed Ogun. LosWorld Ooski is LosWorld TY's brother. And here goes TY, making a song where he's rapping about how it must have felt for the life to leave Ogun's body. These guys are rapping about pissing on graves and then shooting music videos of actually doing it. It's all very disrespectful, Yuri. And this disrespect, it makes so much money."

"It's death, Eddie. The more death, the more money. You are no innovator. As if I have never sold death before. What do you get from this?"

Eddie watched the fat piece of shit dig into the absurd mountain of heart of palm and felt ill.

"You look green, Eddie, my boy," said Yuri. "You've been playing with your nose again?"

"No, man. I'm good."

"You sure, my boy? Not back to sucking the proverbial glass dick either, Eddie?

Eddie felt his bowels clench. "No, Yuri. I don't mess with any of that shit anymore."

"Did you know that heart of palm is the warrior's fruit?"

Eddie felt the snake uncoil inside his solar plexus. "I did not know that."

"People think that the triceratops was a grazing animal, but its jaw structure implied otherwise. A beak, you understand me? It had a beak. Like a fucking parrot. A beak. And like parrots, the jaw is for shredding plant material or, in the case of the triceratops, palm trees."

Eddie rolled an unlit cigarette between his fingers. He didn't know how much more of this performative bullshit he could take.

"So, you see," Yuri continued, "the heart of palm is the warrior's fruit."

"I don't get it," said Eddie.

"Because the first men who ate heart of palm had to fight the triceratops for it!" Yuri leaned back and roared out laughter, long, bass-filled barks that sounded like *hargk*.

Hargk! Hargk Hargk!

Eddie hated this rich idiot. He gave it his all. "Yuri, there's no taxes paid on death benefits with company-owned life insurance."

Yuri shook his head. "Oh, Eddie. How much?"

"I want 20% on every life insurance policy for every rapper I get for you."

"Okay," said Yuri through a mouthful of heart of palm.

"Okay?" Eddie was surprised.

"One condition, Eddie." Yuri wiped his mouth. "I take out this, how you say, key person insurance policy on you."

Weeks later, back at Vonyetta Mosley's Marzipan Palace, Eddie was sitting in the same booth, but with the young rapper from Southwest who went by LosWorld TY.

"When I'mma see this money?" asked TY. "That's all I wanna know."

"Listen," said Eddie. "Everything's gonna be fine."

TY shook his head so that his locks fell in his face. "You not hearing me though. Three weeks is crazy. I need this motherfucking money now, you understand me?"

Eddie brought out a burgundy jewelry box. He passed it to TY. "Open it, man. It's from our investors."

TY opened the box. "It's a watch. So what?"

"TY, my boy," said Eddie, shaking his head, "do you know what this is?"

The rapper sucked his teeth.

"This is an Audemars Piguet. A Royal Oak. Check out the 18-carat gold Tapisserie dial. Baton hands, the finest automatic movement. 416 handmade, hand-finished parts. You don't hear a tick, am I right?"

"You wildin'." TY closed the jewelry box and pushed it across the table.

Eddie swallowed. "So, we're looking good on that new visual. Everybody loves '37thStreetK4L.' It's like, the views are going up and the comments and likes match the views, so there's never any question as to the authenticity of those views and—"

"Yo, Eddie." TY took out a neon orange pill bottle and cracked it open. "You questioning my views, folk?"

"No, never, not that," Eddie said. "TY, my man, please. I'm attesting to the validity of your YouTube views! Other artists will purchase views, so then their likes and subscriber numbers won't match the views because the views aren't coming from real people."

"Don't you think I know that?"

Eddie smiled. "I do, I do. TY, please, forgive my indiscretions."

The rapper swallowed a blue 30mg OxyContin and put away the pill bottle. "You way too slippery, Eddie. Real backdoor type."

"I'm a slippery fuck, yes." Eddie nodded in agreement. "But I'm a slippery fuck that knows how to make money and right now I'm under contract as your slippery fuck to make you money, cause that's the only way I make money, you understand? I'm only here to make you rich. And I'll backdoor anybody if that means it'll get you to the top faster."

TY was tearing up his plate of thinly sliced tenderloin. "Yo, this food is pretty good."

"It's called steak tagliata."

"Whatever," said TY, through a mouthful of food. "It's weird, but it's aight."

Eddie looked around the restaurant. "Did you know that the house this restaurant is located in was built in 1930?"

"Boy, I don't give a fuck about no type of shit. Fuck wrong with you?"

Eddie nervously laughed. "I guess you're not a fan of history."

"You better have my money, Eddie, that's on the set, I'm not playing with you. Get me my money. I don't want no fucking watch. A watch is crazy. I know what an AP is. I'm not pressed about no AP. You act like I've never seen ice. Get me my money." LosWorld TY walked out of the restaurant.

In the overflow parking lot of Vonyetta Mosley's Marzipan Palace, Yuri smoked 2-MMC in the backseat of a black Rolls Royce Cullinan. In the seat next to him was a Chaldean woman, impossibly long legs, pointy knees pressed up against her chin.

"Once there was a girl," he said. "She was so young, truly a girl, but she became something different after they killed her brother. They named the village after her brother. His name became a battle cry. She made sure of this. Their enemies shit all over his name, the name of the village. She killed all of them." Yuri passed the vape pen to the woman.

She put the pen to her lips and pressed the button. Her long black hair reflected light.

Yuri smiled through the blue cloud of smoke. "This girl–this warrior woman–was afraid of no one. She would ride into the neighboring village and attack them every night, at the exact same time. Why would she do this? Endanger herself by moving like clockwork, no? She had no care because she had no fear. She truly lived without fear. They killed her for her fearlessness. When you have something they do not, they will try to take it from you. And when they cannot take it from you, they will kill you in the process of trying to. This is the way of people, no?"

The woman's pupils dilated. Against her dark brown irises, they made her eyes look like black saucers, swirling in the blue glow of the fiber-optic starlight roof. "If you cannot hold onto something, you do not deserve to have it. Is this not what you believe, Yuri?"

Yuri smacked his belly twice and smiled. "Of course, I believe this. I taught you this, I am telling this story how it was told to me. This woman was killed in the most heinous of ways. This is not unorthodox, of course. It is surprising that her surviving family members were not held responsible for her actions, because her actions, too, were truly heinous. So, they killed this woman and her village renamed itself after her, not the name of her departed brother. Change is inevitable, no? I need you to reach out to your brothers for me. Can you do this?"

The Chaldean woman smiled. "Yuri, this is not a problem."

Yuri reloaded the vape with another cartridge of cathinone-propylene glycol-mix and nodded. "Make it so. Eddie and his little friends are taking too long."

Eddie couldn't believe it. The stars had aligned.

"Shoot for the moon," Eddie's dearly departed father used to say. "And if ya don't make it, at least you'll land amongst the stars."

The man was an idiot.

He didn't know that the stars were an impossible distance from the moon and that 12 out of a 15-year stretch is what you get for felony credit card fraud in the state of Maryland.

But Eddie's stars had all the way aligned. LosWorld TY had crossed the threshold. That invisible barrier that bars a rapper's ability to make it to that upper echelon of success. That place where Lil Baby and Cardi B and Drake and Future live. LosWorld TY had made it there. And it happened overnight.

The rapper Kodak Black live-streamed himself dancing shirtless on top of his McLaren 720S to a song by LosWorld TY called "Demon Timing." And then someone shot Kodak Black in front of the millions of people watching.

"TY, my boy, we did it."

TY glared from across the table.

"You, *you*, not we!" Eddie laughed nervously. "You did this. Brass tacks, it's done. You're on, my boy. It's the big leagues now."

"'Cause a motherfucker die I made it?"

Eddie sighed. "TY, come on. You can't think like that. The stars aligned and—"

"Fuck stars." TY wasn't looking at him anymore. "It wasn't supposed to be like this. I don't even know slim."

Eddie tried being firm. "Well, it happened. And it is what it is, and we're here now, and we gotta take advantage of this shit anyway we can, understand me?"

TY said nothing and Eddie held his breath. The sound of glass and silverware clinking came from the kitchen.

"Vonyetta Mosley ain't even a real person," said TY.

Eddie winced. "What?"

"Vonyetta Mosley. The broad this joint was named after."

"OK."

"This place isn't even here. Have you ever seen any marzipan here? Any at all? All of the world's marzipan comes from a small town in Germany called Lübeck. Ain't no almond groves in Downtown Silver Spring. Besides, marzipan is something that look like something it ain't, right? Same with all this shit. None of this is real."

"You sure know a lot about marzipan."

"Shut the fuck up, Eddie, I'm serious."

"TY, my boy, look—"

"Nah," said TY, leaning in closer. "You look."

Eddie looked around. They were the only ones in the restaurant. At some point, the other patrons must have left. But when?

"That's some liminal shit, right?" asked TY.

"What?"

"Like, are we coming or going or what? Is this what's next or what's now or what was? It is what it is."

Eddie felt lightheaded. He was back on the powder and hadn't eaten anything solid for some time. The tip of his nose burned red.

He would stop now. Stop using that shit before it got out of hand like it always did. He had time to quit though. He had only been tooting for a couple days or so, not long enough to get hooked again. No. He needed to quit now. Get rid of the 8-ball that he stashed between the passenger's seat and the center console. He was going to quit, he was sure of it. Things were going to be different this time.

"Why are we doing this again?" Yousif asked.

Jajjo secured the hundred-round drum to the bottom of the Glock 34. "20 racks is why. What the AirTag say?"

Yousif looked at his phone. "They at that weird restaurant. Up the road, not in the downtown part."

"Marzipan Palace?"

"Yeah."

"Let's slide."

Yousif put his phone on the dash and hit the push-to-start. "Have you listened to their music?"

"What?" Jajjo was frowning at him. "Listen to whose music?"

"These rappers. LosWorld and them."

"Why the fuck would I listen to any of that bullshit?"

"Alright, chill." Yousif got onto the Beltway and went east towards College Park. "I'm just sayin', that LosWorld shit is alright. I like it, for real. I'm jackin'."

"Asking me if I listen to this LosWorld and 37thStreet trash," Jajjo fumed.

Yousif laughed. "Ha! You do listen. I ain't even say anything about no 37thStreet."

Jajjo smiled. "What can I say? Maybe I know a little something."

"This guy!" Yousif slapped the dashboard. "I think we're here. Check my phone. See what the AirTag say."

Jajjo checked the phone. "Yeah. This is it. Go time."

Yousif put the windows down and Jajjo flipped the auto-switch on the Glock 34.

Bullets sprayed in an arc out of the car, hitting the restaurant.

The glass storefront shattered, making the sidewalk and bench in front look wet. Screams came from inside. In less than three seconds, the whole drum was spent.

Jajjo threw the gun out the window and slapped the dashboard. "Go! Go!"

The car sped off down Colesville Road. Soft sobbing came from inside the blown-out dining area of Vonyetta Mosley's Marzipan Palace.

Everything changes.

It only took three months before the frilly, antique-furnished joint inside of the historic Tudor home was no more. A piece of yellow police tape hung from a chain-link fence. The fence surrounded the shell of a multi-unit residential space, something with more than eight stories and a garage that would eventually cost $18 per day to park in. The Salvadorian food truck that served *pupusa, tortas del chavo, sope,* and *costilla asada* was no longer at the gas station on Colesville and Dale.

On the other side of Colesville Road, a black Rolls Royce Cullinan with tinted windows idled in front of the Panera Bread that opened a week earlier. One corner of the **Grand Opening** sign had come loose from the brick and hung in front of the storefront, blocking view of the patrons inside.

Yuri sat in the back of the black Rolls Royce in a blue cloud of smoke, the Chaldean woman sitting beside him, one long leg draped over his massive thigh.

"A fox came upon a vineyard," he began. "There was a tall, wooden fence that surrounded the vineyard, preventing the fox from getting inside. The fox circled the fence until he found a small hole, just wide enough that he could push his head through. The fox saw inside—the rows of delicious grapes. But the hole was too small for anything more than just his head. So, what did the fox do?"

"Tell me, Yuri," the Chaldean woman purred.

"The fox stopped eating for three days. He became so thin that he could fit his whole body through the hole, so he slipped inside the vineyard and began to eat the grapes. The fox kept eating, the gluttonous fuck, until he grew bigger and fatter than ever before. Eventually, he wanted to leave the vineyard, but the hole was too small for him once again. So, what did he do?"

"Yes, Yuri! Tell me!"

Yuri laughed. "Once again, this slick bastard fasted for three days and got skinny enough to slip back out through the hole. Do you understand the meaning of this parable, my love?"

"I do," said the Chaldean woman, blowing out cathinone smoke. "Just as a man comes into this world empty-handed, so he leaves it."

"Indeed," Yuri said, reloading the vape with a new cartridge. "And his wins in life are the only fruits he takes with him."

Author Bio

@WholeTimeDavid   /ToppDoggHill

Marylander **David Simmons** has worked as an optician, rapper, electrical estimator, and drug dealer. Simmons authored the Baltimore Duology, where the supernatural and strange grapple with the ever-present past of East and West Baltimore. His work has appeared in *The Washington Post, Strange Horizons, Brooklyn Vol. 1, Another Chicago Magazine, Snarl, 3 Moon Magazine, Bridge Eight, Across The Margin,* and numerous anthologies. He is a regular contributor to Books to Prisoners, a Seattle-based nonprofit that fosters a love of reading and self-empowerment to break the cycle of recidivism.

More From Our Authors

Cabrones Perros is a rum-soaked crime-comedy that can be read as a standalone novel, though it concludes Manny Torres' Dog Trilogy. From Atlanta, Georgia, to Odyssey, Florida, hitmen (and -women) converge where drugs are cheap and human-trafficking is prevalent. Nolin is the ex-con barback who can't catch a break besides breaking necks. Shank is set on revenge against who killed her family. Ambitious gangstress Shady clashes with an Eastern-European crime family. This war on the waterside can only end with scorched sand and severed heads.

Middle Men

By Liv Strom

Nick the Schtick, cook and crook, wasn't the funny egg he used to be. The Big Apple might've been booming, but when the glittering ball dropped at the end of 1927, the lease on Nick's Diner would be up and the building replaced by another skyscraper. His greasy spoon washed away by modernity. That would have been enough, but when it rained, it poured.

Big Timo, whose stature fulfilled his moniker in every direction, slid a Rolex across the counter. Nick slipped it into his apron pocket while flipping burgers on the grill.

Timo gestured wildly while talking. "He didn't even notice, Nicky. These subways are a pickpocket's wet dream, but anything bigger and you've got both the mob and the fuzz sticking their nose in it."

Nick grunted in agreement. "What happened to your cousin? Haven't seen him around."

"Got nicked, he did. Went to rob the Times Square ticket office, should have been in-and-out, but cops were waiting. They're everywhere these days. People getting nabbed off the street left and right."

Nick couldn't argue and poured complimentary coffee tipped with moonshine. There was, in fact, a copper lurking in the corner, listening to this very conversation. Same who sat there when Nick tipped off Timo's cousin about the ticket office.

After Timo downed the burning hot brew without blinking, he stepped out into the November rain and detective Collins, a man in his thirties unable to outgrow the gangliness of his teens, took Timo's seat.

Without a word, Nick handed him the Rolex. There was honor among thieves, but morals had a way of crumbling when stuck between a rock and a hard place, especially those already as fractured as Nick's.

Collins rejected the watch without looking. "This small-time stuff won't do it."

"I'll let you know if I hear anything."

"That's not good enough. If you want Grandma out of lockup, you need to make it happen. And soon."

Nick swallowed his first decidedly impolite response. Blackmailed by the damned pigs. "These are the criminals you hunt these days, are they? Gram's a 90-year-old woman. Can hardly walk with that hip. Mind not what it used to be. And forcing me to betray good peo—" Nick was only warming up to his running rant when Collins interrupted.

"You're a fence and middleman. And the so-called good people are thieves and crooks, and that Grandma of yours was caught with jewelry from half the elderly of the Upper East Side. When arrested, she said they 'weren't using it anyway' and there's evidence you were in on it. So, suck it up, buttercup, and give me a real scoop."

Nick sighed. "I'll see what I can do, but if I bring you something big, I want Gram released and my immunity in writing. On police letterhead, stamped and signed, all official-like. And if you want it snappy, I might need some assistance."

"Just make sure it's a promotion-worthy catch. I'm proposing at Christmas and the in-laws need a shove."

After Collins left, Nick swallowed his pride and got on the telephone. Gram Agnes had raised him, and he would do whatever she wanted to keep her from dying in the clink. She always had a plan, but now it was up to him.

Well, ain't this just the bee's knees? He watched the hot stove, waiting for future diners and the incessant rain outside. No customers, no savings, and Collins tightening the screws.

After the lunch rush the following Thursday, Big Timo was back in his seat, together with Jack the Rat and Jones. Nick handed each a cup that was more moonshine than coffee and joined them while Detective Collins hid behind a newspaper.

"So, you've got a soup job," Big Timo said.

Nick lowered his voice. "Will need the best double you can do. And fast. Have it all planned out."

"Picture?" Jones asked, pinching his words like his pennies.

Nick slid over the photographs of the jewels that would be displayed at the National Museum's Christmas exhibition. Collins had been more than happy to provide them with floorplans to the storage area after Nick told him the plan. Catching famous jewel thieves fell into the career-making category.

"Too risky," Jack said. "There's only a week until the exhibition opens. Planned to take the wife."

"Has to happen Wednesday night. Take of a lifetime, even split. It's a perfect double-deal," Nick said, putting on his best smile while drowning his nerves in moonshine.

"Buyer?" Jones asked.

"Already waiting."

They looked at the pictures again. Even in scales of gray, the stones from some far-off European monarchy glittered. One after another, the men nodded.

The following days were a frenzy of hidden activity, which Collins' men tailed from a discreet distance. Nick fretted and sweated while serving greasy food to the workers who built the monstrosities that cast his diner into eternal shadow.

Early on Tuesday, Collins sat alone at the counter, smiling wider than a copper should. It was the first time the detective had approached Nick since the wheels started rolling and, if something was going to go wrong, it was the time. "All set for tomorrow night?"

Nick served him sinkers and suds with a nod. "If the information you gave me on the security company is right, you'll have your thieves. Sure you don't want to nab them as they go in?"

"Preventing a jewelry heist isn't the same collar as catching the thieves. I have the plan, surveillance on all three of your friends and, when you hand me the stolen stones after the drop-off, there will be enough to put them behind bars for life. Just stick to your part."

"And the agreement? The word of the fuzz ain't enough."

Collins slid over an official-looking form. "It's valid after you hand over the stones and I sign. So don't get any funny ideas."

Sweat stuck Nick's shirt to his back as he broadened his smile until dimples were forced to appear. "I'm all about family. Everything I've given you so far has panned out, right? What's given to me will be handed onto you when the men come here to celebrate at midnight. Just make sure no one spooks them before then."

After the detective left, Nick made a last call to his extended family. Unable to sleep, he stayed until midnight packing up anything of value in the storage. No matter how tomorrow went, his days were numbered.

The next night went off like a well-oiled locomotive, running fast as a heart attack. Biting his nails, Nick waited for the agreed signals. Two rings and a hang-up meant they were in position, supposedly with Collins and his men waiting for the masked robbers to enter the museum warehouse at 11.

Outside, rain swallowed the November night, like God himself was pissing on coppers and crooks alike. Nick made his call, flipped the sign on the door to **closed**, and turned off all but one lamp. In the near dark, he wiped and polished the wood counter until it reflected the light like water. His fingers knew each stain and burn, knew where knifes had been slammed down, where his cousin had broken his tooth in a fight. Behind this counter, he had laughed and cried, proposed and made love. Memories etched into wood soon would be thrown away like trash to make way for the new.

Quarter before midnight, the telephone rang three times. Nick was still alone, though he expected Collins to arrive soon for the planned arrests. *Time to take out the garbage.*

Huddling under his raincoat, Nick placed the black bag in the alley behind the diner, picked up the soaked cardboard box left among the trash, and hurried back inside.

Half an hour later, Collins barged in through the front door. "Where are they? They were supposed to come back here to be caught red-handed! A journalist is waiting outside for me to lead them away in cuffs."

Nick hid his twitching eye behind a large swallow of spiked coffee.

"They called from a payphone. It's the signal that they've been made. Your men were too obvious. They're most likely hiding under their mother's beds right about now." Collins looked ready to pop a blood vessel when Nick nodded towards the sagging box.

"Dropped off the take for me to move, though."

In the blink of an eye, Collins grabbed the box and counted the ice. Nick had already confirmed that every stone taken in the heist was accounted for.

"Their mothers', you said? We'll just pick them up then."

"Does this mean our business is done? No more snitching and Grandma is clear?"

Collins nodded distractedly and signed the immunity deal. "You can pick her up on Monday. As long as you both stay out of trouble and never mention my role in this, we're done."

And so, the detective waltzed out of Nick's Diner with a smile. Only when the door was locked and curtains drawn, did Nick's lips widen in his first genuine smile since Agnes' arrest.

As Nick received the morning's bakery delivery from his aunt, Big Timo, Jack the Rat, and Jones entered the diner with red eyes and crumpled suits. Nick served coffee, for once without a kick, and breakfasts swimming in fat without a question.

"Nothing like spending the night in the clink," Jack said after finishing his first cup. "Squeezed us tight as sardines."

"So, it worked then?" Nick asked, sipping his own brew.

"Yeah, after you called to rat on the speakeasy on 112th, they raided within the hour. Predictable as a fight on St. Patrick's. We made sure to be good and zozzled. First time I've looked forward to being dragged in," Timo said while inhaling his food. "The ice?"

"Where you said. Handed it over," Nick answered. "He counted them and everything and went looking for you. No one suspected we farmed out the job."

"To middle men." They raised their cups and cheered as Nick handed each an equal slice of freshly baked apple pie.

They had just started their third coffees when Collins burst in through the door, slamming it hard enough to crack the glass. "You! I'm arresting you all."

"For?" Jones asked without inflection.

"For the robbery of the National Museum's warehouse last night. I have seen you case it. Saw the robbers going in. The stolen goods in evidence. Don't think you got away with it."

Big Timo rose to his full height, narrowed his eyes, and switched from thug to outraged citizen. "I don't take well to baseless accusations and neither do my friends. We spent last night in your lock-up, with several upstanding citizens who can testify that we entered the bar before dinnertime. Then, taken by your colleagues before 11—think that's what you call an alibi. No law against enjoying the city or family and friends."

Red-faced, Collins turned to Nick. "You handed me the stolen stones. I heard you plan it together. Know that you provided floorplans and guard schedules."

Nick shrugged. "Needed some stones to get Grams out. You should have them tested. I would never commit a crime, and certainly you, as an officer of the law, wouldn't be encouraging me to. Might have had a few conversations. A thought experiment, if you will. Maybe someone else overheard and took it too seriously. Lots of unsavory people eat here. I don't discriminate."

Collins seemed to shrink. "The stones are fake? But you can testify that they were dropped off here."

Nick raised the form Collins had signed the night before. "Seems I have this immunity agreement that says I cannot talk about my role in any hypothetical criminal events such as you refer to. Wouldn't want to risk Gram's release, you know. It's official and everything. And you better stick to your word, or there is no knowing what will come out of my mouth. I wasn't the one requesting floorplans and mapping guard schedules. Seems the one who did that masterminded this whole thing. Lucky for you, I'm no snitch."

The detective was going from pale to green. "I could lose my badge. Put my head on the line... My girl will leave me... I trusted you."

Nick shrugged. "Suck it up, buttercup, and take your sob story elsewhere. I've got to prepare for the lunch rush and ready Gram's belongings before getting her from the Big House. You don't know the trouble she'll give me if everything isn't just so."

Monday, gray, wet and early, Nick picked up no-worse-for-wear Agnes outside the clink. Despite the birthdate on her documents, she looked no more than a well-cared-for 60 in conservative dress and a fox stole. "Was all this necessary, Grams?"

Agnes glowered at his frown. "Don't be a wet blanket, Nicholas. I handed you Detective Collins on a silver platter—all you had to do was chew him up. More ambition than brains, that one. And the stones?"

Nick started the car and offered her a bakery box with a sigh. He knew better than to argue. "The last eighth of an apple pie à la Aunt Marge— extra iced."

Even split eight ways, Nick had enough dough to start over, away from all this modernity and stress. He was packed and ready to go, and after dropping off Agnes, he didn't plan on stopping anytime soon. He'd heard Florida was nice this time of year.

Starting the car, Nick smiled, sure his luck had changed and the '30s would be the best decade yet.

Author Bio

@LivStromWrites /AuthorLivStrom

Swiss-Swedish **Liv Strom** writes speculative and crime fiction, often featuring strong women. Her stories have appeared in *Apex, Hexagon SF Magazine, Gingerbread House, Mystery Magazine,* and *Tor Magazine'*s "Must-Read Speculative Fiction" and reviewed on *Locus Mag.* Her first novel, *The Last Spiritwalker,* is a dark contemporary road trip fantasy where no one is safe. Her Tales of Bones and Roses series retells fairytales in the city of Tal, where epic fantasy and romance meet, like *Stealing Glass,* a story that asks, What if Cinderella was a thief?

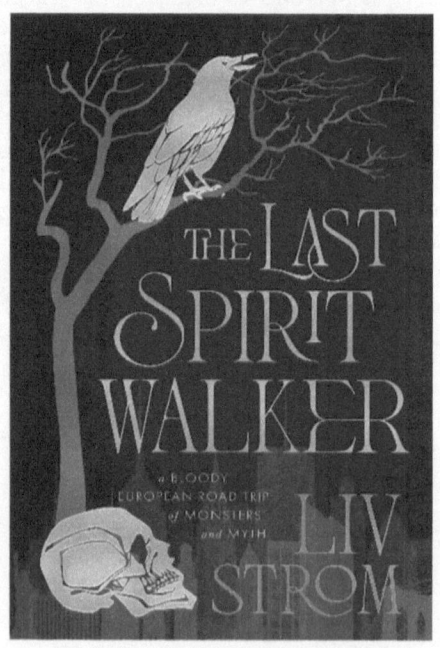

More From Our Authors

Cracker, the explosive sequel to *Poser* is here to answer what *Desperate Housewives* would look like as a noir novel sprinkled with ecstasy pills, pearl-handled guns, and secret alliances. Here, Ambrose fights through jealousy, grief, and a trip to Texas to reconnect with his imprisoned bro, Butch. When Ambrose returns to the Bay Area, he faces a showdown with the mob bosses who've been antagonizing his dominatrix boss and her dungeon, Dover, Inc..

Scar on Scar

By Jon Gingerich

At the slaughterhouse, I was the killer. They put me in the stick pit with a bolt pistol. On a good day, I'd get 20 pigs on the rail in an hour, hang them on a gambrel and run a blade from the carotid to the jugular. Most kids don't have the stomach for it—the smell fogs up your eyes, and pigs' screams sound like children—but by 19 I was the best man they had on the line. Dad put in a word to make me floor manager, but then we had our falling out and I quit and moved to the city. That's when I met Geordie Roe.

Geordie and I worked night kitchen at Pat's, a bar and grille downtown. Everyone called it an Irish pub, which in Central Ohio meant it served Bud Light for humps whose grandparents once owned an Irish Setter. I took my savings from the slaughterhouse and rented a one-bedroom off High Street for three-twenty a month. Geordie smoked me out in his Corolla after a Saturday shift and, when I heard Motörhead in the tape deck, I realized this was a guy who knew where to find trouble. Six months later, he was still the only friend I had.

Geordie was seven years older. He'd been in Desert Storm but was sent home because of an injury. A pink scar sank into his left cheek, made him look like one of those Greek busts that'd been eroded by time. He dressed like someone looking for drywall work, kept a mop of oily hair under a baseball cap and wore an Army jacket with a patch of an upside-down American flag. Geordie got me into clubs even though I was underage, introduced me to his pals, carnies and pawnbrokers who sold downtown brown out of pool-hall bathrooms on the weekends. We'd drink and dash at campus bars, crash frat parties and upper-tank their toilets, piss in the ice trays. We had our own jokes, spoke our own language. We made it impossible for anyone to hang out with us, even if no one wanted to anyway.

Geordie was intimidating. I knew big guys at the slaughterhouse, but they were guy's guys, guys with families. Geordie had a chip on his shoulder. I saw him lay someone out once for criticizing how he racked a pool game. Guys like Geordie didn't knock around with kids like me. He had a fearless nature I'd always wanted for myself, so hanging out with him was like trying out some character role I knew I'd never own.

Gallery Hop, last Saturday of the month. The galleries in the neighborhood stayed open late so yuppies could drive in from the suburbs to gawk at art they didn't understand, and every restaurant on High Street got pounded. Last call was 10 minutes out and I was stringing cling film over the vegetable station while Geordie scrubbed the range with a grill brick. Another night for the books.

"They're sending this back." Gene, the manager, shoved into the kitchen with a plate. "Said the cottage pie isn't authentic."

"Neither are they," Geordie said.

"Kitchen ain't closed, fat ass." Gene grabbed a fistful of onion rings from the fryer basket, dusting the floor I'd mopped with crumbs. Gene was heavy, not fat like me, and had one of those forgettable faces you end up assigning to a dozen people over the years. He gave the impression that this wasn't the life he'd had in mind for himself, and somehow this was everyone else's fault. "A four-top just ordered steaks. Make them nice or make them twice."

As soon as he'd said it, a ticket came through the printer.

Geordie lived in the basement below a split-double on the eastern edge of campus. The walls were exposed cinder brick, a TV and stereo in one corner, a couch and milk crates filled with records in the other. Clothes scattered everywhere and the furniture was mismatched, every item competing for last place. There was a bedroom without a door, just a bed sheet thrown over a curtain rod. Beside it was a glass tank where a rat turned in a wheel.

Geordie got beers from the fridge and put a Sabbath record on the turntable, took his rat out of the cage and let it run laps across his shoulders. He rolled a joint and licked it like an envelope he was sending someplace important.

"Best Sabbath album with Ozzy," I said. "Go."

"Oh man," he said as he picked a bug of wax out of his ear with his keys.

"Trick question. Every album before *Technical Ecstasy* is their best album."

He left the couch and inched up the volume. He was tall and rangy, and his limbs made these jerking movements, like his bones didn't fit right. He passed the joint and I took a drag and let the smoke linger in my lungs.

"Careful," he said. "That's Meigs County kine."

"Best American metal band after 1980."

"I don't know, Jessie."

Grass never had a dulling effect on me; it made everything pronounced. There were colors on the wall I hadn't noticed, and the music felt larger, urgent, like the earth had split open to share a secret.

I chiefed on the joint and passed it back. "How'd you get that scar?"

"Dune coon shot me in Rumaila."

"Were you drafted?" I asked. "Or did you, like, sign up for money?"

"Hasn't been a draft in 20 years, dumbass. Pop was in 'Nam, so it seemed like a good idea at the time."

My relationship with my Dad had grown strained, and we weren't on speaking terms. Dad was conservative; the dial didn't turn to the right past him. Everything was a problem: if it wasn't my weight, it was my hair, or the music I listened to. Dad saw the world in absolutes—a right way to do things, and the way I did them—and he was always over my shoulder, always dressing me down, like I was a project, something to be fixed. As if he'd hung the moon. The year before, the slaughterhouse gave him a ham as a holiday bonus. Anyone else would've considered this an insult, but he insisted we have it for Christmas dinner. The ham looked like a football and, even though he soaked it for days, come Christmas Eve it was so salty that no one would touch it, so we ate the sides Mom prepared as Dad worked away, sweating at the far end of the table. You couldn't help seeing yourself in your parents. They were a cautionary tale, a worst-case version of yourself you swore to avoid, even if you suspected you'd end up like them no matter what.

"Best guitar solo," I said.

"Van Halen. 'Eruption.'"

"Everyone says that."

"Alright. What's the best guitar solo, Jessie?"

"Megadeth. 'Hangar 18.'"

He thought about this. "There's like 10 solos in that song."

"Exactly. Best Metallica cover of a Diamond Head song."D

"Goddamn, Jessie. I'm trying to relax here." He inched closer, reached for his beer. He put his other hand on my leg, and I set my eyes on the floor. Everything looked strange in the light and now my legs felt heavy.

"This grass is strong," I said.

He was stroking my leg, running his hand from the inside of my thigh to my crotch. The music was beating in my ears and then Geordie put me on my back and did his thing on top of me as our shadows made animal shapes against the wall.

It was October, and classes at Ohio State had started a month earlier. The Buckeyes creamed Iowa that weekend and students celebrated by rioting and setting dumpsters on fire. Geordie and I met at a pool hall on Summit and played a few games while Geordie talked a blue streak about all the times in recent memory he'd gotten into a fight. He detailed horrific assaults, like how he'd kicked a guy so hard that he'd crushed the orbital bone above his eye.

"But you know me, bud. I don't start nothing with nobody." He said this anytime he recounted these stories, as though meeting trouble halfway somehow meant it wasn't his fault.

It was late when we walked to Geordies' Corolla. He'd parked on a dark street that dead-ended at the railroad tracks, where the air smelled like a factory fire. I sat on a nest of wrappers in the passenger seat.

"Ever try ketamine?" he asked as he cut up lines on a cassette case.

"Aren't you tired?"

"What can I say. The Devil haunts a hungry man."

He hit a rail and his face bunched up, seemed to tuck into itself.

He passed the case, I took a bump, and the world went soft.

"Got a favor," he said. "I'm so broke I can't pay attention. My transmission failed and getting it fixed set me back on rent. I was a technician for guided missiles in the Gulf and half the time I'm forced to choose between food or bills at the end of the month. Figure that shit out."

"What's the favor?"

He opened his wallet and unfolded a check. It had gold-foil accents, a simple background made to look like parchment paper, monogramed initials in the corner. All the fields were blank except for the amount: two hundred and fifty dollars.

"I run errands for the old man who lives upstairs," he said. "I mow his yard, get his mail. I fixed his toilet last week and he cut me a check. You mind cashing this for me?"

"He left it blank?"

"The guy's senile. He forgets my name, so he wrote in the amount and told me to fill in the rest." He paused a beat. "It'll clear. The guy's loaded. I'll let you keep $50 for your trouble."

"Why can't you cash it?"

"I don't have a checking account. My credit's shit. I cash my paychecks at the Kroger but they won't touch personal checks over $200."

Everything started moving slow and I got tunnel vision. "I suppose I could do that. I'll take it to the bank tomorrow and square up with you Friday."

"I'm kind of hamstrung here. You mind if we find an ATM and settle up? When you make a deposit, the bank usually honors the check and lets you withdraw against it right away."

"There's a branch about a mile up High."

"Anyway, I've got a pen somewhere."

By the time Halloween rolled around, I was staying at Geordie's two or three nights a week. He'd lure me back to his apartment with the promise of drugs, wait until I was completely boxed and pull my pants down and work himself inside me. After he finished, he'd leave me in the dark halfway world of the living room, alone with my thoughts and the deadtime hum of the furnace, the whining wheel of a rat in its cage.

He'd given me more checks from the old man upstairs, and they always cleared, so I never asked what he was doing for the money or why the checks kept increasing in value. I had an idea, but I figured that not knowing was better, and besides, I was making a coin, a couple hundred a week, so it seemed best not to rock the apple cart. Pretty soon, all that cash started burning holes in our pockets. I bought video game consoles and new clothes. Geordie got a waterbed and a guitar. We plundered campus record stores and came home with full crates. We started going to restaurants in our spare time or to the movies. Or we'd hang out at the bar.

Pat the owner had this racket where he ran tabs for the staff. Employees could get as drunk as they wanted, and Pat deducted the drinks from their checks. Everyone considered the tabs a perk, but Pat charged staff full price, so he was essentially turning his employees into customers. I didn't have this problem because the bartenders wouldn't serve me, so most of our time was spent drinking forties of Olde English 800 on Geordie's steps while we caught the neighborhood drama.

A redneck family lived across the street, and when domestic disputes arose, they'd settle their differences in the dirt patch that served as their yard. There was a plasma center on the corner that drew in the neighborhood drunks like flies. They'd sell their bodies to science and hit up the adjacent liquor store, which served as a one-stop-shop to cash their checks and piss them away on pints of Cisco or Wild Irish Rose. Between the rednecks and drunks, there were always fights, which was a lot more entertaining than watching a game at a bar. But my favorite moments were in the quiet of Geordie's apartment, breathing in the warm cellar smells the couch picked up. Time didn't exist down there, and the dark felt like an accomplice, like I'd drifted to some remote hideout at the bottom of the ocean where no one could find me.

Tuesday before Thanksgiving, I stopped at the bank to deposit a paycheck. The teller gave me the receipt and I noticed the balance seemed low, so she tapped at her computer and that's when I found out $700 was missing from my account. The manager ushered me into his cubicle and looked over the charges, then told me the last check Geordie had given me didn't clear because that account had been closed. He said it took a week for the issuing bank to send the check back, but now they'd reversed the deposit and the bank had also slapped on a $40 fee.

I said there had to be a mistake, but he held the line, advised I contact the person who'd given me the check and said, if I deposited another, they might close my account. I was furious but also running late to work, so I told him I was filing a complaint with the corporate office and stormed out. I kicked the door for good measure.

The restaurant was a madhouse that night. There was a steady foot-long truck of tickets on the slide, and we were a man short, so I was plating and running the grill while Geordie covered salads and the fryer. A customer said she'd found a hair in her food and Gene was fit to be tied. Geordie demanded they produce the hair.

During a stretch of downtime, I asked the dishwasher to man the line and pulled Geordie into the walk-in freezer.

"I've got a problem," I said.

"What's up?"

I told him that the last check from the old man had kicked back, and I was on the hook for it.

"I'm sorry to hear that, bud. You need to call the bank and settle that shit. Similar thing happened to me and that's why my credit's shot."

I suggested he come with me to the bank and explain the situation. He didn't seem interested in that, so I said I was open to suggestions but figured it was his responsibility to lend some support, considering I'd done him a favor by depositing the checks.

"I can't help you, bud." He kicked a box of chicken patties with his heel. "Come on, man, quit fucking the dog. I'm guessing you didn't tell the bank about that new PlayStation? We're just going to have to cut our losses, which sucks for me. Not all of us are playing poor until we get a real job."

I thought I was getting the shaft and he was getting the mine, but I didn't want to make things more uncomfortable than they already were, and my nuts were getting frostbite in that freezer, so I let it go.

Sometime before midnight, Dad called the restaurant. We hadn't spoken since I'd left and I hadn't given anyone my number, so I figured my sister Marissa must've told him where I worked, because she was the only one who I still spoke to at home. He did that thing where he used small talk to smooth over the awkward nature of the call, asked how I was doing and if I'd planned to come home for Thanksgiving. He sounded like he'd been drinking. The bartender set his eyes on me, and I could tell he was annoyed that I was standing front-of-house in my apron. Dad said something about how it was a shame they had me working hours when most people were sleeping, and that bugged me, the idea of him calling unannounced to drop his opinions about the place that paid my bills. He asked if I'd gotten the oil changed in my truck and I told him that he shouldn't dial up a business for personal matters and hung up, and this small triumph left me feeling deeply satisfied.

Next morning, I was up at nine, the earliest I'd woken in ages. I drove to the community college downtown, found a stack of course catalogues in a rack by the information desk, and browsed the winter course offerings. I never wanted to go to college, and with the slaughterhouse I didn't need to, but I'd been having second thoughts. I'd made good grades in high school and wasn't trying to be a line cook for the rest of my life, but I had no idea how that ball was supposed to start rolling, didn't know if I had to take certain electives or if I could pick whatever courses I wanted, and the catalogue didn't say anything about tuition or how financial aid worked. I sat at a bench and skimmed descriptions of classes as students passed in the hall. I felt like a stranger, like I'd wandered into someone else's dream, so I put the catalogue back and drove home.

I checked the mail that afternoon, got a letter from the bank with a returned check from the old man upstairs. I burned one and listened to some music, watched an episode of *Star Trek: The Next Generation*. Half-hour later there was a knock at my door and the biggest shit-kicker redneck I'd ever seen was filling out the doorway. There was a distinct, serious look he was giving me, like I'd just plowed his wife.

"You Jessie?" he said.

I didn't get a chance to respond. He grabbed me by the collar and marched me across the courtyard, behind the row of dumpsters at the edge of the parking lot.

"What the shit, man, what'd I do?" I tried to make a break for it, sort of threw my shoulder into him, but he tossed me onto the asphalt, set a knee on my back, and started giving me the business, flailing his arms like a whirling dervish as I buried my face in my hands.

"Where's the goddamn money, shitbird? Forty-five fucking hundred dollars you stole from my Papaw and I'm here to collect."

"I've got some of it," I said. "It's in the bank."

He worked me like a job, beat me until he was hunched over and wheezing in the lot.

"Where's your car, fat boy?"

I was busted up pretty bad, but we walked to the far end of the lot, climbed into my truck, and took Pearl Alley for several blocks until I pulled up at a convenience store.

"The fuck is this?"

I told him there was an ATM inside. He didn't like the idea of letting me out of the truck and said he wanted a bank with a drive-up cash machine. There was a branch a mile north of campus, so we headed up High Street in silence. I drove slowly, occasionally looking into the rearview. The man's eyes were like a pair of burned bulbs and he was red all over, and I didn't know how that was possible, being sunburnt in November.

"How'd you do it?" he asked.

"What?"

"The checkbook, lard ass. You break into his house?"

"No, nothing like that. I mean, I don't know how the guy took it. He wrote me checks and let me keep some of the cash."

"Who?"

"Some guy."

He seemed to lose interest in this line of questioning. "Christ, look at you," he said. "You're like if butter was a person."

Things were fitting together. The old man's family must've looked over his bank records and discovered money was missing, which explained why the last check bounced. It was also obvious why this guy hunted me down himself and hadn't called the cops. He'd probably been skimming from the old man for years, and now the casino was closed. I'd be pissed too.

The bank was jammed, and a line snaked from the ATM through the parking lot. When we got to the cash machine, I got blood on the keypad and some of the bills.

"What's this?" he said.

"That's all it gives me. It only lets me take out $500—"

He slapped me upside the head. "Hand over the keys."

I parked in the lot. My ribs were throbbing, and my jaw was swelling up, which made it hard to get any words out, but I knew that if I told him what he wanted to hear, there was a chance he'd go away.

"Be smart," I said. "You won't be able to sell my truck. And you know where I live. I'll get you the rest of the money. Give me until next week."

He considered this and scratched his beard, shook his head as he stared into the sun. "No, that ain't going to work."

"Tomorrow's Thanksgiving. The banks will be closed. You think I'm going to call the cops? I'm guessing you found me because you've got the statements to prove what I did." If he was processing any of this, he didn't let on. His eyes gave nothing away; I might as well have been talking to the back of his head.

"We'll call it five large," he said. "For pain and suffering and whatnot."

He told me to drop him off at the pool hall on Summit. We drove back to campus without a word spoken and I parked at the curb.

"What's your name?"

"Harlan," he said. And then he beat me some more.

I'd saved a nest egg from two years at the slaughterhouse without rent or bills to worry about, but it wasn't five grand. I wasn't about to tell Harlan that, so I needed to get on the stick and figure out a plan. Whatever I did, I decided it was best not to tell Geordie what happened, at least not yet. Geordie was impulsive, and I didn't want him retaliating against Harlan, or worse, doing anything to that old man. I was willing to cut my losses, especially if it meant keeping Harlan off my ass, so I gave it some thought. My best guess was that I'd have to sell my truck.

Thanksgiving rolled in and a cold snap came over Central Ohio. I called Geordie but he didn't answer, drove to his place but his car wasn't in the lot. I'd wanted to crash there because I'd been too scared to stay at my apartment. I had Thanksgiving dinner that night at a Waffle House near the freeway, went back to my apartment, crushed up one of the Oxies I'd bought from the redneck family across from Geordie's, and watched a *Star Trek: The Next Generation* rerun. As I drifted into the couch's dark waters, a lone voice in the street outside the window yelled, "O-H-I-O."

Saturday was November Gallery Hop, or Holiday Hop, as everyone called it. Busiest Gallery Hop of the year. I heard Pat tell Gene once that Pat's made enough that night to cover a semester of his daughter's college. Day crew prepped for dinner rush all morning and kitchen staff were required to work mandatory 10-hour shifts. Geordie called and asked for a ride because his car was having problems.

"What happened to you?" he asked when he got in the truck.

"Couple frat boys got hold of me outside the Blue Danube." I was having a hell of a time talking through the pain in my jaw. At least I wasn't pissing blood anymore.

The restaurant was packed butts to nuts from the minute we clocked in. Tickets were firing out of the printer faster than we could get them on the slide. Wrong orders, orders that didn't make sense. Someone on the line messed up a plate and a server came into the kitchen and cried about it. By six o'clock, we'd pulled in the busboy to wash dishes because our dishwasher was working the fryer.

I was unpacking the reality of the situation and kept reminding myself I had options. I could sell my truck. I could tell Geordie about Harlan and we could come up with a plan. This was the pipedream scenario, because chances were that nothing we did would amount to five grand. Either way, I felt I'd crossed a doorway with no return. I'd never stolen anything before, and, until that week, I'd been happy living in the city and working at Pat's, definitely happier than I'd been at the slaughterhouse. There's no humane way to handle pigs, any farmer will tell you. You had to dock their tails or other pigs would chew them off. Pigs weren't like other livestock, and not for reasons you might expect. Pigs were smart; I'd play fetch with pigs before I put a rod between their eyes. I'd spent years trying to get away from the life I had, but now the past felt resolved in a way, like I was looking at things with fresh eyes, because, for the first time, those days seemed a lot closer to who I was than where I was headed.

It was seven o'clock and Hell was just beginning. Every inch of the grill was covered, and we were 86ing another menu item every hour, then every half-hour. The heat coming off the burners was unreal, and my legs were rubber and my ribs were killing me and I'd burned the shit out of my thumb. A lot of words were said between us, and more than once I thought about walking out, but that's how it is on a line. In the end, we got through it like we always did: one ticket at a time.

"Great job tonight, Jessie," Gene said as we closed the kitchen.

I took off my apron and made my way to the bar. The Pat's crew partied after shifts, and they were tying one off tonight. The bartenders didn't usually serve me, but they offered to make an exception. I edged into a stool and listened to the servers discuss customers who'd annoyed them or what college courses they were taking. At some point, I wound up in a conversation trap with the busboy, who was several drinks into his tab and muttering something about the O.J. Simpson verdict. The bartenders were arguing over whether Clinton would get reelected. Someone bet the barback 20 bucks to drink a bottle of mustard, which he did, and then he spent the next 10 minutes throwing up in the bathroom.

"Alright Jessie," Geordie said. "I'm knackered. Let's hit it."

I noticed he wasn't drinking, which was strange, especially after the night we'd had. "You want to leave already?"

"I've got a dentist appointment tomorrow."

"On a Sunday?"

"Ya'll motherfuckers are crazy," Geordie announced to the room. "Love, peace, and chicken grease. Catch you on the flip flop."

We left the restaurant and tracked north to campus. It was pissing rain and I was so tired I felt sick. Geordie didn't say a word. I smoked a couple cigarettes, tried distracting my mind from the feeling that something was off. Best Megadeth guitarist: Chris Poland. Worst Ozzy guitarist: Brad Gillis. Best band mascot: Vic Rattlehead. Best concept album: Queensryche, *Operation: Mindcrime.* Best crossover band: D.R.I. Great metal album that's also a great punk album: Misfits, *Earth A.D.* Worst album from a great band: Judas Priest, *Turbo.* Worst solo effort from the former singer of a great band: Paul Di'Anno's Battlezone. Best song that's also the title of an album that's also the band's name: "Iron Maiden," *Iron Maiden*, Iron Maiden.

I stopped at the light on the corner of High and King. For a second, there was just the rain. Then Geordie shifted the truck into park and took my keys out of the ignition. I couldn't get a word out before there was a tap on the glass and Harlan was standing there with a gun to my face.

"Move over," Harlan said. He climbed into the truck and I slid next to Geordie. "One door closes, another opens. It's those dark hallways that scare the fuck out of me."

"You know this asshole?" I asked.

"We just want to talk," Geordie said.

Harlan kept the gun in his left hand and steered with his right. We headed up Seventh Avenue to Indianola and entered the projects. The street was empty, and the asphalt was cratered with potholes, so my knees kept hitting the dash.

"What are we doing?" I asked.

"We're going to Papaw's," Harlan said.

I assumed Harlan wanted me to fess up to the old man about depositing his checks. But then he started talking about how the guy had taken his money out of the checking account and put it in a cigar box he'd stashed behind a slat of particleboard in the cabinet above the stove. Harlan said there was a hammer under the sink. They'd wait in the truck while I busted up the cabinet and grabbed the box. He said I'd have to work fast.

"How am I supposed to get inside?"

"I'm guessing the keys that I'm about to give you will do it. There's one for the back door, so you won't have to walk through the house."

"What if he wakes up?"

"Oh, he'll wake up. Papaw's a light sleeper. That's why my ass ain't going in there. Good news is you can tip him over with a feather."

"But what if he sees me?"

"Then I guess you'd better not get caught if that's a concern."

We turned eastbound onto Eleventh Avenue. I was putting it together as fast as I could. Geordie and Harlan cooked up a plan to steal from the old man by using me to cash his checks. He figured out he was being ripped off, so he closed the account and confronted Harlan about it. Harlan tried to collect the difference from me, but then he and Geordie must've realized they could turn a roadblock into an opportunity, take the old man for even more money, and have me on the hook for that too. It made sense.

"Come on, man. I said I'd get you the money."

"You're really starting to scuff up my Rustlers," Harlan said.

We reached Fourth Street and continued north. As we passed Chittenden Avenue, Geordie dialed up the volume and Slayer's "Reign in Blood" began piping through the stereo.

"Christ, turn that shit off," Harlan said. "Ain't you queers ever heard of Johnny Cash?"

I grabbed a tire gauge from the glove compartment and jammed it in Geordie left eye. He let out a scream and Harlan hit the brakes. Geordie and I tumbled around before I got on top of him and fumbled with the door. Then there was the gunshot and the window over my shoulder exploded.

That's where the story ends every time that I tell it to myself. There's more to it and I know I'm forgetting some details, but that's the way my mind always sketches it out. Then the years go by, and the story fades and I have to tell it to myself again, like words written in sand. I remember running until I couldn't run anymore. I took alleys, jogged west and backtracked east to throw them off in case they were following me. By the grace of God, I chanced upon a northbound COTA bus near Lane Avenue. I couldn't go to my apartment because I knew Harlan and Geordie would be there, so I took the bus all the way to Worthington. It terminated somewhere after the 270 outerbelt and I found a payphone in a Bob Evans parking lot. Then I called Dad.

I was surprised when Dad dropped me off at the house. I figured we were going to the police to give a statement, but he just asked where Geordie lived and said he was picking up Grady Mumm and Zeke Shifflet from the slaughterhouse. That morning, I slept in my old bedroom. Mom and Marissa were having lunch when I woke up. I think my swollen face and the general sight of me scared them and it was the quietest meal I'd ever had. It was almost dinner when dad showed up with my truck. He didn't say a word when he wandered in, just went to the bathroom and turned on the shower.

Later that night, Marissa filled me in on what was going on at school, which was basically just a new version of what had happened when I went there. After she and Mom went to bed, Dad came into the living room, handed me a tumbler of Wild Turkey, and settled into his recliner. His face was soft and pink in the light and his eyes had a hazy look, seemed to float there in the room. I never did get the full story about how Dad got ahold of Geordie and Harlan. He'd only said they'd found them at Geordie's place and my truck was in the lot with a shattered window and to keep my mouth shut if anyone asked about it.

I don't know what he did to them either, but I noticed he smelled like the slaughterhouse when he showed up that night. I'd heard rumors about things that'd gone down there afterhours. Men brought in who never came out. Allegedly, there was a child molester who'd taught volleyball at Worthington High. He'd done something to one of the day crew's daughters and got picked up one night and hauled off to the kill floor. I never gave these stories much thought because the people who'd shared them weren't exactly reliable sources, but I guessed if you wanted to hide a body, a slaughterhouse wasn't a bad place to do it. I'm sure I had questions, but I only remember Dad telling me this was something we weren't going to talk about again.

There were a lot of things I'd resented him for over the years, like the crash diets where he had me eat nothing but All-Bran and lettuce, or that week I had to jog through the neighborhood every morning while he followed behind me in the car. Or when he made me try out for the baseball team and the coach made fun of the way I ran and one of the kids threw my mitt in a urinal after practice. Or the dumb pride in his voice when he bragged to his friends that I'd signed on at the slaughterhouse, which, admittedly, was the one thing I was good at before our falling out over my lifestyle. I'd inspired a lot of disappointment, that was clear, but, for the first time, I wished I could've at least met him halfway, because I owed him that much.

Then Dad broke the silence and mumbled something about local gas prices.

I never bothered to put in my two weeks at Pat's and never heard a word about it. Dad called my landlord, told him to use the deposit as last month's rent, and we moved out before the holidays. The apartment looked the same as it did the day I'd moved in, which was tragic in a way because it suggested nothing had happened. I moved back home. That Christmas, Dad gave me a thousand dollars.

Dad got me rehired on the slaughterhouse floor. I was promoted to manager the next year, then head supervisor just before he retired. When Dad passed away, he left me several hundred acres in Delaware County. I live in a house near where I was raised, keep a boat docked at Buckeye Lake. I manage a staff of 30 and we take a profit every year. I have investments, money in the bank. I never lost weight—in fact, I gained a few pounds—but what can you do.

For a long time, I waited for someone to come after me, got a concealed carry permit and slept with a gun under my bed. I suspected I'd get a visit from Geordie or Harlan and told myself I was ready. I guess I only started taking those old stories about the slaughterhouse seriously after several months, when no one showed up. Then I figured a friend or family member might at least come around, asking questions, but that never happened either. I always thought that was strange. Imagine being so alone that you could go missing and no one would even care.

How long has it been, 25 years? I don't get down to the city very often; work keeps me tied up. Besides, High Street looks different nowadays. Condos everywhere. It seems like a lifetime ago and yesterday at the same time, but the place I knew was gone. The problem with being young is you think life is always going to be that way, and for some of us, it is. Geordie gets to be young forever. He visits me in my dreams sometimes, always the way I remember him, and when I wake up, I feel the ache of this familiar sadness, those memories the body holds onto, buries so deep that we forget they're there.

Looking back, it always seemed I'd lived around my experiences while people like Geordie lived through them. Because I'd lived afraid, because I never felt comfortable in this skin. I thought if I told myself this story enough times, it could change me, that if rearranged the details, I could come up with some version where I'm a stranger, a scenario in which I'm someone other than the person I was. But that never happened. No matter how many times I repeat it, the outcome always ends up the same.

I got out of bed before dawn, drove to the slaughterhouse, and met my nephew Jake at the gate. He's 18, a good kid, but he's been having a rough go since his dad and Marissa split. I gave him a job on the floor last month, figured I'd show him the ropes, let him earn a paycheck while he learns a trade.

I disarmed the security system, and we walked darkened halls to the stock pens. I climbed into the last pen before the kill floor and found a hog shaking in the corner. I pet it a few times while Jake came up from behind with the stunning tongs. Its legs started bucking and we ran chains around the hindquarters and carted it to the stick pit with a wheelbarrow, hoisted it upside down onto the gambrel with the winch, and then I stuck a boning knife in the carotid under the jowls. After it bled out, we rinsed the hog with the hose and scalded it in the water tank, ran it through the dehairing machine and used a hand torch to sear off the stray hairs. Jake cut off the hooves at the hock joint while I separated the head from the backbone and then we eviscerated it, Jake cutting downward along the midline while I removed the guts, the heart, the liver, and the lungs. We separated the backbone and sternum with a splitting saw, sectioned it, and washed it again and brined it with salt and hung it in the chiller, and, by the time the rest of my crew arrived, it was ready for production.

Author Bio

@GingerichJon

New Yorker Jon Gingerich is an editor of the trade magazine *O'Dwyer's* and has penned some of LitReactor's most popular columns on writing. His short story, "Thornhope, Indiana," won *The Saturday Evening Post*'s 2022 Great American Fiction Contest while his nonfiction appeared in the *Guardian*. His debut novel, *The Appetite Factory* (Turner Publishing, 2022), is available on Audible and has been optioned by Sony.

More From Our Authors

Loaded guns, lesbian love, and lecherous mafia-types make this a novella not to forget. Kika was a map of bruises. She was a cicatrix of vengeance, the scar of a wounded mind, the fetid and gangrenous lesion of a town's malevolent psyche. And she's come back to Carbon, Georgia, to find her missing sister.

A Confederate Engaged to a Jihadist

By Nathan Pettigrew

"You can bring home a black girl," Ma had said while eating crawfish, "but don't you dare bring home a Muslim."

This, coming from a woman who'd grown up in New Orleans.

Born and bred amid diversity, Ma had raised me to stand against bigotry, but after 66 years of breathing Southern air, she was yet to become acquainted with any Muslims.

I changed that for her on a Friday night in mid-May of 2020, when most of the country wanted to believe that the worst of Covid was behind us. Restaurants and bars were reopening. People were flying again, so I booked roundtrips from Tampa International to Louis Armstrong, where Ma and Pa were all smiles at the TSA gate.

Nassira hugged them first. "Nice to finally meet you."

"We've heard a lot about you over the years," Ma said.

My best friend of more than two decades had become my fiancée, but neither of us could've imagined falling for each other until Nassira was there for me through a divorce.

With a push from Ma after some trouble, I'd left Terrebonne Parish, Louisiana, in the early '90s to pursue a degree at UMass Amherst. A change in scenery for sure, but the environment was the same. Parties everywhere. I wasn't alone in flunking out, having landed on Nassira and her boyfriend's couch, where they allowed me to crash until I put the pieces back together.

Finding work at a call center, I'd saved enough for a studio apartment and slept around before meeting my ex-wife.

My failed marriage of 10 years had left Ma torn between resenting "that bitch" and wanting me to fly home for a celebration.

Nassira would drop off her Algerian cooking, going through a mid-life crisis of her own.

I'd visited Terrebonne during the final crawfish season before the lockdown to tell my folks that I was seeing Nassira, that it was serious, and, in turn, received Ma's warning about bringing her home.

But there we were a season later, holding hands in the back of Pa's Honda Pilot.

"Y'all eat before the flight?" Ma asked.

"Yeah. Y'all didn't?" I asked.

"We picked up some Popeyes and have leftovers," she said.

"I like their new chicken sandwich," Nassira said.

On and off like this, between fake pleasantries and awkward silences for most of the hour.

Reaching the outskirts of Terrebonne, Nassira couldn't bring her attention back from local businesses that were built like giant boat sheds.

I smiled in Southdown West, where I'd grown up riding bikes with friends and ringing doorbells after dark before hauling ass. Other kids would leave burning bags of dogshit on doormats, but our crew was never that gross.

Most of the brick houses were one-story homes belonging to the more frugal of the upper-middle class. Now retired, Ma and Pa had owned a bait shop that was bought out by a convenience store with gas pumps, and—other than the old man's removal of the swamp maple from the front yard—their house looked the same. The grass was tight, as always, and the dark green paint was still chipping from the wooden bench on their porch.

Nassira and I set our luggage in the foyer, and Ma offered us a choice between Miller Lite and bourbon.

"Susan," Pa said. "It's almost 11."

"Go to bed then, Randy," she said.

I shook his hand. "We won't be up late."

"I'll have what you're having," Nassira said to Ma.

"Same," I said.

Our drinks were strong. Ma settled on the sofa next to Nassira while I fell back into Pa's swivel chair.

"So, tell me about Sharia law," Ma said before taking a sip.

Nassira took a sip of her own. "My family doesn't live by that."

"Don't Muslims want to impose Sharia law on the world or see us dead?" Ma asked.

"Not all Muslims are terrorists," Nassira said.

"Not all Muslims are terrorists, but all terrorists are Muslims," Ma said.

"Well, I didn't know," Nassira said, nudging Ma's shoulder. "I had no idea that Timothy McVeigh and Ted Kaczynski were Muslims."

Trying to take another sip, Ma caught herself smiling.

"Seriously," Nassira said. "'Not all Muslims are terrorists, but all terrorists are Muslims.' Sounds like a Fox News nursery rhyme."

Like a balloon had popped, the women fell into each other, laughing and so loud that Pa hurried into the living room, tying his purple LSU robe. "Everything okay?"

"Fine," Ma said, refusing eye contact.

"See y'all in the morning," he said.

"*Inshallah*," Nassira said.

"I just— I don't know," Ma said. "I'll never believe that most Muslims can be trusted."

Nassira smiled. "Well, can we agree to disagree?"

"Of course," Ma said, clinking her glass and still acting as if I wasn't there.

Nassira slipped into her black-and-gold muumuu after we brushed our teeth. A cool nod to the Saints. "So, this is where you used to jerk your dick?" she asked.

"This ain't it," I said. "This is a freakin' library."

Nature paintings had replaced my Public Enemy and Cypress Hill posters while Southern travel guides from Ma and Pa's store filled the bookshelf where I'd kept my football cards.

"Oh, come on," Nassira said. "It's nice."

I pulled the chain on the fan light. "That could've gone a lot worse," I said, getting comfortable with my bride-to-be.

"She has a kind heart, George."

"Yeah, well. Let's hope it stays kind."

"*Inshallah*," Nassira said.

"*Inshallah*," I said.

Ma was the first to wake up, and I walked in on her loading the dishwasher. "Sleep okay?" she asked.

"Yeah. Got any coffee?"

"Cabinet above the pot," she said. "What does *inshallah* mean?"

I found filters next to the red Community can. "Means 'God willing.'"

"In what language?"

"Arabic. Why?"

"Her English is perfect," Ma said. "I was expecting an accent."

"Told you, Ma. The smartest and kindest person I know."

"Join me when you're done," she said.

She didn't smoke in the house, flicking her ash in the garage when I stepped out in my slippers.

"Her family's good to you?" she asked. "No issues with you being a Southerner?"

"Lot of countries have north and south issues," I said, stopping to sip my warm black coffee. "They get it."

"I'm just glad she's taking care of you," Ma said. "Not like that bitch."

"Why do you hate her so much?" I asked. "'Cause I don't. I'm happy now."

Ma took a long drag before exhaling. "You're right. My anger's misplaced. I warned you about her."

"What do you want me to say, Ma? You never have to see her again."

"We have traditions in the South," she said.

"I get it," I said.

"Well, your father wants to pick up some crawfish for lunch."

"And Nassira will love that," I said.

"You see that nice big one over there?" Pa asked Nassira, pointing to the fattest red on her platter.

We'd dumped 15 pounds of boiled mudbugs on newspapers covering the breakfast table. Garlic potato halves and buttery ears of corn were mixed in, but Ma had ordered the smoked sausages in a separate bag since Nassira didn't eat pork.

"That's it," Pa said. "Squeeze the tail and remember to pinch the end so it's not so tough to pull apart. Good. Now use both thumbs, and there's more meat."

"Don't forget to take out the poo line," I said before sipping my beer.

"Aw, hell," Pa said. "It won't kill her."

"Is it really poo?" Nassira asked, and I couldn't help laughing mid-sip.

"Just slide it out with your fingers," Pa said to Nassira.

The doorbell rang, and Ma reached for a napkin.

"I can get it," I said, standing. "Enjoy your crawfish."

I found Toby and C.J. peeking through the oval glass, both decked out in black-and-gold Saints gear. I unlocked and opened the door, and we exchanged bro hugs.

Toby was the bigger of the two, a former football player who'd given up on his team in tenth grade. "Heard from your brother you were in town," he said. "You weren't going to call us?"

"The fucker knows I'm in town but won't visit," I said. "How is he?"

"Asshole hasn't changed," C.J. said. They worked offshore for the same oil company, and—while my brother had gone on to become their foreman—he didn't trust Toby or C.J. much. Ringing doorbells was one thing—my brother would join us on occasion—but Toby and C.J. had graduated to dropping acid and throwing bricks through windshields.

"Look who's here," I said in the breakfast room, and Ma stood to hug them. A surreal sight.

Like my brother, Ma couldn't stand my friends in high school, but years had changed "the troublemakers" into sights for her sore eyes.

Remaining seated, Pa shook their hands, and they were both visibly surprised by Nassira's appearance when I introduced her.

Toby elbowed me. "Your brother lied and said she was from Africa."

"Born and raised," Nassira said, smiling.

"Let me grab some chairs from the dining room," Ma said.

"We don't mean to be rude," Toby said. "We didn't realize y'all were eating crawfish."

"Why? Y'all up for a ride?" I asked.

"If it's okay," he said, looking for Ma's approval.

She sat and reached into her bag for a sausage. "Y'all have fun."

Toby drove a white Camaro and kept her spotless. C.J. took shotgun, first pushing his seat forward to let us in the back.

"Nice ride," Nassira said.

"Thanks," Toby said, exposing his undying love for Soundgarden's *Superunknown* when turning the ignition.

Leaving Southdown West on Chantilly, he eyed Nassira in the rearview while lighting a joint. "Hope you're not offended," he said.

"Not as long as you share," she said.

Toby caught a red light at the intersection near Southdown Plantation, and two kids on bikes pedaled across.

"Fucking Democrats," C.J. said, striking Nassira as funny.

"He speaks," she said, still laughing. "How do you know they're democrats?"

"Can't drop N-bombs these days," C.J. said, passing back to her. "Too many woke folks lose their shit. So, we call 'em democrats."

"*Interesting*," Nassira said, giving me her "what the fuck?" eyes.

"Y'all hungry?" Toby asked when the light turned green.

"We might be again after smoking," I said.

"I'm thinking Pete & Dee's," he said, bringing back memories.

"No worries," I said to Nassira, taking the joint. "Place is a bit on the rough side, but safe during the day."

Pete & Dee's Diner was an L-shaped shithole on Highway 90 headed toward New Orleans but home to the best and thickest burgers I'd ever put my hands on. The meat was never dry, always perfectly pink, but at no time served with a soggy bun soaked in grease.

Preferring a window booth, Nassira didn't comment on the black-and-white framed photos of slaves on the rosy walls or the questionable characters sitting around us.

This wasn't my old room at Ma and Pa's. The place hadn't changed, still a 24/7 stop for shady business. Whoever owned the diner had cops on payroll, having made Pete & Dee's our high school hangout after long nights of partying. With Toby and C.J., I'd seen lines sniffed from tables, pros allowing drunks to expose their breasts, the homeless assaulted by bikers, and a man stabbed to death.

Back then, a trucker having coffee with a towering man in a dark gray suit slammed his fist on the table before pulling a hunting knife. "Think you can threaten my family, fucker?"

Responding with a .45, the man in the suit smacked the trucker to the floor and holstered his piece. Taking a knee, he picked up the knife and used both hands to drive the blade through his opponent's neck. The sound of a man coughing up blood while ground beef sizzled on a grill turned my stomach. I didn't puke, but nausea had drained my strength.

Standing casually, the suit reached for his pocket square to wipe his hands and made eye contact with no one while exiting the diner.

That cold, black morning marked the first time I'd seen parish patrol cars lighting up the Pete & Dee's parking lot. I'd nearly bumped into a drunk who'd gotten himself knifed in New Orleans during Mardi Gras of '91 but was yet to see a fatality in Terrebonne.

My friends and I were questioned as witnesses and quickly interrogated as suspects in a statewide drug ring.

For months, we endured surveillance and dirty looks in public, but we were never charged.

"Maybe pursue college instead of going offshore with those troublemakers," Ma had said in the garage.

I smoked too at the time. "LSU?" I asked. "Kind of figured that's where you wanted me."

"Not here," Ma said. "Up north."

And that was that. Before Nassira, Ma was my most trusted confidante.

"Can you believe we have Nigerians in Terrebonne?" Toby asked C.J..

The waitress had come with menus. A short brunette with a ponytail and bad teeth, she glared at Nassira before leaving us.

"Sorry," Toby said to Nassira. "I'm just messing around."

"No worries," she said. "George didn't tell me you had Nigerians in Terrebonne."

"What's with Nigerians always scamming folks?" he asked.

"You mean those emails?" she asked.

"Yeah," he said. "That shit comes from a call center or what?"

"Asshole," I said. "It's Algeria. Not Nigeria. She's from Algeria."

"Oh," was all Toby had to say after I'd wiped the smirk from his face while C.J. kept his eyes on the parking lot.

The waitress brought four waters in mason jars. "Ready to order?"

"My fiancé says you have the best burger in Terrebonne," Nassira said.

"I'll be back when y'all are ready," the waitress said.

"Doesn't matter," C.J. said, his attention still outside. "You're a confederate engaged to a jihadist in most eyes."

"Seriously?" I asked.

"They didn't exactly embrace you up north," he said, facing me, "and I'm guessing Nassira gets no love in Sunny Florida."

"You've never been to Tampa," she said.

"Just Destin," C.J. said.

"Well, we love it," Nassira said. "It's why we moved there."

"Jesus," I said. Parish police were flooding the parking lot, all lit up and followed by an unmarked black van.

Sheriff Daigneault hopped out of his car to speak into a megaphone. "George Duval," he said. "You and your party, step outside. Slowly. One at a time, with your hands up."

It had all happened so fast; I reached for Nassira's hand, but adrenaline kept me from feeling her grip.

Letting go, I walked out first.

"Step to your right," the sheriff said. "Okay. Whoever's next."

Nassira followed his instructions, and Daigneault aimed his rifle at her. "To your right with George. Slowly. Do not make physical or eye contact with him."

Her calm demeanor kept me from having a meltdown.

"Toby and C.J.," Daigneault said. "Come out together and step to your left."

They were giggling like they used to in the principal's office.

"On the ground," Daigneault said. "Hands behind your heads."

Three SWAT troopers surrounded Nassira, their AR-15s drawn.

"Wow," she said. "Terrebonne shows up."

"This is no laughing matter," Daigneault said.

"My tampon isn't a bomb," she said.

The troopers consulted their shot caller on radio before asking Nassira to pull the string from under her dress.

"Are you fucking serious?" I asked, taking a swing at one of their face-shields before finding myself gut-punched by the stock of a semi-automatic.

Daigneault placed a firm hand against my chest, keeping me down on my knee.

"Seriously," I said, catching my breath. "What's this about?"

"Got a call about an Islamic extremist," he said.

Facedown on concrete, Toby and C.J. couldn't help cracking up, and I'd never felt so gross, so confused, still finding love in my heart for two old friends who I wanted to see dead.

Our relationship and history. Our families and their histories. Our ties to Islam. Nassira and I were interrogated by ATF and Sheriff's deputies for an hour but kept in our interrogation rooms for two before being released.

Pa had come alone to pick us up, and I let Nassira have shotgun.

The ride on Barrow heading toward Bayou Black was almost quiet, if not for the cool air blasting through the vents.

"Impressive," Nassira said when Pa took the right on Library Drive.

"Right?" I said, admiring the two-story media center. "Used to be a stinky shithole downtown when I was a kid."

"George loved it," Pa said. "He would read in left field during baseball practice."

"Was it built like a boat shed?" Nassira asked, getting him to smile.

"Nassira," he said. "I just want to apologize for—"

"Don't," she said. "It's George who owes the apology."

"For real?" I asked.

"You promised the best burger in Terrebonne," she said, "but Pa delivered when it came to crawfish."

Waiting in the foyer, Ma stepped out to hug Nassira. "I'm so sorry you went through that."

"I'll pray for them," Nassira said, and Ma let go.

"What does that entail?" she asked. "One of those carpets in my son's room?"

"I meant the carpets in our living room at home," Nassira said, smiling.

Flying out the next evening, we packed without speaking and scrubbed each other down in the shower, keeping it light on kisses.

"Well?" I asked when drying Nassira off.

"Think we're all talked out for one day," she said.

We brushed our teeth, and Nassira allowed me to hold her when it was time to get comfortable.

"So, we're good?" I asked.

"It's just funny your mother's the one you were worried about."

"What can I say, Nassira? We'll never see them again."

"*Inshallah*," she said.

"*Inshallah, habibti.*"

I heard Ma unloading the dishwasher, opening my eyes. Nassira was snoring, and I rolled over to kiss her forehead.

After using the bathroom, I found the kitchen empty, and Ma flicking her ash in the garage. "Morning," I said.

"You're no longer welcome here," she said.

"Calm down, Ma."

"I am calm, George, and serious. What did you expect?"

I reached for one of her cigarettes, and Ma lit me up for the first time in almost 30 years.

"You haven't changed," she said, disrupting the orgasmic exhale of stress from my nerves. "Always putting yourself and those you love in danger."

"Only in fucking Terrebonne," I said. "Wasn't my fault."

"Doesn't matter," she said.

"Look," I said, stopping for another drag. "I'll call you after we land."

"I'll answer your calls, George, but that's it. You can't come back here."

"And Pa's good with that?" I asked.

"He'll have to be," Ma said.

I tried to take her hand.

"No," she said. "Don't make this harder. I warned you, but you continue to defy me." She stubbed her filter and left me to smoke alone.

I was five when Ma jumped into the YMCA pool to save my life. I couldn't swim in the deep end without a kick board and had lost my grip—splashing and splashing until Ma pulled me to safety. She'd come to my rescue a second time when sending me away from Terrebonne, and again when warning me about my first marriage—but this morning felt different, and final.

Like three strikes and I was out.

Author Bio

@NathanBorn2010

Nathan Pettigrew was raised an hour south of New Orleans, and currently lives by Tampa with his loving wife. His stories appear in *Deep South Magazine, Cowboy Jamboree,* and *Nasty: Fetish Fights Back*, as spotlighted in a 2017 *Rolling Stone* article. Anthologies he features in are Crack the Spine'*s The Year,* Stephen J. Golds' *Gone*, Bristol Noir's *Savage Minds & Raging Bulls*, and Outcast Press' *Mirrors Reflecting Shadows.*

More From Our Authors

Craig Clevenger has written four novels, most recently *Mother Howl*, and most notably *The Contortionist's Handbook*, which Chuck Palahniuk, author of *Fight Club*, praised as one of the best books he's read in a decade. Much of his work is about on-the-lam men living under new identities while on the brink of intoxication and incarceration. Clevenger also featured in *In Filth It Shall Be Found* and regularly crafts workshops to help writers delve into the darker truths of their storytelling.

Two Boys in a Diner

By Dino Parenti

Uncle Harry bought it last summer. An overdue coronary while sunning his townie hide in the middle of the worst Miami heatwave in memory. Two months later, I was swizzling bad coffee in the Adirondacks, staring at a slo-mo confetti of snow through a grimy diner window, wondering when the last time was that I'd seen the white stuff fall so pure and plump.

Pop was flirting with the end himself, someplace in New Jersey, but he wasn't done course-correcting the fortunes of people he hated and loved, and, in any case, it was Uncle Harry who'd been weighing on my mind of late. He was Pop's younger brother by six years, and, though he would end up having three more brothers, Harry was always his favorite. It wasn't even close, and it only further convinced me that whoever laid claim that there was no favoritism when it came to blood was either a straight-up liar, or a terminal peacenik, and the world already had too many of both.

I was mostly thinking of Uncle Harry 'cause the old man who sat at the corner booth when Jimmy and I first walked in was a dead ringer, down to the Karl Malden honker, Henry Fonda baby-blues, and Dolly Parton man-cans. And like Uncle Harry, that coot's mug lacked all lines. A chubby newborn's face. As if no beef, worry, or humor ever made it to the surface, but instead white-watered, unseen, through his veins.

Uncle Harry's one expression was a glare so cold that it froze the piss in your bladder—the inverse of Pop whose puss was an aerial view of terraced rice-paddies. His was an open floodgate holding back nothing. Except for gratitude. Oh, Pop would bear-hug and hair-ruffle and kiss you like no one's business—if he took to you—but lots of luck prying a "Thank you" or "Nice job" out of the man. In that sense, he and Uncle Harry were mirrors of one another.

Maybe there was something beautiful in that, but I wasn't qualified to see it.

Anyway, Uncle Harry and his baby-butt face were gone, and so was his double because he'd vacated before I sat down, and the first snow of the season started to fall 20 minutes ago, and that's where we were, a handful of quiet monkeys gathered in a remote diner, wide-eying nature's wonder the way our harrier forefathers must've gawked at comets.

My kid brother, Jimmy, finally strolled out of the can after 10 minutes. He said he needed to piss, but it was a ruse. The way a kid would claim he was only trying to cool you off during a swelter after you'd caught him fishing the tub of ice cream out of the icebox. Jimmy just wanted to change, which he did, looking spit-shined and polished, even in a parka. He had a white shirt on underneath—not the plaid number he wore when we walked in. He always carried an extra shirt in the car, and it was always white, and it was only so people would think he was bulletproof to spillage and sweat.

He strutted back to the counter in his best Jack Elam and waited by his stool, hands on hips, a quarter-inch of tomcat tongue poking past his lips. Jimmy always gave every new roomful the same showy once-over. He even did it at Uncle Harry's wake, putting the stutter in the priest's paid, prepared lies regarding the deceased's generous ways.

I wanted to keep staring at the snow—search out some ultimate pattern in its drift that related survival to vanity—but we didn't have all day, so I said a terse, "What's the word?" before gulping more coffee.

Jimmy diddled at his chin cleft. I used to tease him that he could stash a gym-bag of swag in there, and the cops would be none-the-wiser. "I say we take 'em for all they're worth," he said.

Until that moment, I thought that stuff about blood forming psychic links across space—like with twins—was nonsense, but I swear I could've felt our father's neck tendons go piano-wire taut right then.

I said, "Pop would pass his spleen, he heard you say that."

What started as a sigh ended in a double-barreled nose blast from Jimmy. "We'd be out in two minutes flat, Vic. How about it? For old time's sake?"

I saluted him with my cup. "Take a load off for a bit, huh? Watch me finish my joe."

He stopped poking at his chin-hole and asked how long I planned to be. I told him, "10 minutes." He asked if that was wise, and I told him the diners weren't going anywhere—that they hadn't even started their eggs yet, to which he fiddled some with his watch before drilling mother-superior eyes at me.

"I'm timing you," he said.

"They got any maps here?"

"I haven't asked."

I glanced at my watch as if mattered. "We'll need a map."

His ass kneaded bacon farts out of the stool vinyl and soon his hands were crumpling invisible sheets of paper on the countertop. Jimmy, for whom patience was only a virtue for surfers and saps. 30 seconds into it, and he fired an off-the-cuff wolf-grin at the mousy, old biddy a table over, whose blue, saucer-big irises had locked on him with a loud blend of surprise and disapproval. The locket perched on her thick knockers winked like a third eye, eager to help cast judgment.

"That's a nice piece of gold," Jimmy muttered through a smile.

"Not what we came for."

Jimmy lip-farted and called me a killjoy. "They can't take it to the grave with them, you know." Jimmy always reminded people of something, even if it was nothing.

"Pop would beg to differ," I said.

"Says you. And you got nine minutes."

I wondered, did Jimmy know that, at 22, he'd only just begun to shed his juvenile skin? That the theory of manhood was a cakewalk compared to its practice? 15 years floated between us, and, within that stretch, Pop had spit out five others. But only Jimmy and I sparked, split, and ripened in the same womb, and maybe that was enough for me to suffer his random moments of stupidity without losing my cool. Which was why I made no fuss when he started spinning around on his stool, completing two-and-a-half orbits before tossing back his elbows on the counter to probe the room again.

I'd gotten the full gist of the place 10 seconds in: mountain roadside diner, writ large. A tiny upstate joint that whiffed of fry grease and Bengay from the mostly long-in-the-tooth clientele, most of whom had come in the charter bus outside. Some weekend seminar down the valley on reversing the aging process through meditation and diet, all for the low, low cost of one bible-thick book, plus a year's supply of miracle vitamin tonic. The brainstorm of some 30-something latent flower child who'd been to India and back without losing his nose to leprosy.

Jimmy started humming, and humming was his engine gauge tipping into the red and about to peg out. I watched his eyes toggle from face to face, assessing, calculating, fussing, and, a moment later, he said, "Would it be too much to ask they appreciate at some point the virtues of self-offing?"

That was a new one. "A bit extreme huh, Jimbo?"

"Really?" He frowned at the nearest diner who paid him no mind. "A man should know when his usefulness is at an end. That he's become just another mooch in the world, ergo, he should do the noble thing and take one for the team, and so forth."

Listening to Jimmy wax introspective tested the spring in my nerves, but to have called him on it was to deny him his fool's paradise, and we all had a right to our own version of it. "You're proposing seppuku," I said. "As a kind of...national mandate?"

"What? What's that? Sounds Hawaiian..."

"It's Japanese. Loosely translated, it means honorable suicide."

"Huh. Ain't that something?"

"Used to be, a dishonored samurai, he would take his own sword and gut himself with it."

Jimmy scowled at another unmoved diner at the end of the bar, one who seemed to hide behind the tray of clean root beer float glasses left on the space next to him. "The Japanese do that?"

"No, Jimbo, not all of them. And not for a long time."

"And you said I was being extreme."

"To the Japanese, old age is something to honor. They don't get bent out of shape about it the way we do here."

"And this impresses you?"

"What we went to war for."

He chewed on invisible taffy before batting the air back at me. "Bull, you don't know. Seven-and-half-minutes to go, genius. What do you got, bourbon in that cup?"

I wondered, did Jimmy know that we always spoke in similar, trivial bursts with Pop? That our entire conversational life was a long string of wind-swept isles in a sea of dumb silence?

Jimmy had spun himself back to forward, and we both poked some at our respective oatmeal while Don McLean griped on the juke about Jack Flash and dying days—until Jimmy decided to kibosh the peace by letting his spoon clang into his bowl.

Jimmy, always the first to destroy a perfectly fine tranquility. Silence terrified him the way large crowds did others.

"Is Pop old to you?" he asked. Practically whispered it, so I paid extra heed.

"I don't know what that means."

"I mean, does he seem...to be winding down?"

"Pop? Hell, Jimbo, Pop's Pop, you know?"

"Yeah, I know. I mean, do you see him for the age he is? Or the way you always saw him growing up? Tough, you know? Indestructible?"

God, I loved the kid, but Jimmy's non sequiturs were free-floating lodes of peanut butter I was always strip-mining from my upper palate. At such moments, I would let my thoughts drift to mayflies and dragonflies—any creature I could think of with short lifespans.

About a year for chameleons and octopi, if I remembered right.

A drone bee lived about a month, but what a productive month!

"Remember that first stroke," he went on, "we drove to Syracuse to be with him? Saw him jacked into all those tubes and wires. I swear, he looked the smallest I'd ever... That's the first time I realized how much bigger I was than him. Hell, I'd been bigger since I was 16, but…you know what I mean?"

I'd noticed that some of Jimmy's oatmeal had catapulted onto my shirt cuff, and I got to flicking off the morsels as if they were a line of ants. "Stop putting him in the ground, Jimbo. Wasn't for the cancer, he'd look a hell of a lot healthier than these coffin-dodgers."

"Except he ain't that much younger than most of these coffin-dodgers."

"Yeah, but you can't quantify Pop in terms of elapsed time. Tough-ass bastard—ask his competition if they think he's old."

Jimmy glazed over all of a sudden, as if he'd just taken some jilted broad's right hook to the chin. "Five minutes down, five to go," he said, jittering back to earth.

"Next gas station, we should stop and get a map."

"Yeah, a map, sure. Hard to know where to go on a mountain. Up or down."

"Do you remember if we hit the 11 first or the 22? 'Cause I don't know about you, but I don't want to wind up in fuckin' Montreal, saying, '*Merci*' to every teenager smoking a cigarette who gives us directions." Another raspberry.

I wondered, did he grasp yet all the particulars of coping? All its shades? Was he privy to the humbling mechanisms people turned to on a daily basis just to get by? That while most men clung to every last scrap of their youth, some fought tooth-and-nail to forget theirs? That some might actually resent their longevity?

Something was burning in the kitchen. That, or they'd over-brewed the coffee. Neither challenged to overtake the stink of muscle ointment though, and that jolted me into realizing I'd been stealing looks at the old man with the angel-hair beard and suede blazer who sat at the counter's elbow, under the wall clock. More to the point, the obscenely large gold crucifix around his neck, inset with a pearl the size of a baby's eye at the junction. The gaudy thing stirred all kinds of new and interesting odiums in my belly. But there was something else about him I couldn't place exactly until I mentally shaved the bush from his face, at which point it all clicked and I nudged Jimmy's arm. "Now that there is the Amish version of Pop. Tell me it isn't."

Jimmy, whose mood had ticked down a few more degrees, smile-gazed at the geezer a bit before shrugging. "Pop's a hard man to talk to," he said.

Yeah, I was in for it. The kid would not be deterred. "Pop comes from a world of bricks, Jimbo. Of sledgehammers. An open book, he is not."

More stool-dancing from Jimmy, until the constriction finally got so that he had to chuck his parka. "Naw, man, that ain't it."

My turn to let the spoon drop, and I took even more soggy shrapnel on my arm. "What's the problem? Seriously, you've been ball-breaking all day. I told you to hit the sack early last night. Didn't I tell you?"

He fished out his lighter and got into his groove of popping the lid up-and-down with a thumb. He'd been trying to quit for months, and he once explained how the scratch of the flint wheel was sometimes enough to fool his lungs, and, if that didn't work, he wasn't above holding his palm over the flame until the burn took the urge away.

I worried that he was about to try it right there and then, but he pocketed the Zippo and raked fingers through his hair.

"Jesus, Vic, is this gonna be us someday? This heap of mealy, broken-down meat? I mean, look at 'em."

But I didn't look. I didn't want to get sucked further into one of his panic spirals, so I focused down on my own face as it floated in the muddy pool of my coffee. Sometimes it was just easier to carve a universe out of the 18-inches of tabletop your cone of vision provided.

Chuck Berry's "My Ding-A-Ling" had overtaken "American Pie" on the Wurlitzer, and, when I figured he'd settled down some, I risked a look at Jimmy. Jimmy with his full lips and almond eyes that the ladies couldn't stop smiling at, and I wondered, did he know about all those years that I resented his looks? Looks that greased wheels and opened doors better than crowbars and hard work? Did he know about schadenfreude in the objective sense? That when cast-off lovers and spurned colleagues tried to take a piece of that face, that not everyone in the world felt sorry for him?

"I wouldn't sweat it, Jimbo," I said. "You're cinder block tough, Brother. Everyone knows that. But one thing you're not beating is a clock. We're all time's sorry, collective punk. All we can do is grab ankles or fight back. Like Pop."

His return smile was Paul Newman handsome, and a small part of me that I'd thought long dead cried out a final time before wilting. "Like Pop," he echoed. "Just a hair under three minutes to go, Vic."

A pair of lumber-heavy semis thundered by, rattling flatware and kicking up gales of brown shoulder snow that spritzed all the way to the front windows. I wished one of those truckers would've stopped and chimed the bell over the door to swap out the air with something less congealed, but it was just as well they hadn't.

Jimmy giggled quietly to himself out of the blue, dragging a slow finger across his belly. "Wonder if I can do it," he said. "When the time comes, of course."

"Do what?"

"You know. Self-off. Like the Japs."

And in that moment, I had an epiphany: that Jimmy's simper was my acid reflux trigger.

"I think when the time comes, shitting yourself and dribbling pea soup on your crotch will look like a million bucks compared to dragging a blade across your gullet." He stopped his slicing, and, with the same finger, got to scribbling words in the air. His inhale before a confession. "I ain't as tough as you think, Vic. Not like you are. You got a handle on things. You've had more time to get ahead of the curve. It's why Pop trusts you the most of all of us. You got his best love."

Christ Almighty, did Jimmy know that he was gas lighting, or was it just a reflex? Did he know that the first kid is the guinea pig, and that the guinea pig got force-fed not just all that new, raw love, but all the neurosis and misplaced expectations?

That first wasn't always best?

He spun back around to face the diners and soon fell into a detailed inventory of every face in the room, as if to record them for some future group doodle. In due time, he said, "Wish this wasn't necessary. I mean the goddamn mess…" Jimmy, at long last, found his bearings and dealt with the issue at hand.

"Yeah," I said. "But Pop wouldn't last in prison, Jimbo." And like Jimmy, I twisted myself around and let my eyes hang on each face for a moment, as if somehow the act alone would've spooled back the film to before we'd walked in, and a different tactic might've pried loose from one of our brains and prevented our excess. But no such double-backing came to pass. No bullet reversed its flight back into the muzzle, and each face stayed as dead as the next: the bearded old man who looked like Pop, the mousy old lady with her locket, Uncle Harry's twin, who'd slumped under the booth, trying in vain to plug the air leaving his lungs with dispenser napkins.

"No, he wouldn't," said Jimmy. "But still…"

Their blood had begun to pool at their feet or in their seats, or slithered down the walls behind their heads. Some still dripped from the ceiling. You fought enough wars, shot enough people, and you could start to match a victim by the distance and intensity of his splatter. Older people had weaker jugulars, weaker blood pressures. They tended to just spill.

It was the young ones who sported geysers.

I shrugged. It's what I imagined God did when cruising by our world on his slow laps of the universe. "State's star witness is on the bus, we follow the bus. They don't provide us photo ID, we're left but with one option, and that's to be thorough. Like Pop would've been."

"Yeah, like Pop," Jimmy said. He started breaking down the M3s with downcast eyes, and I wondered, did he know that, like napalm or chemo, sometimes you had to lay waste to entire mass areas just to eliminate a few nuisances? Or just one?

I got up and worked my way to the kitchen, which had started to smoke something awful. I turned off all the burners and opened the back door, mindful not to slip on any of the spilled buttermilk, broken glass, or the cook's brain matter. On my way back, I glanced at the shattered wall clock, frozen forever at 8:14AM. Just about the same time to the minute that Little Boy revealed the soul of the universe to 80,000 unawares people of Hiroshima, Japan, freezing clocks, watches, and shadows alike, and I thought again of all our patterns and cycles, and the wisdom or fallacy in trying to break them.

In the end, maybe blood wasn't always thicker than water, but it would always be harder to clean.

Greaser guns safetied and packed away in my old navy duffle, Jimmy strolled up to the bearded man kitty-corner from us and finger-traced a crude constellation out of the dime-size holes punched into his neck, cheek, and forehead above the left eye. "I see it now," he said. "Clean him up some, and he'd look just like Pop."

"Yeah, like Pop." I downed the last of my coffee and sleeve-wiped my mouth. "You done good today, Jimbo. Good control. Better than my first time."

I had to admit, Jimmy's sheepish grin warmed my heart for a change.

"How we doing on time?"

"Minute-and-a-half?"

And just like earlier, I practically felt Pop's grip on my neck at our childish loitering, and I got to wondering what, if anything, the drawing corners of my mouth were doing on his end. Pop once told me that he'd had kids because he'd lost his sense of self-preservation—his fear of death—but I didn't think he ever had one. I doubted that we helped.

Outside, the wind had picked up and the snow had started to swirl and eddy, and I wondered if we would make it back down the mountain unnoticed. Wondered if it was still hot in Miami, and if Pop would make it another year or, for that matter, Jimmy.

Either way, I was certain to outlive them both. Testimony was my goddamned lot in this whirling mud ball.

"Hell, why not?" I said. "Let's bag their fuckin' loot. You collect the gold, I'll collect the brass."

"Hot damn!" Jimmy whooped, clapping his hands and checking his watch. "Okay, okay… 90 seconds. We can do this. Then we can go get your dumb-ass map."

"Dibs on Amish-Pop's cross," I called out, and started scooping up .45 casings.

Originally published in *Shotgun Honey,* September 2012

Author Bio

&@DinoParenti

L.A. author Dino Parenti specializes in dark literary and speculative fiction. He is the winner of the first annual *Lascaux Review* flash contest and features in the Anthony Award-winning anthology, *Blood on the Bayou*. His short-fiction collection, *Dead Reckoning and Other Stories*, is out now (Crystal Lake Publishing, 2018).

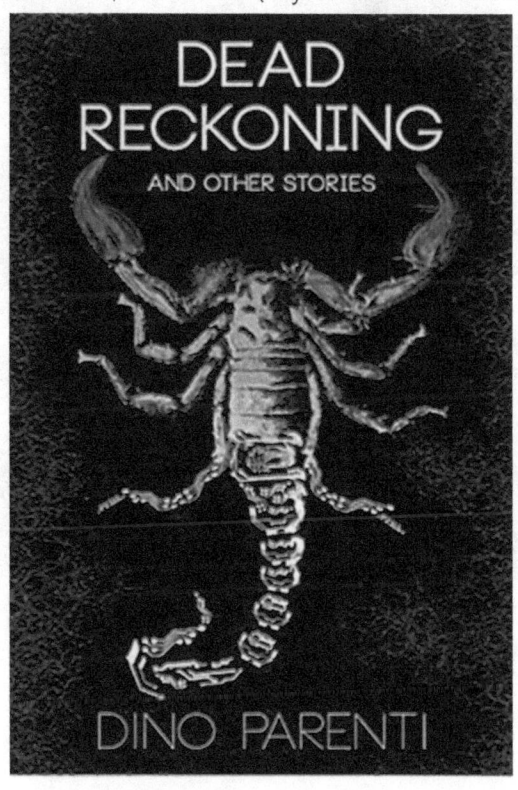

Atomic Getaway

By Jesse Bethea

The trick of it is, you never know when a bomb's coming. The Air Force never tells anyone when they run one of their little tests, so if you want to see it, you've got to spend a whole day watching the desert. You've got to have the time. I have the time. Cold beer, good book, I can spare a day. Just me and the empty edge of America and whoever else comes upstairs for a look. A whole family today. Good people, seems like. Probably came in from the suburbs or passing through on a grand western tour. None of them have sunglasses so they're saluting the sun. Little boy is getting antsy, wants to see something big and deadly.

Ah, there it is.

Even at 60-something miles, an A-bomb is quite a show. The light comes first and fills the horizon like a flashbulb, smacks my eyes through my Aviators. Must hit the family pretty good because they all gasp and *ooh* like it's the Fourth of July. Then the white clears up and there's this gorgeous golden orb in the middle of the mountains, and there, all around it, are the smoke trails they send up so they can watch the shock wave, following the smudges. Then the gold turns to a black cloud looming over the plain. No sound, not this far away. Just the sight of it, that's enough. I draw in cigarette smoke and puff up a salute. Welcome to the world, you big, beautiful monster.

And that's the show up here. I leave my seat, walk to the stairs. Family still watching. That little boy looks like he finally knows God. It's a spiral staircase back down into the café and the dark air is nice and cool enough to button up almost to my collar. Might as well look professional. Decent midday crowd here at the Getaway. Maria serves lunch here, but nothing to write home about.

Don't give me that look, she'd say so herself. She's over there, behind the bar, the bigger gal in the black skirt, pink diner shirt—**THE ATOMIC GETAWAY, LAS VEGAS, NV**. Her parents started the joint back in '47, before they started the tests in the desert. Mostly only drunks came back then, same as now. Figured out they could go up to the roof and watch all those flashes out on the range. So, Dave and Donna just decided to let them do it. Put chairs and tables up there, changed the name of the place, made up some drinks, "Fission Fizzer," "Manhattan Project Manhattan," that sort of thing. For the tourists, you know? Ones that come here every day just get beer. Dave and Donna died in a crash a couple years ago, so now it's all Maria's.

I crawl up to the bar and smash my cigarette in the ashtray. Maria doesn't always like the sight of me, but it seems like other things are on her mind today.

"Whadduya want, Kent?" says Maria. "Beer?"

"Coffee," I says. "Business lunch. Gonna grab a table too, you don't mind."

"Don't mind, don't care," says Maria. "Lucy, grab some menus."

Girl in the corner behind the bar, in the same pink shirt, startles so easy that she drops a coffee mug. Good thing she didn't lose the pot with it. Bigger mess, you know? Not that Maria cares.

"Damnit, Lucy," she yells.

"I'm sorry," says the girl. "I'm real sorry, I'll clean it up." Girl disappears somewhere, looking for a rag. Maria picks up the pot and pours another mug, slides it over, me smirking the whole time.

"New girl?"

Maria just rolls her eyes. Guess that's what's on her mind. I hold the mug around the rim and amble over to a table halfway between the bar and the door. I like to see who comes and goes. New girl brings a couple menus and I light another cigarette. I pull out my notebook and look at what I've got so far. Never liked waiting.

I got hired by Vincent Bolling—you know, the Hollywood bigwig? It was about a month ago. Mostly, though, I'd been working with his wife over the phone. She broke the news that Vince wasn't long for this world. He was never in good health, even back when I knew him, five-or-so years back. He's a jolly old dope, Vince. Latter-day Falstaff. Used to throw soundstage parties and get all the actors drunk. Invited me too. Liked my war stories. Never met his daughter, though, or Juliet, the wife. Juliet bred and took care of horses, I think, and Louisa, the daughter, was always in boarding schools. Just a kid back then. Now she's 19 and missing.

They didn't want it all over the Los Angeles papers, you know, so they didn't tell LAPD. Never tell LAPD nothing you don't want in the papers next morning. Vince sent me a letter, along with a down payment, and told me Louisa ran away in the night. She'd been living at home, that hillside villa

Vince bought after the Crosby picture was a hit. Young lady had potential, I read. Blew all the critics away with that musical a year or two back. Then she up and ran off to who knows where with who knows who. Never liked musicals.

Vince wrote how he couldn't understand it, didn't make any sense, all that stuff the parents always say. Just worried about his little girl, you know? Anyway, health went after that. Whenever Juliet phoned, she would tell me more about how far he'd sunk. Also saw it in the L.A. papers I still keep up with. The Hollywood beat said he wasn't out and about as usual. That kind of lifestyle always calls in debts. Forswear thin potations, and all that jazz. Nothing stings like consequences. I look up and down his letter again. Handwritten, you see? Neat and tidy. Heartfelt words. Can almost feel just how much the scribe wanted to find Louisa.

The little bell over the door rings. Oh my, would you look at that? Don't have to overthink this one. That's definitely her. Smart, cream dress with navy lapel trim. Peach neck scarf, probably silk, and white driving gloves pulling those pearly, swoopy sunglasses to the bridge of her nose. Golden hair all over the shoulders. She's got to be all L.A.. None of it belongs in LV. I should jump over and shake her hand. She's gonna be lost in this place otherwise and probably never recognize me. "Juliet Bolling?" I say in my sweetest client voice. "Hi, I'm Kent Collum."

She's got that little finger pinch handshake rich people use when they want to limit contact. "Mr. Collum," says Juliet Bolling. "Thank you ever so much for inviting me."

"Of course," I say. "Please sit down."

She pulls out the other chair and sits in front of the menu, wincing the whole time. Southern accent, don't you think? But not too southern. Kentucky, maybe. Horses and whatnot. "I'm sorry we've never met before this," she says. "You're not quite what I expected from a private detective."

Heard it before. Bogie set a high bar, you know? Best to laugh it off. "Yeah, stopped cutting my hair sometime after Okinawa," I say, tugging on my shirt collar. "And the whole hat and coat bit doesn't work much in the desert."

"Well," she starts, searching for something to say. "It's quite colorful."

"Yeah, it's Hawaiian."

No, not Kentucky. Virginia. No holler in that voice.

"Thank you for coming all this way," I say. "I'm afraid there's a lot to talk about and I didn't want to do it over the telephone."

Her face gets grave much too fast. "Thank you, thank you Mr. Collum," she gushes. "Vince and I are both ever so worried about Louisa."

"From what I can find," I say, "there was no foul play. It seems she ran off on her own accord. And as far as I can track, she came here."

"To Las Vegas?" she asks.

"Yes ma'am."

"But why in heavens would she want to come here?"

"Oh, all kinds of reasons, Mrs. Bolling," I say. "Some maybe you don't want to know about. This city collects runaways like..."

"Yes?"

"Well, I'm not sure," I say. "I never really collected anything. You?"

"Yes, pre-war French dressage saddles."

"Okay, yeah, like that."

"I'm just ever so frightened," she spouted. "You say there was no foul play, but what has she gotten into here? My heavens, the characters she might have fallen in with."

"A worrying prospect, ma'am."

"Drug addicts, perhaps?" she says right through me. "Sex fiends, or...or...Mexicans?"

"Mmm," I say to my watch. "Yes."

"I mean no offense, Mr. Collum, but I do not feel comfortable in this sinful place," she says. "I was ever so nervous about coming, I even took this from Vincent's office." She holds up her purse and pulls out the rear end of a tiny revolver, gloved thumb and index finger pinching the edge of the pearl grip.

"Oh my," I say. "I hope that won't be necessary."

"You don't like guns, Mr. Collum?"

"Love guns," I say, sipping coffee. "Elegant, simple, beautiful machines. It's bullets I don't much care for, and even that's just a matter of velocity."

She shoves the thing back into her purse, a little harder than might be recommended. "Will you continue searching for her, Mr. Collum?" she asks.

"Of course," I say with a reassuring hand. "I know she's in the city limits, only a matter of time. Checking with my contacts in...well, certain circles."

"Oh, heavens!" she cries, her pretty face planted in a driving glove.

"And please, call me Kent," I say. "Mr. Collum is my uncle's name."

She looks up, cocks her head. "Don't you mean your father's name?"

"Don't know my father's name."

New girl comes up and looks at us both, still nervous and fidgety as a boy waiting for an A-bomb. "May I take your orders?" she asks.

Juliet flicks open the menu and then flicks her big blues around. "I will have..." she says, slowly, like choosing a spider to pet. "The cheeseburger." Then she smacks the menu into the new girl's palms and looks away.

I smile at the poor girl. "I'll have the same, please. With fries."

The girl takes both menus and slinks away, head in her chest. Meek, and ready to inherit the Earth. Reminds me.

"Is there an inheritance?" I ask. "When Vince passes?"

"Oh, yes," says Juliet. "Quite a sum. But I don't like to talk about money."

"Rich people never do," I say. "I saw in one of the L.A. papers it was around four million."

"Morbid, morbid," she says. "Why can't they stay out of our business? But yes, it is substantial. And that is why Louisa must come home."

"I take it two of those millions are hers?"

"Yes, of course," says Juliet. "Vince wanted to make her comfortable as she started her career. But what is far more important is that she must come home before her father passes. My heavens, she might not even know he's sick. Think of the shame!" She touches my left hand with her right. "Tell me you will find her before that happens," she pleads.

"I will do my best."

"And promise me," she says, squeezing my hand. "Promise me you will call me first when you know where she is. Not the police. We must keep it from the papers. I must be the one to bring her home."

Never liked promises.

"I will do my best," I say.

I pull a cigarette from my shirt pocket and make her an offer. She accepts and I shove my Zippo over to her. Left glove covers while the right glove lights up and the new girl comes back with our food. Don't know if Juliet's ever eaten a cheeseburger before. She knows enough to take the gloves off.

"I knew you were the right choice, Mr. Collum," she says. "Vince was always so fond. He said you did such great work for him in Los Angeles."

"Yes," I say. "Different work than this."

"Oh?"

"Vince liked my stories," I say. "From the war, the Occupation and from the newspaper."

"Why did you leave California?"

"Too dry."

"And now you live in Las Vegas?"

"Vegas, Reno, Carson City, Flagstaff," I say. "I keep on the road, and I keep busy."

"Would you ever like to come back to Los Angeles?"

I smile. Not the first time I've heard it. "No ma'am," says I. "There's no place for me but the desert."

She doesn't seem very hungry and we finish in silence. Never liked talking and eating. New girl brings the bill. I pull out some cash but Juliet puts up a hand.

"No, no, Mr. Collum, I insist," she says. "You've been ever so helpful."

She pulls out a checkbook and a pen and starts writing. See? Right hand. I light another cigarette.

"Just as well," I say. "I'm left-handed, you know. Same as Vince. We used to joke about smudging everything we wrote longhand. Both of us. Looks like he cleaned up his act, though."

I hold up Vince's letter to me. Not a smudge to be seen. She looks at it, then at me. Then back at it. Ah, there it is. She gets it now. She could give me something. There's ways out of this, you know? Oh yes, he dictated, and I wrote it, blah, blah, blah. But she can't. Sometimes a person bakes a big lie so long they're just not prepared to sprinkle any little extra lies into the mix. Eyes just keep getting bigger and bigger and brighter. Flash in the desert. Something to say? No, no. She's got nothing. Swallows and throws the check down. Gloves on and storms out. Nothing stings like consequences. Bell over the door rings and dry, hot, desert air gushes in and then she's gone.

I'm standing up by now, watching her rush to her baby blue coupe, and the new girl walks over. She picks up the check and stares at it while I puff smoke.

"So you saw her kill him, then?" I say to the new girl. "Caught her in the act and then ran off before she could do you too?"

New girl just looks at me. Doe eyes. Same big blues as her mom.

"Four million," I say. "Yeah, maybe I'd do it for four million. Not my own kid, though. Not Vince, and I ain't even married to him."

I crush the cigarette in my coffee mug and start making for the door. Not before leaning in.

"Hitherto shall I come, but no further," I whisper. "Here shall my proud waves be stayed."

She looks confused. What, they don't teach kids the Old Testament no more?

"Whatever you do is whatever you do," I say to her as I leave.

And wouldn't you know it, the next day I come driving up in my old Studebaker and the cops are crawling all over the Getaway. Never liked the Vegas cops. They're also not big fans of me, as you might imagine. That guy, walking right at me, that's Detective Herman of the illustrious homicide division. That's what we in the business call a clue, boys and girls.

"What the hell'd you do, Collum?" he barks.

I walk past him and toward the baby blue coupe parked outside the Getaway. Uniforms all around and one sweaty suit taking pictures. Juliet Bolling is spilled out of the driver's side, big blues up at the sky, kitchen knife in her neck.

"Witnesses say you met her here yesterday," says Herman.

"She's a client," I say.

"Yeah?" says Herman. "Well, the desk girl at her hotel says she got a call last night. Someone left her a message, told her to meet here."

"Huh."

"And do you want to tell me why your client brought a gun in her purse?"

"Do you want me to do your job, Detective?" I say. "Murder ain't my speed."

"Yeah, and where were you?"

"Out on the Strip all night," I say. You know me, you know where to check."

He pushes back his jacket and puts his hands on his hips, chin up and tongue almost clucking at the top of his mouth. I've got about a foot on Herman, so he's got one of those Napoleon attitudes, only Napoleon conquered Europe and Herman has to share an office with one of the armed robbery guys.

"I will check, Collum," says Herman. "But until then, you're staying here."

"Don't mind if I do," I say, lighting a cigarette. "Should be about that time, anyway."

She must've found my name in Vince's records after she did him and after Louisa took off. Probably figured I was a good fit. Just the right bloodhound to lead her to her daughter and all four million. Led her to a knife in the neck instead. Bad way to go. Not that there's a good way. My apologies, Mrs. Bolling, but you did have the advantage. I knew I got a bad feeling from that gun. I figured maybe she was telling the truth about being scared. But no, it was always for Louisa.

I walk across the road to where Maria is standing, smoking, and staring across the desert.

"New girl show up for work?" I ask.

"Lucy?" asks Maria. "I ain't seen her."

"Didn't think she had it in her."

"Kent," she says. "When they're gone, you're gonna tell me exactly what happened here."

"You're gonna love it," I say. "Promise."

A white flash washes over everything and clears out just as fast. We squint out at the sand and watch that brilliant, golden star turn ashy and orderly, climbing into the sky, announcing itself to the desert. Hello, beautiful.

Originally published by *Tell-Tale Press,* 2019

Author Bio

@JesseCBethea   /JesseBetheaAuthor

Award-winning journalist and videographer Jesse Bethea is a resident of Columbus, Ohio, along with his wife and three cats. His first novel, *Fellow Travellers*, won the 2019 Great Novel Contest as a time-teleporting adventure equal parts crime, conspiracy, and comedy (Bellwether, 2021). Keep up with his latest projects at JesseBethea.com.

More From Our Authors

20 dark short stories by debut and veteran subversive writers like Craig Clevenger, Greg Levin, Lauren Sapala, Stephen J. Golds, Paige Johnson, & more! Everything from serial killers and speculative cannibals to strippers and smack addicts.

Denim

By Joseph S. Walker

At just past 11:30 on a Saturday night, the Argos Diner was not quite busy enough for Ollie to feel guilty about holding a booth as he read his book. Andy topped off his coffee every half hour or so and left Ollie alone otherwise. Ollie's tip would more than justify the space he was taking up.

Half a dozen people sat at the counter, most alone, absorbed in their phones. Couples and small groups, fresh from the theater or on their way out to the bars, took up booths and tables. A slippage hour. Some ending their days, some starting a new one. Some just stitching the time together any way they could. Like Ollie.

His booth was in the farthest corner, his cane hooked over the table to his side. Farthest from the door, near the restrooms. He sat with his back to the room. Once in a while, a voice rose above the general murmur and his eyes flicked to the mirror he was facing, then went back to the book.

He was starting to think about leaving when a woman slipped onto the bench across the table from him. She took his Mets cap off the table and put it on, pulling it low over her eyes. Ollie had just a glimpse of short dark hair and wide brown eyes before the brim cut off everything above her lips. A denim jacket draped over her shoulders, the sleeves hanging empty. She pushed herself back into the corner, as far as she could get from the aisle.

Ollie marked his place with a finger. "I'm sorry, miss," he said. "I think you've got the wrong table."

"Be quiet," the woman said. Leaning back, she let the jacket fall open so Ollie could see her arms crossed in front of her. Her right hand was holding a small, shiny handgun, an automatic. Her left was clutched tightly to her side. She was wearing a blue T-shirt, and the part of it underneath her left hand was covered in a vivid, dark red stain.

As soon as he saw it, Ollie caught the coppery scent of blood.

"I'm going to sit here for a few minutes. You do anything I don't like, I'll start shooting people."

Andy appeared at the side of the table as the jacket closed. "Get you something to drink?" he asked the woman.

"Water," she said. She didn't look at him. Her eyes were fixed over Ollie's shoulder.

Ollie put his bookmark between the pages as Andy hustled away. "You're hurt," he said. "Can I get you some help?"

"Just stay quiet. Anybody asks, I'm here with you. I'm your niece or something." Her left hand, stained red, snaked out of the jacket. She pulled a wad of napkins from the dispenser and brought them back under her jacket, wincing as she pressed them against her side.

Ollie folded his hands. "If you're my niece, shouldn't I know your name?"

"What?" For the first time, the woman looked him full in the face. She was in her thirties, Ollie thought, though freckles spreading across her cheeks made her seem younger. "Whatever. Fine. Call me Helen." Her gaze went back over his shoulder.

Ollie grunted. "At Argos with Helen. I think I can remember that. My name is Ollie."

Andy put a glass of water on the table and looked pointedly at the menu propped between the napkins and a ketchup bottle. "Anything to eat?"

"No." Helen still didn't look up at him. "I won't be here long."

"Andy, this is Helen," Ollie said. "My niece."

"Pleasure," Andy said. "I'll check in on you in a bit."

Ollie watched in the mirror as Andy crossed the room and began taking orders from a rowdy group of college-age men. When he looked back at Helen, her mouth was tight.

"Don't call attention to me," she said.

"I've been coming here for years. Andy would expect me to introduce anyone sitting with me."

"Fine. But don't push it."

Ollie finished his coffee. He set the cup at the edge of the table, where Andy would see it. "Won't it look odd if we're just sitting here quietly staring into space?"

"Fine." There were beads of perspiration on her face. "Talk."

"Are you waiting for someone? You seem to be watching the door."

"I didn't say ask questions. Just talk." She glanced at the table. "Tell me about the book you're reading."

"It's a novel about the first World War."

"Yeah? Who's winning?"

"I don't think there was a winner. Just a prolonged time-out."

Andy walked by, one hand holding a pot of coffee, the other under an enormous tray balanced on his shoulder. He barely broke stride as he filled Ollie's cup.

Ollie tore open two packets of sweetener and poured them in. "You're not really listening to me."

"I've got things on my mind."

"Were you shot?"

She let out a deep breath through her nose. "Stabbed."

"By somebody still after you?"

"Stop trying to get a story out of me," she hissed. She looked over her shoulder at the short hallway to the restrooms. "Is there a back way out?"

"There's a door past the toilets. I assume it goes outside. I have no idea if it's locked."

"Fuck."

"Are you in pain?"

"I said, stop asking me questions." Helen's breathing was rapid and shallow. "Just talk. Tell me about yourself."

"There's not much to tell," Ollie said. "I was an engineer. Now I'm retired. I was married. Now I'm widowed." He sipped the hot coffee. "My life is heavy on *was*."

"Everybody's got a story," Helen said.

"What's yours?"

She just shook her head.

"Tell me anything," he said. "Tell me this. If I end up reading about you in the news, would I be happy about you getting away, or happy about you getting arrested?"

For the first time, Helen picked up her water, drained half of it in a few hurried gulps. When she put the glass down, the condensation was tinted pink with blood.

Ollie took a napkin and wiped it off.

Helen watched him do it. "I'm not going to be on the news."

"I did say *if.*"

She wouldn't meet his eyes. "I'm going to sit here for maybe 10 minutes, Ollie. If nothing happens in that time, I'm going to get up and leave. You'll never see me again or know anything about it."

"Hmm." Ollie cupped his coffee. "That sounds frustrating."

"Life can be that way. Tell me something else. You got kids?"

"No. Eleanor couldn't. We talked about adoption, but it never happened." Ollie stopped talking because Helen wasn't listening.

She stiffened, then slumped further into her corner, a tiny slice of her eyes visible under the brim of the hat.

Ollie looked at the mirror.

A tall, solidly built man stood just inside the door, scanning the room. His hair was blond and cut in a tight military buzz. He was wearing a leather raincoat, the belt tied loosely at his waist.

"You look like you're hiding," Ollie said. "Don't slouch that much. It's not natural."

"Shut up." She straightened a little. "It's not going to make a difference."

The blond man's gaze had almost reached them.

Ollie saw Helen's right arm, the one with the gun, twitch. "You don't want to do that in here," Ollie said. "All these people."

"Not my call."

In the mirror, the blond man saw Helen. He smiled and his hand went inside his raincoat, but, at the same instant, the door opened. A uniformed policeman came in. He had to step around the blond man, and there was a little pantomime of *excuse me* and *no problem* between them. The blond man's eyes never left the corner where Helen was sitting.

"The policeman can help you," Ollie said.

"No. He can't."

The cop went to the counter and, loudly asked for a coffee to-go. The waitress was new. Ollie didn't know her name yet. The blond man stood for a moment, uncertain, then took a stool a few feet to the cop's right. He swiveled and looked straight at Helen. His smile was broad, taunting. He took a toothpick from the dispenser and stuck it in the corner of his mouth.

Helen was pale.

Ollie scooted a little closer to the aisle. "I'll go tell the cop you need help."

"No." Her voice was urgent.

"This guy your boyfriend? Husband?"

"Don't make me sick." She was looking straight at the blond, their eyes locked.

"I think I deserve to know what I'm in the middle of," Ollie said.

"Probably. You know a lot of people who get what they deserve?"

The counterwoman handed a cardboard cup to the officer, who seemed impossibly young to Ollie, like someone wearing a costume in a school play. The cop said something to her, and they both laughed. He slapped the counter and turned away, heading for the door.

Helen scooted to the other edge of the bench, almost hanging off it into the aisle.

Ollie sat very still.

The cop went out the door.

The instant it closed behind him, Helen was on her feet. She pivoted and pushed through the swinging doors to the restrooms, moving as fast as she could manage.

Ollie watched the mirror. The blond man was coming this way, not quite running. One hand was inside the breast of his raincoat. As he came even with the table, Ollie grasped the head of his cane and tilted it toward him. Its long, metal body angled out into the aisle, between the blond man's legs, and was jerked out of Ollie's hand as the man stumbled and fell forward, his hand tangled with something inside the coat. His shoulder struck the doorframe hard enough for Ollie to feel the vibration.

There was an immediate silence as everyone turned to look for the source of the crash. Ollie had a piercing memory of being in a school cafeteria, hearing someone drop a tray of silverware, the same shocked, confused silence as everyone took stock.

He leaned into the aisle. "I'm so sorry, sir. I didn't see you. Are you all right?"

The blond man rolled onto his back. Ollie had a glimpse of some kind of long gun held against his side before he pulled the raincoat closed. His face was twisted with rage, but, before he could do anything, Andy was kneeling beside him, making apologetic noises, and reaching for his hand to help him up.

"I didn't see him, Andy," Ollie said again.

The blond man pushed Andy away and got to his feet, moving awkwardly. Most of the people watching probably thought he was hurt. Ollie knew he was trying to keep the gun hidden. When he was standing, he rolled his shoulders and winced. The look he gave Ollie was venomous. "You're lucky I don't have time to deal with you, old man."

"Hey," Andy said. "There's no call for that, now."

The blond man shook his head. He turned and went through the swinging doors.

Helen had not reappeared, so Ollie guessed the back door wasn't locked.

"What an asshole," Andy said. He picked up Ollie's cane and handed it to him. "You okay?"

"Just shaken up," Ollie said. He took a twenty from his wallet and pressed it into Andy's hand. "Take care of my check, will you? Keep the change."

"Sure," Andy said. He took Ollie's elbow and helped him stand. "Hey, where's your hat? I don't think I've ever seen you without it."

"Oh." Ollie felt the top of his head, as if checking that the hat was really gone. "I guess Helen took off with it. She can be a little flighty."

"Seems like it," Andy said. "She forgot her jacket, too." He picked up the denim jacket and held it out. "You can get it back to her, right?"

"Sure." Ollie draped it over his arm. He wondered how much blood he'd find when he looked it over at home. "I'll see you tomorrow night, Andy."

"I'm off," Andy said. "But I'll see you Monday, yeah?"

Ollie nodded.

On the sidewalk outside, he paused, listening for shots, or yells, or running feet.

There was nothing. It was getting a little chillier, fall definitely coming. He thought about putting the jacket on but didn't.

Probably, he would never know if he'd just done a good thing.

But he'd done *something*.

He ran a palm along the tough fabric and turned for home.

Author Bio

 @JSWalkerAuthor

Joseph S. Walker lives in Indiana, where he teaches college literature and composition courses. His stories have appeared in Alfred Hitchcock's and Ellery Queen's respective *Mystery Magazines*, *Tough*, and many anthologies. Walker won the Bill Crider Prize for Short Fiction, as well as the 2019 and 2021 Al Blanchard Award. His novella *Two Black Bean and Shrimp Quesadillas and a Pink Ruger* (Down and Out Books, 2022) is part of their Guns + Tacos series.

Watch Yourself

By Gordon Dunleavy

"I need to talk to you about something."

Jerome takes his eyes from the front door of the diner after what seems like hours. He squints at his comfortably dressed partner across the table from him while his eyes adjust. "What is it? Is it about what Boss-man has us doing?"

"No... I don't think so anyway."

"Then I don't care."

Louie sighs. "Well, I'm going to tell you anyway. Last night, I was watching a movie. A foreign one with subtitles. Korean, I think. Beautifully filmed. But there was this one scene in particular, had some loud background noise in the shot while the two actors were talking, and—"

"Where're you going with this? How is this relevant to now?"

"Well, I did something I've never done before. Something that has me worried about my cogstinance."

"You mean cognizance?"

"Goddamn it. What the hell is happening to me?"

"What the fuck, Louie? What's going on? If this is something that'll compromise the reason we're here, you need to tell me now. Like right. The fuck. Now."

"I turned the volume up."

Jerome's anger obliterates any awkwardness in the silence. "Say again?" Jerome had no trouble understanding what his partner said. He just wanted to make sure Louie caught how ridiculous his words sounded.

"I told you. I turned the volume up on the movie."

"Louie, we're at this diner for business, not to record a podcast about your boring life." Jerome checks his watch as he goes back to staking out the front door. "Jesus, get your mind on what we're doing here. I don't want to hear any more about you turning the volume up on a flick with explosions or some shit. None of that should be of concern right now, and it's certainly nothing that should be said aloud to anybody...ever."

"But they were speaking Korean in the movie... I don't speak Korean."

Jerome's head falls into his hands.

"My mind's going, Jerome. Who in their right mind needs to turn the volume up to read the subtitles better? There's something wrong with me."

"Something? As in one thing?"

Louie cocks his head.

Jerome continues. "I've worked with you for over a decade. I could name you 10 somethings that are wrong with your head if you'd like. And only three of them have to do with that fuck-face you were born with."

"That's cold. That's hitting below the belt. I'm trying to open up to you, Jerome. I'm trying to be real and talk about how fleeting time is on this Earth, and you just shut me down." Louie turns the dinner knife on the table 'til his reflection shows. "Have you ever thought about what we're doing with our lives? Are we making the world better or worse?"

"What the fuck are you talking about? You backing out on me? On this mission? Are you gonna make me do this solo?"

"No. God. I'm just...talking."

A waitress in a frilly, greasy apron approaches the table. Her voice graveled from too many cigarettes. "One coffee. Black." The first cup clinks to the table. "One chai latte, soy, no foam, with a zest of cinnamon." The last cup drops in front of Louie. Most of the contents stay in, but more than a dribble splashes onto the table. The waitress turns toe and plods to the next customer before Louie or Jerome confirms the order.

Louie and Jerome say, "Thanks," to the back of the waitress's head.

Jerome sips his coffee. "Maybe your mind is declining."

"What? Why?"

"Your order? Fucking chai latte with soy?"

"With a zest of cinnamon. Yeah? What of it?"

"We're sitting in Spoony's Diner. A fucking hole of a restaurant. They don't have that shit you ordered. The waitress was pulling your leg. You're not sipping on a chai latte, Louie. What you got in front of you is a mug full of fuckin' Folgers and a squirt of whole milk."

"This has dairy?"

"100% it has dairy."

Louie shrugs as he takes a sip.

"What're you doing? You're lactose."

"I need the caffeine, and I have no intention of accusing that lady who just walked away of lying."

"Jesus fucking Christ, Louie. Once we're done here, we're stopping at the next Target to button up that asshole of yours so tight, even the Kool-Aid man won't have a chance of breaking through."

"Not funny. You always take things too far." Louie shakes his head and checks the time on his watch. "He should be here by now."

"Yeah. I know. He's late. I'll give it a few before—" The front door dings open. "Well, well, well."

"What? What is it?"

"Big Roy. Goddamn. He's…big. Way bigger than the pictures make him out to be. What Boss-man told us does not do him justice. It's one thing seeing six-foot-seven, 350 pounds on paper, and it's another seeing it with my own two eyes. Goddamn. Looks like that guy could bench press a Bradley."

"What's he wearing?"

"Louie. You've seen his pictures. Plus, he's six-foot-seven, 350 pounds? That won't stand out to you? You need me to describe his shirt's floral pattern in order for you to pick him out?"

Louie grunts.

"Okay, he's sitting down. I—"

"Where did he sit?"

Jerome exhales an annoyed sigh. "He's a mob boss in a shit-hole diner. Where do you think he's sitting?"

"That corner booth in the back? The one nearest the kitchen?"

"Good job. You get a gold star. Now keep your eyes on the reflection in the window to keep up with the rest of the class. We're going to make our move soon. Don't screw this up, Louie. You know how important this is."

"There's a lotta people here. You sure we should do this?"

"You gettin' soft on me, Louie?"

"No. I—"

"Then shut up and get your head on straight. Don't forget, his guys are carrying. It ain't anything out of the norm, but they always have heat on 'em. Even Roy's carrying. Usually something small on the ankle. You got it? Now throw some money on the table to cover our tab. We're moving."

Jerome pushes himself up from the table. Louie does the same after tucking a $50 under his coffee mug.

Nobody in the restaurant takes any notice of the two men walking to the back booth, but that's about to change.

"Hey, Roy!" Everyone in the diner, except Roy, stops what they're doing to see who shouted. Jerome continues in the hushed silence. "You got something of ours we're gonna need back."

Two pillars of sadistic muscle plant themselves between their boss and the newcomers. The silver butt of a snubnose gleams from an inside shoulder holster of the man on the right. Big Roy never addresses Jerome's accusation. Just takes another bite of the country-fried steak that was waiting for him when he sat down.

Jerome's growl crescendos to a yell, "You're going to want to fucking listen to me, Roy."

Roy still refuses to pay him any mind, refuses to let his eyes leave the greasy slop sitting in front of him.

Jerome pulls out his weapon from his waist and explodes the kneecap of Big Roy's right pillar, toppling him to the ground. When the guard on the left reaches for something from his back waist, Jerome doesn't give him a chance for show and tell, but he does give him a 9mm slug to the knee like he did his comrade.

Every patron, save for the ones with holes in their knees, writhing in pain, sits statue-still. Even the drunks have enough wherewithal to stay silent.

Big Roy shovels another forkful of fried meat into his mouth. His eyes never meet Jerome's or Louie's. "A real pity," Big Roy says to no one. "I had such hopes for my men. Looks like I got a couple of open spots on the roster again. And these ain't jobs you can put up a **Help Wanted** sign for."

"Sorry about putting you in that tough position, Roy. I really am."

Roy takes his eyes from his plate for the first time to see what angle Jerome is playing.

"I'm going through a minor crisis of my own. You see, I can't stand the number 13. And after the two shots I used to take your men down, 13 is the exact amount of rounds I have left in my magazine. So, I was thinking, since you're not cooperating with us, how about I use one more between your eyes? Then I'll have an even 12 sitting in my reservoir, and you won't have to worry yourself about starting up anymore 401Ks." Jerome's gun sits rock-solid in his left hand, outstretched. He looks to Louie, who hasn't even pulled his gun.

Without a word, Louie reaches to his waist and mimics his partner. His gun isn't as steady, but it's aimed at the same spot.

"So, what do you say, Roy? Wanna talk to us, or do you want your mama kissing a pile of mush at your funeral next week?"

"Fuck," Roy chews four bites of greasy steak before saying, "you."

Jerome looks to Louie to signal that he's at the end of his rope. It's time he takes the reins of the conversation, just like they've done all those times before.

"That watch on your wrist, Roy," Louie says. "That belongs to our employer. I believe it would be in your best interest to hand it over."

Big Roy stops chewing. He wants to swallow, but he can't. His throat is bone-dry. "You're... You're Bruno's men... Aren't yo...you. Why didn't you tell me?"

"I'm glad you've heard of our employer," Louie says. "And that he frightens you as much as he frightens us. Now, hand over the watch to my partner."

Jerome walks forward with the palm of his non-gun hand up. Only the perspiration on Big Roy's forehead moves.

Louie wasn't sure if fear or stubbornness had frozen him. So, he finishes his request with a "Please."

The watch rattles on Big Roy's wrist while he peels back the latch, and hands it over.

Jerome looks over the watch and shows it to his partner. Louie exhales.

"What's with the sigh?" Big Roy asks. "You have the watch. There aren't any scratches or dings on it. The thing's fucking cherry. What are you complaining about?"

"That watch is not 'fucking' cherry, Roy." Louie keeps calm despite the disrespect shown to him. "This particular timepiece, before you stole it, was never worn. It had a serial number on a piece of foil attached to the back. But when you slipped this once-immaculate 1971 Rolex Oyster Cosmograph onto your wrist, you rubbed off that foil, halving its value. Now instead of it being a goddamn Van Gogh, it's a fucking tchotchke—albeit an expensive tchotchke—that tells time. So, to address your concern, Roy, you are mistaken. You didn't give us the watch you took from our employer. You gave us back something completely different."

"That's bullshit. How am I supposed to know about some goddamn sticker on the back of the watch? That ain't on me. You can't fuck me over on a technicality."

"That technicality, Roy, is worth a lot more than the town we're standing in." Louie puts his gun back in his waistband holster. Jerome's jaw drops ever so slightly. Louie wasn't supposed to do that. Guns don't get holstered 'til the threat is neutralized. They both know the rule. They've both abided by it for the last decade.

Something's up with Louie.

Roy's as unsure of Louie next move as Jerome is, and he wishes the revolver on his ankle was closer than it is. Roy shifts in his seat, peeling his sweat-soaked back from the vinyl of the booth. "Now, I'm not as much of a heavyweight in our line of business as your employer Bruno is, but I can still do things he might not be able to."

"We're listening."

"I know a guy. I've used him before. He's top-notch. He can put that foil thing back on the watch and everyone will be happy."

"Do you really think Bruno would go for a forgery?" Louie asks. "A guy Elmer's Gluing on some tinfoil to the back of the *Starry Night* of watches sounds like a good idea?

"No, I never said—"

The grip Jerome has on his gun tightens, but Louie holds up his index finger, asking for a little more time. "You're fucked, Roy," Louie says, "and you know it. But today is your lucky day because now is usually the time in our little show where we use our guns to…flash you our brights, so to speak. But today… Today is not one of those days."

The glare Jerome gives Louie tells the entire diner Louie's going off script.

"You owe my employer. There is no doubt about that. You took something from him that cannot be returned. And since he's made more money in the time that we've been talking than you have all year, any monetary compensation you offer will be humorous at best."

"If he doesn't want money, then what the fuck does he want?"

"That's easy," Louie says. "Bruno wants what everyone else in this world wants—to not be fucked with. That's why he sent my partner and me here to pick you up and deliver your body…your dead body, to him. Does that properly address your concern, Roy, of what the fuck my employer wants?"

With a gun pointed at his head, Roy knows the only response to a question like that is silence.

"But like I said, we don't have to go that route if you don't want to."

Jerome has to clench everything to keep from shouting at Louie. He wants him to stick to the plan. The plan that's always worked. But Jerome doesn't say a word because insubordination in front of the people they're trying to intimidate will do nothing but cause problems.

"I always prefer plans where my heart is still beating at the end," Roy says.

"Fair enough. I'd be the same way too."

Jerome shifts his stance. His gun still sits rock-solid in his grip, pointing at the man they came for.

"Now, I didn't come to this diner planning to do what I'm about to," Louie says. "I had every intention of throwing your body in the trunk and having you buried in a field of nothing. But right here, just now, when I drew my weapon, my own mortality came to mind as well as the deaths I've caused before you. How many bodies have I killed, and how many more would I have done in the future? I couldn't help but think how short all our lives are. So today, you are a free man."

Big Roy stands to leave.

Jerome can't hold it any longer. "What the fuck are you doing, Louie? Why are you trying to save this asshole?"

"Jerome—Cool it. I got this. And Roy, sit back down and listen a bit more, because freedom, your freedom, will come at a cost."

Roy does as he's told.

"Now if I were to set you free, my employer would be upset with me, and I can't have that happen. He's trusted me for years. He's helped me put a nice roof over my head and a few other extravagancies that have made my life pleasurable. So, in doing what I want to do, I will have to make him happy while also not killing anyone, including yourself. So, here's what you're going to do—"

A hole blasts through Big Roy's head. His blood and brains paint the wall behind him red. His giant body slumps the length of the booth he was sitting in. His wrist, tan-lined from the Rolex watch, goes limp.

The front doorbell jingles. Everyone in the diner turns to see two well-dressed men with their guns at the ready and Bruno. Right there, next to them, holding his own gun. Cordite smoke trickling from its barrel.

"You didn't think you'd get away with this, did you, Louie?" Bruno pays no mind to the others in the diner. His full attention is on Louie. "Jerome warned us you weren't acting right. Talking about abandoning me and whatnot." Jerome couldn't take his eyes from the floor since the big man keeled. "Any update since our last communication, Jerome?"

"Louie said he had no plans to kill Roy or anybody else."

"Is that true, Louie?"

"The thing is—"

"Yes…or no… Did you say those things?"

Louie hangs his head and answers, "Yes."

"You don't want to kill anyone anymore?"

Louie shakes his head no.

"You mean people like this guy?" Bruno's gun rises to a Q-tip view of a man in a silk shirt. A pair of gold Ray-Bans, folded, sit on the table in front of him. The gray streaking his hair shines under the fluorescent lights. And after Bruno pulls the trigger, the shards of bone and sinew left hanging from his jaw and skull shine even brighter. The woman opposite the silk-shirted dead man lies doubled over in the four-person booth, sobbing, screaming for the nightmare to end.

The entire diner gasps.

Bruno continues, "You wanted to save one life? Now I've taken two. If you would've just done your goddamn job, you would've saved a precious life. Now, look at you. I don't know what's come over you. But whatever it is, we're done. My trust in you is broken." Bruno turns to his men next to him. "Take that piece of shit outside."

The punch to Louie's stomach knocks him to his knees. The elbow to his face makes his world go black.

Gravel digging into his back wakes Louie to a splitting headache. Louie wants to scream from the pain, but his body only allows him to moan. A single cloud floating through a blue sky takes up Louie's entire field of vision. Under different circumstances, he might've thought it beautiful. Louie lies on the ground surrounded by people he'd rather not be.

Bruno is the only one standing without a drop of sweat on his brow. "Did you really think I'd be okay with what you did? That I'd thank you for changing the plan and let you be free to go about a life not under my employ?" Bruno circles Louie's body. He stops when his own shadow lays across his prey's chest.

Louie squints twice to look his employer in the eye, but the glare of the sun is too much. Everything is too much. But everyone, including Louie, knows the pain won't last much longer. Words struggle out of Louie's mouth. But if he's going to survive, his voice is all he has. "I wasn't trying to go against you, Bruno. Honest. You've given me everything. Everything that's made me happy in my life is because of you. Please. Give me another chance." Louie rolls to his side to get up, but the pain is too much.

A calm comes over Bruno. "With our lives, the lives we have chosen, you know I can't let you go. We have chosen to chase that almighty dollar, to forego a 9-to-5, to become rulers of our little square in the world. You have helped me on my journey, and I, no doubt, yours. So, when you went against my wishes, you, like Big Roy, stole from me. Though what you took wasn't a material object like a watch, it was still something precious to me. You took my power...my clout. You stole my fear, a tiny swatch of terror I worked so hard on instilling in those trying to bump me out of my path. That Louie, that is more valuable than any watch ever crafted. If people in this game of ours think for even one second that I am vulnerable, that there's a chink in my armor, then the life I have worked so hard to create will deteriorate. And Louie, that can't happen. Not yet. Not at your hands. My time will come. I'm not naïve. But that time is not now. Your time, on the other hand..."

Tears won't stop rolling down Louie's cheeks. "There's gotta be another way."

"I don't know what you expect me to do. You sealed your fate the moment you went against me. All I'm doing is completing the circle, crossing the Ts and whatnot. If I don't do this, others will come after me. People much smarter and stronger than you."

"You won't get away with this. My family, my friends, they won't let this stand. They'll come after you if you do this."

"I expect things like that to happen. The cost of doing business and all. But in your case, Louie? I'll be fine."

Louie finds the strength to sit up.

"You have no one, Louie. It's always been that way. Ever since you came to work for me, you've been alone. You go home to an empty house.

You work holidays and your birthday. We've been keeping tabs on you. We know your story, Louie. No one is coming after you."

Louie starts to say something, but Bruno cuts him off.

"When you went against me, you cut every last tie, every lifeline you had. Nobody's coming to save you, Louie. No one loves you. You will not be missed. This is the end of your path. This is your goodbye."

"I'm begging you. Please—"

A single shot echoes off the diner and down through the canyon on the other side. Bruno falls to the ground. His body becomes still in the oil-stained asphalt of the near-empty parking lot.

Jerome walks up and looms over Bruno's dead body. Waves of heat from his gun barrel ripple in the sunshine. "May you not pollute the next world like you did mine." Jerome spits on Bruno's face. "No one may love Louie, but he doesn't deserve to die for finding a set of morals." Jerome readies his weapon and fires again into his chest just in case Bruno has one last flail of hate in him.

Bruno's two bodyguards take a step back from the chaos. Their hands hover over their holstered weapons.

Jerome shouts at them, "Any of you two got a problem with what I've done?"

They both shake their heads.

"Then take Bruno's car, take his wallet, take his fucking head, for all I care. You have done a day's work, and you both deserve to be compensated for your time."

One guard says, "You want us to leave anything for you? Would hate to be greedy and take it all."

Jerome fingers the Rolex in his pocket. "No, man. We're square."

With Bruno's pockets picked clean and his car on its way to a chop shop in the city, Jerome nods to Louie, who's now sitting on a curb stop. "Come on. We got a long ride ahead of us."

A million words flood Louie's brain, but all that comes out is, "Thanks."

Jerome shakes his head. "Didn't do it just for you, Louie. Selfishness had a lot to do with that outburst of mine. I figure, if I'm going to live in this world, I'm living in a place with people like you, and not that asshole Bruno." A smile crawls across Jerome's face, but he turns his head to hide his joy. "Come on, Louie. The cops will be here soon." Jerome rounds the hood to the driver's seat of the black sedan.

Louie struggles his way to the passenger's side.

Before Jerome unlocks the doors, he asks Louie, "You okay?"

"Yeah, I mean that elbow to the face rang my bell, but I'm getting bett—"

"No, I don't care about that. I'm talking about all the dairy you had earlier. I was going to stop at the closest pharmacy, but I'd prefer to get a few miles under our belts before pulling over."

"There's no need to stop."

"Louie, I told you. That's not an option. You've just had a head injury, I get it, so I'll give you some slack, but we're stopping at a place if I have to drag you by the hair to do it. Don't make me regret saving your ass."

"Jerome, I had a psychopath hold a gun to my head with every intention of pulling the trigger. I don't need the pharmacy because everything lactose that was inside my body is now streaked somewhere between Roy's booth and the asphalt we're standing on. But if you want to stop for a pair of briefs and some stretch pants, I'm all for it."

"Goddamn it. I should've let Bruno take the shot. At least with him—"

Louie tries the locked handle of the car.

"What are you doing?" Jerome asks.

"I'm trying to get in."

"That's cute, but you're not riding shotgun…or even backseat."

"What? Why?"

"For the same reason they keep dumps on the outskirts of towns. Ain't no one want to smell your shit-stained britches for the next eight hours.

"Well, where am I going to sit?"

Jerome clicks the fob on his keychain and the trunk pops open.

"You son of a bitch. I'm not riding back there."

"If you don't strip and get in the trunk and wipe every part of you down with the Armor All wipes back there, you're walking the fuck home."

Louie sits on the edge of the trunk and disrobes, reminding himself he's lucky to even be alive. When he wipes down his first leg, he throws it inside. "If you spot a nice, pleated khaki when you're buying me pants, I'd appreciate something in a lighter tone."

Jerome puts his hands on the lid of the trunk while Louie cleans the rest of himself. "You're getting fucking sweatpants and a bill in the mail. The only way you're getting anything different is if the tarps are closer to the front door."

Louie, naked, lying on his side in the trunk, props himself up on his elbow. He can't help but smile when he looks into Jerome's eyes. "Thanks again for what you did. You're my only best frien—"

The trunk shuts closed, slamming Louie on the head with a hollow *thud* before his last word. Jerome smiles as he turns back to the driver's door. He whispers, "You're mine too."

Author Bio

@GordonDunleavy

Dual citizen of Ireland and the United States, Gordon Dunleavy is an affiliate member of the Horror Writers Association. He has a short story published in Amazon's #1 best-selling horror anthology, *Night Terrors Vol. 3.* (Scare Street, 2020). He's currently working on his third novel, *The Glow Before The Storm*, when he's not hiking with the cutest one-year-old in the world strapped to his back or exploring the world with the rest of his family.

Stuck In The Middle

By Karen Keeley

Driving on a wing and a prayer the last 30 miles, his luck about to run out, when he spotted a filling station, a miracle if there ever was one. He angled his Chevy Impala toward the pumps, coasting to a stop. His vehicle gave a last gasp, a sputter, and it died. The old-timer sitting out front, his vintage ballcap pulled low over his brow, lifted his chin and gave the driver a hard stare. He left the boardwalk, hands in his pockets. "Fill 'er up," he asked, more of a statement than a question.

"Is the Pope Catholic?" said the guy driving, a wave of relief washing over him; then, "Where the hell am I?"

The old-timer lifted the nozzle and removed the gas cap, his movements quick, fluid. "Nowhere, to hear others tell it, but me? I been here 30 years, give or take."

"You're a sight for sore eyes, I'll give you that," said the driver; then, "You got any grub inside? Maybe a sandwich or two, a cold beer? I can pay. I'm not expecting charity."

"O' course you'll pay," said the old-timer. "Gas ain't free either." He took up the squeegee and made a half-hearted attempt to clean the windshield, it spatted with bug guts, using what little water he had in a bucket.

The fella driving, now standing in what little shade there was under the canopy, looked off toward the horizon, not a breath of wind. "Anywhere I can wash up? Take a piss?"

"Around back. Got me an outhouse with a bucket of water by the door."

"Christ," muttered the driver, shoving his eyeglasses up the bridge of his nose.

The old fella finished up with the squeegee, dropped it back in the bucket. He gave the nozzle a shake, hung it at the side of the pump, asking, "Where you headed?"

"Puget Sound, home to saltwater, seaweed and crabs."

The old fella chuckled, offered his take on the destination: "Peptides and riptides," a feeble attempt at a joke.

The guy driving, he wiped the back of his neck with a soiled handkerchief, got back behind the wheel and cranked the ignition key, angling the vehicle toward the boardwalk. Only then did he notice the window off to the left, what he took to be a diner.

He killed the engine, climbed out of the Impala, slamming shut the driver's door. He didn't bother to lock it. Anything of value was in the trunk: one suitcase and a leather billfold containing a cool grand, a thousand smackeroos—the better part of a year to earn that money, now headed to Seattle. For what, he didn't know. A reconciliation maybe. Or a showdown. That depended on Brenda, the little witch.

He headed round back, made use of the outhouse and the bucket of water, a bunch of dead flies floating on the surface, drying his hands with the soiled hanky. He returned to the diner, noticing two newspaper articles, both framed, hung side by side in back of the cash register. One read **Aliens Captured by US Agents** and the other **UFO found in New Mexico**, more than three decades since that story caught the public's attention.

He paid for the gas, 15 bucks, glad the old fella hadn't gouged him, hadn't charged him double. He could've done that, been one mean son of a bitch, but instead, he proved to be a straight arrow after all, not like Brenda.

The old fella said he had a loaf of bread along with the fixin's, he could rustle up a couple of sandwiches. "You be wantin' ham or roast beef?" He was headed toward the diner side, swapping out his grimy ballcap for an apron as filthy as the hat.

"Make it one of each," said the driver, sliding his sorry ass onto one of the bar stools, his mind occupied by that kewpie doll he'd seen earlier in the day at a roadside pullout, looking to stretch his legs. He'd left the Impala idling, a stupid thing to do, using up gas while walking in circles, and that's when he saw it, that kewpie doll laying in the dirt, its face smashed in. He couldn't help but think someone wacked the doll's face against a fencepost. A kid maybe? A disgruntled parent? Too many miles cooped up, going squirrely, trapped like a rat. After he got settled back behind the wheel, he'd cranked up the air-conditioning, knowing he was probably shooting himself in the foot, given the readout on the gas gauge. He wanted to put the image of that broken doll's face out of his mind.

"What's your story?" asked the old-timer, cutting thick slices of bread from a loaf he'd pulled from the icebox, the fixin's, too.

Overhead, a ceiling fan rotated slower than the second coming, no relief there. "You wouldn't believe me if I told you."

"Try me," said the old fella. "I ain't deaf yet."

"Blessed be the saints and them what loves 'em," said the driver, thinking of his ma, a firm believer in leprechauns and that elusive pot of gold at the end of the rainbow, as if that did her any good, dying without a nickel to her name. He'd been toying with his car keys and now shoved them in a pocket. "I get home from work one day and Brenda tells me she's horny. Just like that, out of the blue. Any other red-blooded American, he'd have jumped right on that, you know? But not me. Oh, no, not me! I'd had a bitch of a day, the boss on my tail, grousing about how expenditures were up and productivity down, and me? I wasn't pulling my weight, according to him."

"What job was that?" asked the old-timer while slathering butter on them thick slices of bread, four slices.

"Don't matter. I quit that lousy job three days ago, hit the road. So there's Brenda, telling me she's horny, and what do I do? What do I say? I tell her, I'm not." He helped himself to a toothpick, a half dozen sitting in a shot glass near the napkin dispenser. He fiddled with the toothpick as though it would give him some kind of insight. "Brenda loses it, flashes them dark eyes at me. You know them kind of eyes what look like they belong to a Senorita. All sultry like that? She accuses me of getting it elsewhere, and me, I'm royally pissed, so I say, sure, I'm getting it elsewhere, and she goes ballistic, calls me one mean son of a bitch." The fella driving snapped the toothpick in half.

"Next thing I know, she's storming down the hallway toward the front door, putting on that little hat she had, some contraption she'd found at Walgreens. It had a daisy and a bumblebee attached to the brim. I tell you, what kind of a woman wears a hat like that?" He took a bite out of one of the sandwiches, not realizing he'd picked up the ham and cheese as he kept on talking while he chewed. "I asked, where're you going? And she said, out to find a man who could give her what she wanted. I asked, 'What's that?' And she said, 'A one-woman man,' and I laughed. That's what I done. I laughed. And again, she called me one mean son of a bitch while I'm telling her, there's no such thing as a one-woman man, all men cheat. Well, let me tell you, she goes ever-loving apeshit when I say that. She makes a hard left and storms into the kitchen, scrabbling through the knife drawer with them lacquered fingernails of hers, and the next thing I know, she's grabbed a carving knife and she throws it at me. Imagine that, a carving knife coming at your head. Damned near took my ear off. I heard it hit the doorjamb, *thwang*! Like she'd been taking lessons from Daniel Boone or Davy Crockett. You remember them two?"

The old-timer nodded, snapped open a Schmidt's, and handed it over, foam dribbling down the sides of the can.

The driver pulled a napkin from the dispenser, wiped mayonnaise from his lips while dropping his half-eaten sandwich back on the crockery used for a plate. He took the lager and asked the old fella, "Why does that happen? You crack open a can of beer, and the damned suds. They been in the fridge, right? Cold, right? So why the suds?"

"Why'd God make little green apples?" asked the old-timer, wiping the counter with a dirty rag, it too about as grimy as the apron, bypassing a dead fly as if it had a right to be there, like that particular spot on the counter was its final resting place.

"You asking me straight or is that a rhetorical question?"

"I'm asking you straight."

"Because all the red ones were spoken for," said the driver.

The old-timer laughed. "Hell of an answer. I never thought of that before."

"Makes sense, don't it? All the red ones spoken for."

"It surely does. All the red ones spoken for." The old-timer couldn't stop laughing.

"It's not that funny," said the driver.

"No, it's not that funny. But it got you thinkin' about apples. Took your mind off of that Brenda gal, a woman who's obviously torn you to shreds."

"Torn me to shreds. Yeah, that'd be Brenda." The guy driving, he hung his head, toying with the roast beef sandwich, peeling back an edge as if looking at the guts of the thing would reveal more insights into his lousy existence. "The thing of it is, mister, I am a one-woman man. Never cheated on her a day in my life. Not even after she left. Can't even look at another woman. I even dream about her."

"And now she's moved on, left the county, as it were."

"She surely has. Came home from that lousy job two days later and she'd hightailed it out of there, just like that." The driver snapped his fingers. "She cleaned me out, not a nickel left in the joint savings account. It's taken me the better part of a year to save up enough money to go lookin' for her. Got word through an old friend, she's in Seattle."

"So that's where you're headed."

The fella driving nodded. "Can you imagine? Seafood and the Space Needle, and for what? Just so as she can watch them sea-lions sunbathing on rocks. Imagine the stink coming off a colony like that, thousands of them critters."

"Maybe she found another fella," said the old-timer.

"Ah, Christ! Don't say that. If she's found another fella, then I'm making this drive for nothing. Might as well have run out of gas there on the savanna and let the coyotes have me."

"It's not a savanna. It's a prairie."

"Same difference," said the driver. "It's the goddamned middle of nowhere." A sudden movement caught the corner of his eye, some motion taking place beyond the picture window. He leaned back, sunlight blinding him, his eyeglasses nothing but a damned nuisance, squinting. "Who's that?" he asked.

"Who's who?" asked the old-timer, having finished his beer.

"That guy snooping around my car." The fella driving slid off his stool and went to stand by the big picture window. It was hotter than a lit firecracker, standing by the glass. He broke into a sweat, scratched his scalp, itchy all of a sudden like ants were crawling all over him. Before leaving home, he'd bought himself a seersucker suit for the trip. Realizing that had been a waste of money, he left the tie and the jacket lying on the backseat of the Impala, the heat sucking any sense of sanity right out of him.

The old-timer joined him. "That guy? He's nobody. Goes by the name of Fergus, no last name. He's a drifter. Travels up 'n' down this stretch of road, sleeps under the mesquite bushes."

"Isn't that dangerous? I thought there were rattlers out there."

"Sure, there's rattlers out there, but they know better than to go messin' with Fergus. He's one ornery son of a bitch. Even meaner than me."

"I don't like the way he's looking at my car."

"Fergus ain't likely to hurt it. He likes cars. What you'd call a fetish."

Christ! The driver headed toward the door to intercept this dingdong called Fergus, to tell him to keep his grimy paws off his car.

The old-timer beat him to it, fast as a rattler the way he moved, coiled and ready to strike. He pushed opened the fly-specked screen door and hollered, "I got one on ice for you, Fergus. Why don'tcha come on in, join the party?"

Fergus turned, his thicket of matted gray hair sticking out from under his cowboy hat, a ratty old thing made of straw, his clothes scruffy, a beat-up knapsack slung over one shoulder. "There's a party?" he shouted.

"Could be," said the old-timer. "Don't three make a party?"

Fergus turned away from the Impala and climbed the few steps onto the boardwalk. "I'd like me a cold one, Chester. Sure, that'd be nice. And a party, why I guess, I'd like me that, too."

So that was the old fella's name. Chester. The driver eyed this Fergus character as he came through the doorway, the fly-specked screen door slamming shut with a bang.

Fergus stepped on over, held out his hand. "Pleased to meetcha. I'm Fergus."

The fella driving, he didn't know what to do. He had no desire to take the drifter's outstretched hand but, then again, he hated to be rude. Rudeness cost him Brenda, getting all uppity with her. He shook Fergus's hand, hoping the guy wasn't contagious, wasn't gonna pass on some parasite or, God forbid, headlice. "Derek O'Sullivan. Just stopping by, got me some gas and some grub from Chester here."

"O' course you did," said Fergus. He'd slid onto a stool as if he owned the joint, plunking his hat and the knapsack on the counter. Chester went back behind the counter, brought out three more beers. Fergus helped himself to the first one.

The guy driving, now known as Derek O'Sullivan, helped himself, too.

And Chester, why, he just smiled, the cat who ate the canary. "Fergus used to be a journalist. Worked out west in Tinseltown for one of them highfalutin tabloids. One of them paparazzi, taking a bite out of the rich 'n' famous, leaving just enough flesh to come back for another bite when needed. Ain't that right, Fergus?"

"Awe, why'd you'd go and say that?" Fergus shifted his skinny ass on the stool, looking uncomfortable. "You know what that does to me? Puts me back in that place I been running from, bringing up my past like that."

"Derek here, he has a past too, don'tcha, Derek? We had us a mighty fine chinwag before you showed up. Derek quit his job, now headed for Seattle. Thinks he's gonna find the wife. She run away on account Derek wouldn't perform like a trained seal. Ain't that right, Derek?"

Derek's face reddened, feeling truly embarrassed. "I wouldn't put it that way."

"What way would you put it?" asked Chester.

"It's like this," said Derek. He'd swiveled sideways on his stool, looking Fergus square in the eye. "You being a journalist and all, you'll love this. One winter, Brenda takes this night school class, some journalism course, like she's going to be the next Barbara Walters, and one of the students comes in late. A confident guy, an older guy, not particularly good-looking but there was something about him. He comes in, expresses his regrets for being late but he does it with finesse, with humor. I forget Brenda's actual words, but she said the guy was funny. Soon the class is chuckling, they like the guy. He's got a certain appeal. You know what I mean?"

Both Chester and Fergus nodded, keeping up with the tale.

"And that guy, why, he's humiliated the teacher," said Derek. "A pompous ass, according to Brenda, no one liked him. The class figured the teacher deserved to get cut down a peg or two. And the teacher, he tells the guy to take his seat. The guy, more 'n' six feet tall..." Derek glanced at the length of his own legs, thinking he'd failed in that department too, damned genetics, blind as a mole, built like a leprechaun, prone to sunburn and psoriasis, having to use a ruddy prescription shampoo containing tar, smelly as all get out. "...That guy, he's hamming it up, lifting one leg over the desk like a dog about to take a piss, swinging himself into the desk in one fluid motion." He looked at Chester. "Like what you did with the nozzle and the gas cap, I never saw anything like it." Derek scratched his head, thinking about that loaf of bread, too. How in blazes did Chester slice four slices of bread without him noticing—*bang*!

There they were, on the cutting board.

"Then the guy's in his desk, leaning back, his long legs sticking out in the aisle, ankles crossed, studying his fingernails like he's bored out of his mind, which further upset the teacher. Brenda said it was one of the most spectacular things she ever saw, why couldn't I be more like that? A guy with chutzpa. A guy who could enter a room and take command, instead of the lousy schmuck I'd become."

Chester went back to wiping the counter sticky with the lager.

Derek said, "Imagine saying something like that to the man you married. Some guy comes strolling into a classroom and Brenda thinks he's the cat's ass, the King of Siam." Doubt crept in. What in blazes was he thinking? Charging off to Seattle, the idea Brenda could be rescued, him the one to save her from saltwater, seaweed and cracked crab when he was the one cracked—cracked right out of his ever-loving skull!

Fergus helped himself to another Schmidt's, snapped the tab on the can, suds spurting forth.

Derek figured there was something hinky with the beer, the way each can exploded with foam, too much pressure built up and then *kaboom*! "You work your tail off, and for what?" asked Derek. "Just to have your boss rip you a new one 'cause you're not bringing in the revenue. Then you go home and there's the wife throwing it in your face, why are we always flat broke? Nothing but lies, nothing but broken promises. Where was the fancy house, the fancy car, the nice clothes, 10 years in, and it still hadn't happened, so she hits me right where it hurts, right in my manhood. Where's the fairness in that?"

"Life ain't fair," said Fergus. "I learned me that a long time ago. It happened to me, too. I had me a wife, prob'ly just as pretty as yours. Always after me to be home by six, dinner on the table when she knew it was my job to go lookin' for the story—nose to the grindstone, keep the public informed. Fact is, I was the one what got taken. The wife, she cleaned me out, and then she run off with some Fuller brush salesman. Like he was better than me."

"Can't trust a salesman as far as you can throw 'im," said Chester, poking the dead fly with a toothpick he'd taken from the shot glass.

"Wait a minute," said Derek. "That's low. I was in sales. I was good at my job despite what that lousy no-good son of a bitch boss thought. Every Friday, after work, he'd sit there behind his desk, crunching the numbers. He crunched 'em alright. Skimmed what little profits there were, betting it all at the track. Tried to make it sound like it was my fault, not bringing in enough dough to keep the business solvent. Nothing fair about that."

"Here, have another beer," said Chester. "It can't hurt none."

Derek wiped a sweaty brow with the back of his hand. Christ, it was hot. "I need to be leaving," but then—all of a sudden, he felt sleepy, his eyelids weighing heavy, like trying to blink through treacle. How'd that happen?

"Just one," said Chester. "Take your mind off your troubles."

Derek relented, slurring his words. "What the hell?" Maybe Chester would let him sleep it off in the corner. He could prop himself up at one of the tables, put his feet up on a chair, take a load off. He hadn't slept well in that fleabag motel the night before, the bed too hard, the pillow too soft, the traffic outside his window keeping him awake until almost dawn. "I got a fact—fact is, I have been a schmuck. Thinking I could drive across country, go and find Brenda when she's prob'ly got some other dope in her life. Women. Can't live with 'em," and then, he lost that train of thought, his mind all a muddle. He laughed. "Sure, give me another. Like you said, it's a party."

"A damned fine party," said Fergus, clinking cans with Derek, giving him a friendly slap on the back. As for the foam dribbling down the sides of the cans, no one seemed to care about that anymore, the diner stinking like a brewery.

Derek asked, "Fergus, is that your real name?"

"It is now. Back when, you'd've recognized my name in them funny papers, but I got tired of skulking behind bushes, hoping for the money shot. That's what cost me the wife."

Derek drank his third beer or was it his fourth? He squinted hard at the remains of the two sandwiches sitting on that grungy piece of crockery, both partially eaten.

Fergus took up one of the sandwiches, folded it in half and popped what was left of it into his mouth, making chewing noises like it was the best damned sandwich he'd had in years. "Mighty good, Chester. I sure do like me your sandwiches."

"Happy to oblige, Fergus. But Derek here, he's the one paying. Ain't that right, Derek?"

"Sure," said Derek, pulling his leather wallet from his back pocket. His fingers wouldn't cooperate, swollen and numb, as though they'd been shot full of Novocain. He dropped the wallet. Dropped his keys, too. He slid off the stool, leaning sideways, reaching for the wallet and his keys when Fergus came out of left field, kicking him hard, right in the gut.

Derek toppled backward, cracked his head on the floor, thinking he'd be sick, the beer and the sandwiches rising like gorge in his throat, threatening to erupt. "What the hell?" he groaned; the wind knocked right out of him. "Whatcha go and do that for?"

Fergus told him, "I figure whatever you got in that trunk of yours, it's a sight more appealing than what I got in this here knapsack. And that

'62 Impala, why—once we get that delivered to ol' Hank down in Sin City, Chester and me, we'll be splittin' the spoils. Am I right, Chester?"

Chester nodded. "Right as rain, Fergus. You always had a flare for stating the obvious."

Derek was struggling to understand, tears in his eyes. Christ, that kick in the gut hurt. He then remembered the newspaper articles framed, hung side by side behind the cash register. Those damned aliens found in New Mexico. He pulled himself into a sitting position, cradling his stomach, taking note of the sad state of the diner. He saw it for what it really was, nothing but filth. If anyone stopped for gas or to top up their oil, they wouldn't have eaten here. He wondered if the bread was as stale as the rest of this place? If only he'd opened his eyes to look, clued into his surroundings. He asked, "You gonna take my car, take my stuff? What about me? You gonna leave me stranded, stuck out here in the middle of nowhere?"

"Don't worry about that," said Fergus, tossing Derek's keys like he'd won them in some state fair lottery. "Me and Chester, we're gonna carry you to what we call the State Line." Fergus laughed, a sinister sound. "We're gonna drag you out back behind that outhouse. Chester's got a nest of vipers back there, mean sons of bitches. The authorities, if they do show up, we tell 'em it was most unfortunate. You headed out back after drinkin' one beer too many, needed to take a leak, put one foot wrong and stepped smackdab in the center of that damned fool rattlers' nest." Fergus then moved like a rattler, giving no indication he'd strike. He grabbed Derek by his ankles, flipped him again onto his back, pulling him toward the door of the diner.

Chester skedaddled from behind the counter, wiping his hands on his apron. He took one leg, Fergus the other, and they pulled in tandem, Derek screaming bloody murder, nothing to grab, no one to hear. The doorjamb, too, slipped out of his grasp as he made one last attempt to save himself. The fly-specked screen door smacked the back of his head when it slammed shut.

His head also took the brunt of the beating as they dragged him down the steps, *plunkety plunk plunk*, his glasses gone. What the hell happened to his glasses? They'd cost him plenty, a goddamned fortune. In his panic, Derek realized it was all an act, these two working in tandem, him stuck in the middle, and what about that kewpie doll? What kind of person would smash in a doll's face, and why? The doll was innocent, an inanimate object. It never harmed nobody.

Author Bio

(f) /Karen.Keeley.77

Karen Keeley fell in love with a good who-done-it when she stumbled upon Rex Stout and his Nero Wolfe novels at a used bookstore in northwestern Ontario. A proud Canuck living north of the 49th parallel, she has two stand-alone publications, *Sticks and Stones: Three Murder Mysteries* and *There Goes the Neighbourhood: Syd Malloy, Private Investigator*. Other stories have appeared in anthologies like *Crime Wave 2: Women of a Certain Age* (Sisters-in-Crime, Canada West).

www.KarenMKeeley.BlogSpot.com

The Eternal Flame Diner

By Meredith C. Kurz

Hell's Kitchen sits on Manhattan's West Side, running down Amsterdam Ave., a north-south thoroughfare, meaning the ambulances screaming up to Mt. Sinai and the fire trucks wailing down to Chelsea interrupt your thoughts. At any time. It's a few blocks from the haughty real estate and squatting but not quite lying down in the bad area blocks.

Hell's Kitchen is where workers go to eat, with its cheek and jowl takeout joints and cheap pizza. Sometimes the Lincoln Center après opera crowd will drip down, but for the most part we're left to ourselves.

There's a double doored entry and, when you're past that, there's that yellow-orange spinner of desserts, the lemon meringue making a sexy pirouette, its platinum blonde pompadour tempting. Sure, there's the solid brick of carrot cake, and the body parts look of rice pudding, but that meringue sucks me in every time.

Nearest the door and at the end of the counter, there's an old-school cash register and a new-school card scanner. The counter's seen about 15 layers of Formica, and the seats and barstools have been covered even more. The Bunn dual brewer slips into mud come 4AM.

The whole shebang dates back to the 1940s. They're open 24 hours.

The menu is thick and heavy with multiple vinyl-sealed pages where you'll find everything from spanakopita to eggplant parm. I bet the menu hasn't changed much in 80 years. The eggs model in a variety of poses, a multitude of clips and colors and additions. Then come the pancakes, waffles, home fries. Ice-cream sodas, burgers, fries. The kitchen refrigerator walk-ins must be huge.

The waitress Ruby, who's our favorite, knows her job. No stopping. Separate checks? No problem. My people, well the people from the area, we all know one another and started out in separate parts of the diner and then just slowly started to coalesce, you know? Over the years. So now we have a pod of booths and whoever comes, comes.

Ruby swipes the table with her worn cloth, unthinking, and I wonder, who is she? Is she the owner's sister? Is the owner the great grandson of the original owner, or did he buy it in the 1980s when the crime bit Hell's Kitchen in the ass?

People always need to eat at 3AM after they get out of the bars, near Times Square. They need to soak up the alcohol.

They need to woo their girl.

Speaking of which, curled up in a corner is a young woman, makeup smeared a bit. High heels plucked off swollen feet under the booth. A curious hand trying to navigate her thigh. She looks more real in this fluorescent light. Her partner looks less shaven. Glazed. Hungry.

A young busboy is studying his ESL textbook on the barstool at the counter. He bends over and bends over, and then his head bounces against the book as he dozes then wakes.

Greek music purrs in the back of the house. Johnny the executive chef runs the radio stations and it's always the same.

The fluorescents have fly specks, but the stainless-steel counters are clean. The walls have yellowed and the chef leans against the door jamb leading to the trash bins, smoking, squinting through the smoke at the light.

There's only one order, so the sous chef whips it up. They are ready for us, day or night. They are ready for a dead night or a flush of 50 seats.

So, when the man, the desperate looking man, comes in, he just seems a little too drunk. Nothing unusual.

"Just one?" murmurs Josey the hostess. People's voice hush in the late early hours.

He's looking over Josey's head, stretching his neck. He's looking for, then sees them, their tongues tasting coffee in coffee, bodies curled in full crotchal probe under the table. "Lucy!" he screams.

Everyone's heads turn in unison.

The young woman who I'm guessing is Lucy has her mouth in an 0, her lipstick mostly gone, the top button of her blouse almost off. Her partner lazily pulls back and gives a stony stare at the caller.

There's a silence, that pause like the moment before one of those Jones Beach waves beats the crap out of you.

"You bitch!" and he pulls out a gun with a wavy arm that sort of points in the general direction of the back booth. Maybe we're jaundiced, but it seems more like a threat. He's wavering.

The men in the diner are transfixed. Frozen.

Josey grabs the man by the neck with two hands, hands that have squeezed and hauled more than many a man, and I'm betting she's getting a good choke on him.

Then his gun goes off.

The girl screams.

The bullet hits a fluorescent light, and it pops off, leaving a gray shadow in the middle of the diner.

Josey lifts her knee, jams in into the back of the man, who yelps like the anemic he is, and forces him to the floor. I mean, a yelp! This shooter has nothing to offer that girl in the back booth.

Finally, the counter guy brings himself out of sanctuary and leans down and, grabbing the gun, sits on the man's back. And he's heavy, I mean, counter guy? I wouldn't want him sitting on my back.

"Call the cops," Josey says, looking at Johnny who's standing by the kitchen door, cigarette hanging on one side of his mouth (Johnny who's loved Josey off and on for years, we all know it). Johnny (who falls in love with her all over again but can't show it), nods.

They all wait, the frothy girl, her beau who finally says, "I'm getting outta here—"

"You can't." Johnny's voice is Marlboro and fire.

"You're a material witness," says Ruby, who's seen enough TV to sling that term in. "Plus, you haven't paid your bill. In fact," she adds, "you better pay it now."

I mean, if he's ready to bail now, he might be wanted himself.

The groper sits down again, next to the girl. Now they're like two virgins on their first date, hands clasped in front of them. The girl scooches down her skirt, adjusts her bra for the crime scene tableau. Dabs at her now-gone lipstick.

A couple walks in—sees the man on the floor, the gun on the counter, and make the moves to leave.

"Hold up—I'm sure the cops are coming," says Johnny.

"Isn't this a crime scene?" the man asks in midflight.

"Almost. Not quite," says Johnny, smiling at the couple and then glancing at Josey.

"I'll put you in a back booth," offers Josey, grinning at Johnny.

Author Bio

 @WriteNY

Meredith C. Kurz is a Manhattan freelance writer primarily covering the city and modern artists. She had a business byline in the Long Island newspaper *Beacon Record*, and produced children's plays that ran through the '90s as a one-woman show. Her speculative short fiction appears in *The Secret Lives of New Yorkers*, about discovering a should-be-extinct bear in a cave carved from one of the glacial erratics in Central Park's Ramble. In her words, her writing "leans more espresso: dark, short and bitter." Find more of her work at www.MeredithKurz.com

More From Outcast Press

20 short stories that explore the ironic side of the adult entertainment industry by transgressive writers like Kristin Garth, Stephanie Parent, Natalie Nider, Sebastian Vice, Paige Johnson, & more! Peruse every echelon of prostitution and fetishism, the world of pantie sellers to cross-dressing diplomats, scag-seeking street-walkers to doted-upon sugar babies.

The Bigger Man

By Jim Thomsen

First, they scraped several trays full of sloppy joes into a trash can.

Then the five of them emptied their milk cartons into the can. Then they reached into their backpacks and pulled out cans of cat and dog food. And emptied out those on top of that.

Then they smuggled out the stinking mess from the school cafeteria and snuck it into the bushes behind the gym.

Then, from the P.E. closet, they dumped in a couple of buckets of golf balls.

Then, after the final bell, they added the piecé dé resistance:

Me. Headfirst. Snatched as I walked past the bushes on my way to my bike.

Then they tilted the can on its side and rolled it down the hill to the middle school. Half the length of a football field. To the bus loop. And the big ditch just before it. Where a few hundred of my fellow high school freshmen were watching and waiting. And then, whooping in delight.

Boom.

A flying apocalypse of balls and milk and sauce and blood and byproducts.

And me. The by-byproduct, you might say.

That's how I remember it across several thousand nights of sweat-soggy dreams.

And the last thing I remember, every time I relive this moment every night since, is Rob McMurdo bending down just before the big push and bugling into my ear:

"Taste it, fagwipe!"

I wish I could deny that I did.

Remember those DirectTV commercials? "When you wait a long time for the cable guy, you get bored. When you get bored, you look out windows. When you look out windows, you see things you shouldn't see. When you see things you shouldn't see, you blah blah blah…?"

My life's been like that.

When you get publicly humiliated before the entire school, you don't return to that school.

When you have parents who blame you for what happened and won't help you get to the nearest other school, you don't return to any school.

When you don't return to any school, you do whatever you have to do to fill your hours and fill your wallet.

When you do whatever you have to do to fill your hours and fill your wallet, you get busted in an undercover police sting.

When you get busted in an undercover police sting, you do two to five with a cellmate who owns your puny punk ass as the price of staying alive.

When you get out of prison after your puny punk ass is owned as the price of staying alive, you do whatever you have to do to fill your hours and fill your wallet. And you go back to prison.

When you do whatever you have to do to fill your hours and fill your wallet after doing time three or four times, you finally figure out that maybe you shouldn't spend your time doing things that make you do time.

When you finally figure out that you don't want to do any more time, you're 44 years old. And working split shifts and mopping out the back of the Petey-Pie diner after midnight, when I don't let it all hang out. That covers Top Ramen, rent, and not a whole lot else.

As you might guess, I don't have cable TV. Let alone DirectTV.

Like every diner these days, or so I read in the newspapers that our customers sometimes leave behind, the one I work in is short-staffed and then some. Kids won't work in them anymore, not even as summer jobs. So, seemingly, will no one else with any better options. So that leaves me, and not enough people like me. People whose resumés include work in prison kitchens. Not that there's much art or craft to dumping freezer-burned leftovers in a pan, baking them into a black brick, and serving them as nutraloaf.

But I avoid those people now. They have a look to them, a look that says, Do I know you? Do you know anyone I know? Do you know anybody who can set me up with a sweet score? Do you realize I'm not going to stop eyeballing you and eventually bracing you until you bear yourself to me one way or the other?

My life might not be much. But it's much better not being much outside of prison than it is being in, no matter how much people mark my time on my face.

I try to remember that. Especially when I get angry. And it seems that I'm always uncomfortably close to angry. Check that: I am angry; it's the expressing of it that I'm always uncomfortably close to. Especially when I'm back in my hometown, like I am now, hating it even more than I did when I was 14, especially since I'd sworn to myself about 40,000 times that I was never coming back.

And hating it even more because I had to come back when my mother went into memory care, because my father was already gone and I was the only one who could or would handle things, and then I found out after all the sellings and signings that there was nothing to inherit, or even turn into quick cash, after getting Mom sorted—for a short while. And that without cash, I had nowhere to go. And as much as I should, and as much as I wish I could, I couldn't leave Mom to be dumped out into the street in six months. No matter how much I hated her.

I couldn't have any more defenselessness in my life.

When I think about all that, I think about the things I used to do for money. And think about getting the hell out of town on the next Greyhound anyway. And then I take a deep breath. Or maybe a few hundred deep breaths. And remind myself, as many times as it takes to bury itself into my prison-broken brain, I don't want to know anybody I used to know. And I especially don't want anybody who I used to know to know me now. Thank god my mother doesn't. Not anymore.

One way to deal with that is to keep oneself too busy to think. To keep my head down if only because it's the only way to cleanly breathe.

It's not much. But it's all that keeps me from exploding.

So, on a Sunday just after noon, after a five-minute smoke break spent staring at the seagulls swarming the dumpster in back and wishing I could afford smokes, I go back inside the Petey-Pie. I swipe at a soup spill with a mop from a bucket of water darker than day-old coffee. I quickly wipe down a six-top, schlep a tub of mostly uneaten scrambled eggs and sausages and soggy waffles to the dish station, and snatch a fresh rack of glasses, and stash them under the front counter, and slide the rack back to the dishwasher for a fresh load of coffee cups.

All in a minute's work at the Petey-Pie. All just in time to sprint to greet the group of six who had just scooted their polo-ed backs and khaki-ed bottoms into a back booth because nobody had been at the front to greet them.

And not just a back booth. The back booth.

Church was out. And so, apparently, was the latest in a human turnstile of hostesses, more of whom quit the millisecond they found something marginally better-paying. Like handing out snack-food samples at the Sav-Lots or slitting chicken throats at the local poultry plant. Jobs, by the way, that I tried to get but couldn't.

I pour waters, I set napkin wraps of water-spotted silverware, I take a couple of requests for decaf coffee and Dr Pepper. And I steal a glance or two. Almost as much as a prison yard, the Petey-Pie is a great place for people-watching, and there's something about these six that bore a bit more of my bemused meditation than usual.

Three generations of a family, I figure. All glowing with great health and gleaming prosperity and glistening Christian goodness, more so than usual here in what I sometimes hear the locals call the Bible Chastity Belt. It seems impossible that any of them, in the Land of Fluoridated Water Is a Communist Plot, had ever missed a dental checkup or even heard of the word "orthodontics."

I picture them piling up carbs here ahead of a happy afternoon of pulling weeds from the periphery of their voucher-funded Christian private school property. I see them hammering nails for the new Boys & Girls Club, or maybe the junior Oath Keepers rifle range. I get a perfect image of them pausing for sips on Black Rifle frappuccinos, singing and swinging scythes to particularly singalong-y songs from a personally curated Jesus station on Spotify. Or serving up cold turkey at the weekly church supper before a busy evening of book burning and screaming at school-board members. Or something equally Q-gasmic.

They remind me of the families in *Sears Wish Book* catalogs from my childhood, the ones in which everyone wore identical smiles in identical sets of sleepwear.

"Where we sleep one, we sleep all," I muttered to myself.

Childhood…

Something squirms at the back of my skull, and slithers away into the blackness before I can get a grip on it.

From the coffee station, I sneak another peek, wondering what that skidmark streak of a thought was all about. And I quickly pick up on the dynamic: the dad, about my age, blond but starting to gray in a TV-lawyer way at the temples; the mom, who smiles as though she's been trained since she was a toddler to smile because, *you know, sweetie, Jesus gave her a beautiful smile*, which she does indeed have, as well as two barely adult kids, sounding out the menu with Gerber-strained patience to two squirmy grandchildren.

Pretty typical for a Sunday here in my small hometown, and I don't see anything unusual about it, and usually I don't see people like them at all. Any more than they see me. Things move pretty fast here, and you gotta watch your six and keep your head on a swivel, like the Army guys who come through here like to say. Or maybe they're just guys who like to make you think they were in the Army. I can relate, having been one of those guys once it became clear that my rap sheet was going to keep me out of the military and the life that built that rap sheet meant more swivel-heading and six-watching than any six people any non-criminal would know.

But, these people. I'm seeing them. And I wish I knew why.

It isn't until I follow up their requests for decaf coffees and chocolate milkshakes and Petey's legendary cherry-pecan-peach pie that I realize two things: 1. Only one of the kids, the blonde goes with the blonde mom and the blond dad; and 2. the blond dad is Rob McMurdo.

30 years have made him pinker and thicker, as if he was vacuum-packed in a freshly trimmed layer of medium-rare, extra-lean roast beef every day. But, hell, I look like I get vacuum-packed every day in the fat trimmed off that roast beef, so, you know, good on him for hitting the elliptical or the exercise bike every morning. In his polo with its real estate franchise logo, he looks to be prosperous on first blush, and pleasant, and perfectly content with his life. As does his wife, and his daughter, and his grandchildren.

And I think on that and something inside me goes a little bit soft and loose.

Rob sees me looking at him a beat too long, and he narrows his eyes a little, as if he thinks I'm cruising him or something—and wouldn't that be something?

Do I know you? Do you know anybody I know? Do you know—

But, thankfully, there's no sharpening light of recognition in them.

I shouldn't find it surprising. Rob's merely gotten older; I've gotten unrecognizable, often to myself. In ninth grade, I was shrimpy, all headgear braces and flyaway Farrah Fawcett-feathered hair. Today, my hair is thin and the rest of me is not, and, anyway, most people, I suspect, can't see past the deep and sandpapery scar, all five inches of it, under my left eye.

The scar I got when my face skidded on the gravelly asphalt of the bus loop, at something like 30 miles-an-hour, 30 years before.

All because Rob McMurdo tried to touch my dick and I said no, and I shoved him and ran away, and he decided to deal with it by telling the world that I had tried to touch his dick. And because he was a golden god and I was, well, not a golden god. You can guess how that played out when I tried to speak out.

I serve their food. I refill their drinks. I clear their plates. I ask them if they want anything else, which they don't, and I do it all as invisibly as possible. Invisibility is my superpower, perfected in prison and on probation and a lifetime of being pushed around by the people who read **prison and probation** on your face as if it were tattooed there in poisoned ink.

And I watch.

Rob's wife, beneath the sedimentary layer of Southern megachurch makeup, has a slightly unfocused shine in her eyes. One that speaks of an overstuffed medicine cabinet. Same with the daughter; there ain't no way to hide Dilaudid eyes (take it from someone who used to deal in that stuff between prison stretches). The son-in-law, handsome but short and flyweight-skinny in a way that reminds me a little bit of ninth grade me, speaks little and mostly stares straight ahead.

And the kids, merrily oblivious, happily crayon everything in sight, including the walls, and I'm going to have to clean those afterwards.

I feel the anger surge back.

I watch.

What to do, what to do?

You know, against every bit of good sense, of which I'm always in short supply, a part of me wants to do it. To confront Rob, in front of his family, in front of God and everyone, which are acknowledged to be about one and the same around here. To take every ounce of anything remotely sloppy joes-y from the kitchen and dump it on his head. And then...

To let the anger fly. To let him figure out why. To toss the pan or the pot behind me like a mic drop and walk out and...

And... Well, what?

Go to jail? Go back to prison? Or, if I'm lucky, go straight back to my crappy little rented room? Where I'd no longer be able to afford the rent, let alone my mother's, after losing my job? All for a petty act of revenge on someone who has no idea who I am or why I did what I did as witnessed by dozens of people who wouldn't care about either? Maybe after, I could hang myself from the shower rod with my apron strings, with a big smile on my face. Maybe I could cover myself in dog food first and scrawl **TASTE IT, FAGWIPE** across the mirror as I think about what I have to do in prison just to be present for this particular shining moment.

It's scary, how much that scenario appeals to me.

Things continue moving fast. I direct a foursome to a table and deliver a platter of Peteburgers and Pete-loaf to another table and dump a heaping bus tub next to the dishwasher for about the fiftieth time today. And I duck into the bathroom.

I splash some water on my face and stare at my unrecognizable self. And I think: What if…there is a different path to dealing with my demons, with the decisions and non-decisions, that formed the course of my dirtbag existence? What if I just let go of the cold rage that seems to constantly coil and uncoil in my cold gut like a chamber full of cottonmouth snakes?

What if Rob had prospered precisely because he'd outgrown his ninth-grade self and put the past properly behind him? What if I grant myself the serenity to accept the things I cannot change and get on with my life, such as my life is, instead of grinding it out on my hot-place face?

What if I were…the bigger man?

I splash some more water on my face.

I feel so much better.

I step back out into the dining room.

I watch as Rob's wife and daughter and grandkids slide out of the booth and stroll to the door. I listen as Rob touches the son-in-law on the back of his hand and tells the others that they will be along "in a minute or two."

I hear Rob say to his wife, "Man talk, you know."

She nods, mechanically. She knows. Whatever that means, she knows.

I get Rob's check ready. I place the check in a folder. I resist the powerful urge to pen a poisonous postscript below the tip line.

I take a step back to the table.

Then I see it.

And I shift into the shadows burying the bus station.

I do it as high-noon slashes the sunlight in two, through the Petey-Pie's bent blinds.

I see Rob look around, and I see him not seeing the invisible me. I see him lean forward and whisper something into his son-in-law's ear.

I see Rob's hand reach, again, under the table. More clearly this time. And I see him stroke the son-in-law on his inner thigh.

I see the son-in-law go as still as a statue. The very same way I had when Rob touched me in that same booth 30 years before, after we scarfed down fries and cherry-pecan-peach Petey-Pies after school. Back when we were friends, or maybe that's something that geeky me and golden-god him wants to believe, each for our own reasons.

Only this guy, trapped in the booth—and trapped in the McMurdo family—can't run away.

I turn away. I step toward the back.

I catch sight of myself in the bathroom mirror once more.

I see my bulging gut under the blue apron. And the unpuny muscles boiling out of my shirtsleeves, borne of three different prison exercise yards. Where I did what I had had to do to survive three different stints with three different cellmates who wanted to own my puny punk ass.

And I decide that I was going to be the bigger man.

That is, when Rob least expects it.

Author Bio

@JimThomsen

Jim Thomsen is an editor for Blackstone Publishing, a manuscript editor, and former newspaper reporter. His crime-centric fiction and nonfiction have appeared in *Switchblade Issue Sixx, Mystery Tribune, The Rap Sheet,* and *Noir City Magazine.* This very story is an expanded version of what he performed in 2021 at The Alibi Room in Seattle's legendary Pike Place Market. A fan of all things Pacific Northwest, noir, and 1970s, Thomsen works on his first novel that bridges all those obsessions, tentatively titled *EVERYBODY HAD A HARD YEAR.*

Pickup At The Main Street Diner

By Margaret S. Hamilton

Motion-activated spotlights flicked on as Dolores Lopez pulled into the empty diner parking lot. She needed an hour to brew vats of coffee and heat the grill before her usual six o'clock opening.

Fran, her talented day cook who'd put the diner on the local foodie map, pulled in next to Dolores. Fran's two daughters would eat breakfast and wait for the school bus while their mother cooked eggs, hash browns, bacon, and sausage for the early morning breakfast crowd.

Black shadows moved behind the dumpster near the rear kitchen door. Dolores put on her cell phone flashlight and held it in front of her. "Hello, anybody there? You're in a safe place. No one will hurt you."

A woman groaned and pulled herself upright, enveloping two small children in her long parka.

"Fran, why don't you and the girls get started while I chat with our visitors?"

Fran nodded. A few years ago, she had been the woman huddled next to the dumpster with her children awaiting help.

Dolores shined her flashlight on the woman. "You're hurt, aren't you?"

The woman sniffled, her face dotted with emerging bruises. "Yes."

"And your children?"

"Cold and hungry," the woman said. "We walked for hours through the woods last night."

"Let's get you warmed up," Dolores said. "You need medical assistance and a place to stay."

"No police," the woman said.

"I understand." Dolores held out her hand. "I'm Dolores. Let me help you inside. What's your name?"

"Mary." She hesitated before she added, "Mary Schneider."

When Dolores had been on the run from her abusive husband, she had yearned for a women's shelter near the small Ohio college town of Jericho. 10 years later, after having helped establish the local shelter, Dolores volunteered her diner as the in-town pickup point for women in need.

Dolores called her morning waitresses in early. Fran's daughters helped by lining up coffee mugs, milk and sugar, and boxes of donuts on the counter, and setting the tables with napkins and silverware. The morning regulars knew the breakfast menu.

Dolores ushered Mary and her two small children to the second floor, which was set up as a temporary dormitory and playroom. She bolted the steel door at the base of the stairs.

"Breakfast coming up. No one will know you're here." Dolores checked Mary's face. "Bruises, no lacerations. How about a bag of frozen peas for your face?"

"Thanks. You can get us to the women's shelter, right? I don't want anybody to know."

"As soon as possible. Though, depending on your situation, we might have to wait until tonight."

"He wanted me to sign papers giving him my house." Mary buried her face in her hands. "It belonged to my parents, and now it's mine. He beat me before he threw me out. We ran for the woods and made our way into town."

"Your husband?" Dolores asked.

The woman grimaced. "Nope. All sweet talk until he realized I wouldn't put his name on the deed. He... He even called me an unfit mother and threatened to take my kids away."

"Does he have a name?" Dolores asked.

"George Baxter."

"Do you know how to reach the children's father?"

"In the wind."

Dolores frowned. Like so many other deadbeat dads. "I'll need your cell phone," Dolores said. "In case George tries to track you."

Mary fumbled in her parka pockets. "I... I must have dropped it in the woods."

Dolores carried soft, buttery scrambled eggs, juice, and toast up the stairs. She gave Mary an ice pack wrapped in a towel and left her with her daughters tucked into cots, the blinds drawn against the morning sun. They were asleep before Dolores took their dishes downstairs.

Dolores stepped outside the kitchen door and locked the gate to the parking lot. She alerted the women's shelter director about Mary's situation. The director agreed that it might be safer to move Mary and her kids after the diner closed in the evening. After she bolted the kitchen door, Dolores warned the waitresses and Fran to be on the lookout for George Baxter hunting for Mary and her children.

The morning rush lasted till 9, when the associates who worked in the Main Street shops ordered takeout coffee and breakfast sandwiches. Fran cleaned the grill, and started a tall pot of vegetable soup while she baked quiches and pot pies for the ladies who lunched. Most of their regulars preferred heartier fare—burgers and fries, or the Wednesday special: hot meatloaf sandwiches.

After the waitresses cleaned the tables and swept the linoleum floor, they took a late breakfast break. Dolores sat in a red leather booth with her coffee and scrolled through video footage of the diner parking lot. She spotted the skunk who usually dropped by the dumpster around midnight, but no raccoons or coyotes.

She continued to scan the surveillance footage. Before dawn, a pickup truck turned off its headlights and circled the parking lot. Dolores slowed the video and watched as a woman in a long parka lifted two small children out of the truck cab and hid behind the dumpster. Mary Schneider had lied about walking through the woods. Dolores tapped her phone on the Formica tabletop. Mary's face was bruised, but her injuries weren't consistent with someone as large as George Baxter throwing punches.

Dolores rubbed her jaw. She still bore the scars from her ex's damage to her face. She spent several months in hiding while she recovered.

Around 11, a rusty F-150 turned into the parking lot and stopped, blocking the entrance from the street. Dolores fingered her phone. Trouble. She tapped **911** and alerted the county dispatcher, then texted Fran to lock the door from the dining area to the kitchen.

A burly man stalked inside and approached Dolores. "You've got my wife, and I want her back." He was unshaven and reeked of bourbon, his pot belly bulging over his jeans.

Dolores placed her coffee mug on the table and dabbed her lips with a paper napkin. "First I'm hearing of it. I'm not married, and neither are my employees. You're at the wrong place."

The man, who must have been George Baxter, lunged for Dolores, pounding his ham hock fists on the table. "My wife has some papers she needs to sign." Spittle hung from the corner of his mouth.

Dolores rested her chin in her hand while a Jericho police SUV stopped next to the blocked parking lot entrance. Officer Bethany Schmidt spoke into her shoulder mic as she and her partner climbed out of the cruiser.

Perfect timing, Dolores thought. Tow his truck. The diner lunch crowd needed access to the parking lot.

Officer Schmidt entered the diner. "Morning, Dolores. Other than the truck blocking your parking lot, anything else I can help you with?" Bethany glanced at the ceiling and winked.

Dolores gave her a quick nod. Bethany was the liaison officer with the women's shelter. Dolores pointed to Baxter. "Please escort this man off the premises. He's not a customer."

"She's got my wife and kids hidden here," the man said. "I know it for a fact."

"Nobody's here except my employees, who are trying to earn a decent living," Dolores said. "You might do the same."

"Let's take a ride to the department where you can explain your actions," Bethany said.

"You can go to Hell, lady. I ain't going nowhere without my wife's signature on those papers."

Bethany's partner shoved the man against the counter and cuffed him. "Nobody talks to Officer Schmidt like that." He checked under Baxter's jacket. "Bethany, he's carrying."

"I don't allow guns in my place," Dolores said. "Get him out of here."

As soon as the police pulled out, Dolores emailed Bethany the security camera footage. She was sure Baxter had dropped off Mary and her daughters.

With George Baxter off the premises, Dolores alerted the shelter director and Alice "Atilla" Hunsacker, the family lawyer who represented shelter clients.

"Atilla, his name's George Baxter. Mary Schneider, the woman he lives with, says he assaulted her, demanding that she sign over her parents' house." Dolores paused. "Something's off with Mary's story. She told me she walked with her small kids through the woods all night. Not true. I sent Bethany Schmidt surveillance footage which shows someone driving a pickup truck dropping off Mary and her daughters just before six this morning."

Atilla was organized for action. "Sure, I'll have my investigator sniff around Town Hall. She'll check the property deeds, and also find out who pays the property taxes."

"Do you have access to marriage and birth records? It's not that I don't believe Mary, but I'd like to make sure she's not married to Baxter and didn't take his children. He referred to Mary as his wife."

"Of course," Atilla said. "Why did Baxter come back to the diner this morning?"

"He or Mary must have known about my arrangement with the women's shelter."

"Are you still part of the Main Street coalition?" Atilla asked.

"Yes," Dolores said. "If a woman in need asks for help at any of the shops or local businesses, they give me a call."

"If you have time, it might be worth checking with your contacts. A new hire might have learned about the referral system and tipped off Mary or Baxter."

Holiday errands and sunny weather brought shoppers in droves from the surrounding area. The diner sold out of quiches and pot pies. Dolores helped assemble triple grilled cheese sandwiches with cups of tomato basil soup for the latecomers.

After the lunch rush, Dolores tiptoed up the stairs and found Mary and her daughters still sound asleep. She left a plate of sandwiches and bottle of water before she returned to the bustling diner.

Mid-afternoon brought more shoppers in search of coffee and dessert. Dolores doubled her usual pie delivery order from the local bakery. After her dayshift workers left, Dolores was on her own until the evening grill cook and waitresses arrived.

Atilla, the shelter lawyer, arrived after having taken the precaution of parking a few blocks away, behind the Main Street shops.

Dolores greeted Atilla at the entrance and locked the door behind her. "Any news?" she asked.

Atilla accepted a mug of coffee. "Mary Schneider is who she says she is. She owns her parents' house free and clear. The property taxes are paid twice a year from her mother's IRA. Don't ask how I know."

Dolores nodded. Atilla had her sources. "And her children?"

"The birth certificates list Mary as the mother, but no father." Atilla looked through her notes. "Mary doesn't have a job right now, but previously worked in several Main Street shops."

"That's how she knew to come to the diner," Dolores said.

"Right." Atilla sipped her coffee. "George Baxter is a local resident using his parents' address for his driver's license. He's self-employed as a handyman."

"Which could mean anything," Dolores said. "This morning, he carried a gun."

Atilla made a note. "Not good."

After the employees for the evening shift arrived, Dolores and Atilla climbed the stairs to the second floor. They found Mary huddled over a cell phone while her daughters watched cartoons on TV.

Dolores introduced Atilla and said, "Mary, you told me you'd lost your cell phone. Someone could be tracking you."

"Don't make no difference now," Mary said. "I know the police arrested George."

"The police let him go hours ago," Atilla said. "You specified no police involvement. Until you give the police your statement, they have no reason to hold Baxter."

Mary turned off her cell phone and tossed it on the cot. "When's my ride coming for the women's shelter?"

"We'll need to get a few things straight before you leave," Atilla said.

"Like what?" Mary asked. "George Baxter hit me and threw me out of my house last night. See my bruises?"

"What time did he hit you?"

"The girls weren't in bed yet. Maybe 7 or 7:30."

"And you walked through the woods all night with them?" Atilla asked.

"Yeah, pretty much." Mary said. "They got tired, and we had to stop and rest."

"Did you get lost?"

"No, there's a path through the woods to town."

"You're lying," Dolores said. "Did George drop you off this morning?"

"What? No way." Mary's forehead was beaded with sweat.

"Is George Baxter your live-in boyfriend?" Atilla asked.

"More or less."

"Has he ever hurt you before?"

Mary sagged to her cot and shook her head.

"When did George tell you he wanted his name added to your property deed?"

"I told you. Last night, before he started hitting me."

Atilla said, "To clarify, the fact that you own your home never came up before that?"

"No. My parents took good care of me. They left me their house and a bank account to pay for property taxes."

"May I ask how you pay for food and medical care?"

Mary sniffed. "What business is it of yours?" She clasped her hands and sighed. "George pays."

"Tell the truth. Did George Baxter give you the bruises on your face?" Atilla asked, her tone stern.

"No. I...I gave them to myself. I banged my face against a door."

"And you weren't out all night, fleeing from George Baxter?"

"You know George dropped me off."

"Why did he threaten me this morning?" Dolores asked.

A tear slid down Mary's cheek. "To convince you that I needed protection in the women's shelter."

"Why?" Atilla asked. "The shelter is for women seeking emergency housing, not free room, board, and babysitting."

Mary scrolled through her phone and tapped an email before she handed it to Atilla. "A woman I've never met—Michelle Gruen—claims we're half-sisters because of the ancestor DNA test she did." Mary continued to snivel. "Michelle checked the deed register and found my name on my parents' house. She told me that I had to sell it and give her half the proceeds."

Atilla frowned. "Ancestor DNA tests are based on statistical probabilities, including whether you and Michelle are half-sisters or first cousins. My guess is cousins." She started taking notes. "Do you have siblings or cousins?"

"No, just me. Mom had some miscarriages after I was born."

"Aunts and uncles?"

"No. My grandparents died when I was too little to remember them."

"Were you adopted?"

Mary frowned. "I don't know. My birth certificate has no father listed. I thought maybe I was born before my parents got married."

"Are you named as their daughter in your parents' wills?"

"Yes."

"Then you don't own this Michelle person a thing," Atilla said. "How did Michelle find you? Did you do the same ancestor DNA test?"

"Yeah, after my parents died," Mary said. "Nobody cared about me. I was alone."

Atilla completed her notes. "Any idea why Michelle is at the women's shelter?"

Mary sniffled. "She didn't say."

"Did you know she was at the women's shelter when George dropped you off this morning?" Atilla asked.

"I... I don't remember." Mary dabbed her eyes with her shirttail.

Atilla was in full courtroom mode. "Did Michelle Gruen come to your house yesterday and tell you she was your half-sister? Did she demand half the proceeds from your parents' house? Was George upset enough to hit or threaten her?"

Tears slid down Mary's pudgy cheeks, dark with bruises. "I tried to stop him, but he wouldn't listen. He went crazy. When Michelle took off in her car, George followed her in his truck. I didn't know what he'd do if he found her, or what he would do to me when he came home." Mary held her head. "George came back, roaring with anger. He followed Michelle to the police department. He parked way down the road and watched a cop drive away with Michelle. George figured Michelle would hide out at the women's shelter and claim he hit her."

"He assaulted her, didn't he?" Atilla asked. "Sounds like Michelle has a good case."

Mary licked her chapped lips. "I figured out a plan. I knew about Dolores running the diner pickup and told George to drop us off. I figured we would get a ride to the women's shelter, and I could try to talk some sense into Michelle."

"When you communicated with Michelle today, did she threaten to press assault charges against George unless you paid up?" Atilla asked.

Mary looked at her sock-clad feet and nodded.

Atilla looked at her watch. "I'll pick you and the girls up in 10 minutes. We'll drive to the police department, where you'll make a statement. You put your daughters in danger, which means Child Services will become involved."

Atilla handed Mary a business card. "When Michelle first contacted you, a phone call to legal aid would have set you straight. Next time, don't open your door to strangers. And get George's gun out of your house before someone gets hurt."

Dolores stood at the kitchen door and watched Atilla drive away with Mary and her children. Dolores had opened her diner and heart to women in need. She gave the shelter clients job-training and referrals. She'd never had a woman lie to her. Still shaken by the events of the day, Dolores checked the area around the dumpster one more time. Empty, with a faint whiff of skunk in the air.

Author Bio

@Margar_Hamilton @MargaretSHamilton

Margaret S. Hamilton of Cincinnati, Ohio, has published over 20 short stories in various anthologies and online publications, including "Black Market Baby" in *Masthead: Best New England Crime Stories 2020*. She is querying her first traditional novel, *Curtains for the Corpse*, and is a member of Mystery Writers of America and Sisters in Crime.

Help Wanted

By Wil Dalton

10 minutes. Pull it together. Owner acted impressed at the mall. Said you had peacock personality. After Lily kept you up all the night before with her coughing and crying! This interview is just a formality. You can do this. Good days ahead.

Still.

I tilt the rear-view mirror and rate my face. It's an eight. Easy. The eyeliner suggests bubbly and smart, but I should have passed on the eyeshadow. No one tips extra for raccoon eyes. I check my teeth. Reapply lipstick. Eddie says my lips bring him back after every escape. Says kissing anyone else feels like kissing the dirty, sticky floor.

Let's pray Eddie stays long gone.

Lily deserves a dad who reads her to sleep and whispers when she's napping. A dad who enjoys wiping poopoo out her little butt because it means more time together. Ha! In a perfect world, Lily would also get organic bananas and one of those mechanical baby rockers. Maybe then she'd actually sleep at night.

Can you make it through this interview on one Excedrin?

Two, it is.

And, of course, you dribble water on the stupid shirt from the back of the closet Andrea insisted you wear. Too thin. Too tight on your mom bra. The bra that Andrea told you to ditch and let your clown-nose areolas promise to show up early to every shift and remember every order and sell double the specials. Start them this weekend!

Sweet Andrea. Cooing over Lily. Pep-talking you out the door with her, "If this guy said you could be a great waitress with next-to- nothing experience, he's only hiring you because he thinks you'll attract repeat customers."

I leave the bra on the backseat and hold my head high as I walk towards the restaurant. A plastic bag blows across the empty parking lot and tangles around my ankle. I kick it away and hope the owner isn't watching through the tinted windows stenciled with jumbo white letters spelling the words: **Fun. Food. Friends**.

Let's go, Excedrin.

Let's go, Diva Cup. You should have backed it up with a pad. Why didn't you back it up with a pad? Periods are the cruelest curse.

I pull the handle. I push. The door stays shut. Through the glass, tables sit empty except for the little caddy with napkins and ketchup bottles. Ocean memorabilia decorates the walls. Back behind the tables, a shadow crosses the floor. I knock on the door.

A short woman hurries to the front, wiping her hands on the front of her apron. Her broad shoulders look perfect for a child to rest her head upon. She opens the door and flashes a warm smile like an aunt on Christmas. Until her eyes move from my face to my chest. Her lips thin. The wind whips my curly black hair across my face.

Her wiry hair is pulled back into a loose bun. "Can I help you?" she asks, straining to return her lips to a smile.

Pulling my hair back, I say, "I have an appointment with Andrew?"

"Do you?" She eyeballs me like I've stashed the salt and pepper shakers in my handbag. "Andrew isn't here." She starts to shut the door.

I put my hand on the frame and ask, "When will he be back?"

"He didn't say." She eyes my hand still on the door.

I tighten my grip. "Andrew said you just lost two waitresses."

The woman shrugs and points with her nose across the parking lot to my car and says, "We'll be fine. You should go."

Lily deserves jackets that aren't labeled with some other kid's name. Lily needs those toys that teach math physics.

I edge my foot closer to the threshold. "Sign says you're hiring."

"For a cook," she says.

"I can cook," I say.

The older woman narrows her eyes. Resistance drains from her face. She steps away from the door and motions me in.

"Okay," she says. "Make me an omelet." She leads me behind the serving counter under the giant net and anchor decoration and into the kitchen. She points to the large silver door of a walk-in refrigerator and says, "Most everything will be prepackaged and cut already. You don't need to go past the fridge door. Please don't over-salt."

"Do you have an idea of when Andrew will return?" I ask.

She stops and stares, and the temperature in the kitchen drops.

Goosebumps ripple my arms. "I'm sorry," I say. "I didn't ask your name."

She shakes her head and returns to the dining area to sit across from the large window.

Don't you worry. You got this. It's omelet time!

Should you wear gloves? If only you knew where everything's stored.

The kitchen is spotless and organized and upscale department store spacious. Large, non-stick skillets hang from ceiling hooks over the stainless-steel prep table. Metal spatulas magnetically stick to the backsplash, arranged by size. A photo of Andrew and the woman, younger and laughing and riding a boat, hangs over the server counter.

The burner clicks. Flames fire.

I warm a skillet. "Is Andrew your husband?" I yell.

The woman nods, stays looking out the window.

Several aprons hang from a rack by the walk-in refrigerator. I drape one over my braless chest and tie it around my waist.

Inside the refrigerator, several containers of cut vegetables are stacked on wire-rack shelves. Mushrooms on top of peppers on top of onions. A large bag of shredded cheese is tied off beside several gallons of whole milk. The eggs sit on a large flat of 50 or more, about eight flats deep. Who knew you could buy that many eggs?

I grab five and cradle them in the apron back to the prep table.

As the onions start to sizzle, the woman yells, "How long have you known my husband?"

"Wouldn't say I know him," I shout back. "He saw me at the mall a couple days ago. Said you needed a waitress who could start immediately."

She shakes her head. "That's a sweet lie."

I toss in the peppers and mushrooms. Shake some salt onto the pan. The smell of sautéing onions fills the kitchen. The mushrooms shrink and brown.

One of the eggs rolls off the table and cracks beneath my feet.

"No use crying over spilled milk," I say softly then apologize to my braless chest and the many nights of pumping. You've cried plenty over spilled milk.

At home, I would wipe the egg off the floor with a cloth, but this is an interview, and I want to show how thoroughly I clean. So, I try the door past the freezer, looking for a bucket and mop. When I pull it open, as the light brightens the dark, a pair of legs are revealed. They sprawl across the floor. As I open the door more, light unveils the owner's face.

I stifle my scream. I crouch, tap his leg and whisper, "Andrew? Andrew!"

His cheek is cold. His skin is pale. A small hole above his eye leaks a thin red line down his nose that trails over his lips, past his chin, and onto his chest.

I close the door.

You can pretend you didn't see anything. This has nothing to do with you. Lily needs her mom to come home now. Better days ahead.

On the table where Andrew's wife is sitting, is my handbag. But beside the server window, a black phone hangs on the wall. The wife continues to stare out the large window. I carefully lift the phone off its handle, dial 9-1-1, and set the receiver on the counter, out of view. Dispatch will trace the call and send someone to investigate.

That's how it works, right?

Should be quick. I passed a police station a few blocks before the restaurant, at the light after the affordable pedicure place.

I grab a dishcloth and wipe egg off the floor. I scrape the mushroom and pepper and onion loose before adding the other eggs to the skillet.

The wife calls out. "I had hair like yours when I was younger. Andrew would brush it when we watched movies together. Run his fingers through the curls. He had real stamina for making me feel loved."

The wife laughs and says, "Like I was the only girl in the world."

Relax. Breathe. Grab a plate and spatula out the eggs. Say you forgot your list of references in the car. Run out the door. Floor it out of here.

I set the dish on the table before the wife.

She glances down and says, "This looks like a scramble."

Beside her, my handbag rests on the table, holding my cell phone and keys.

"How does it feel?" the wife asks.

"Good," I lie. "I need to learn where everything is kept, but I've worked in kitchens similar to this before."

"No," the wife says and reaches for a fork. "Not to cook. To take what's not yours."

"Excuse me?"

"Did my Andrew brush your hair?" The wife takes a bite.

I reach across to snatch my bag, but she grabs my arm and holds it tight.

She grits her teeth and says, "Answer me. Did my Andrew brush your hair?"

"Please, let go," I say and pull back.

The wife slides her hand under her apron and pulls out a gun. "Sit."

I plop into a chair at the next table.

She places the gun beside her plate of eggs. "You're not showing as much as I expected. Not in the belly. Not yet." The wife sizes me up, recalling my shape under the apron. "But your tits…"

"You're making a mistake," I start.

"Andrew already had a family," the woman hisses.

Past the glass, the only car in the parking lot is my own. But any moment now, police cruisers will skid to a stop outside the restaurant. The blue and red lights will strobe through the large window.

"Andrew told me you already had a name for his baby. I'd like to hear it," the wife says. "Poor child. Her soul, I'll pray for."

Where are the sirens?

By now there should be sirens.

"Help," I shout back at the kitchen, at the black phone out of view.

The wife slaps her hand on the table.

I jump up and the chair crashes to the floor behind me. "Please, no, no, no…" I cry.

The wife leans forward and spits at me. The slop of spittle lands on the floor between tables. The wife stands and picks up the gun and points it at my head.

I hold out my hand and shut my eyes. I want to see Lily smiling up at me from her crib, but all I can recall is the hole above Andrew's eye. I trip backwards over the chair. My legs flail and I kick the chair away. I scoot away from the wife. I hold my breath.

The wife wavers. She says, "There's blood on your pants."

I gasp. Tears run down my cheeks.

She says, "You leaked a little."

"I'm not pregnant," I say between wheezing breaths. "I got an 11-month-old daughter."

The wife covers her mouth.

"I can't handle more," I say. "I can barely handle her."

The wife sets the gun back on the table and pushes it away.

"I met Andrew last weekend in line at the pretzel stand," I say. "In the mall. He said he was hiring. That's it. That's all I know about him."

The wife shakes her head. "I think I thought you were someone else."

I rise, steady myself, and grab my handbag. "I should go."

The wife nods and returns to her seat by the window. She picks at her omelet as I open the front door.

A rush of warm air hits me as my eyes adjust to the sun. I want to go home and shower and change. Hold Lily close. Never let her go.

Absolutely zero police wait in the parking lot. No sirens wail in the distance. On the other side of the glass, the wife slides her hand under her apron strings and rubs her neck. Her nails are cloudy and cut at toe-clipper angles. I wonder if she knows about the mani-pedi place not far from here.

I walk back into the restaurant. Return the black wall phone to its receiver. Text Andrea that I will be a little late to pick up Lily.

Then, I start a pot of coffee.

Author Bio

@WilDalton

Wil Dalton is an AmeriCorps*NCCC and Peace Corps (Bulgaria) alum. He earned his master's in student affairs and worked several years in residence life. He currently parents three beautiful children. You can find him at WilDalton.Substack.com where he posts speculative fiction and personal essays on travel, faith, parenting, and living a worthwhile life. He even writes serialized humor romance there as Walt Darling and releases excerpts from imaginary novels and joke magazines. Most recently, his pre-k Halloween slasher features in the horror anthology, *Shallow Waters*.

Thanks for reading! Find more transgressive fiction (poems, novels, anthologies) at: Outcast-Press.com, CraigClevenger.com

Twitter & Instagram: @OutcastPress, @OutcastPress1, @CraigClevenger

Facebook.com/OutcastPress1 and /CraigClevenger

Book at Amazon, Kindle, Target, Barnes & Nobel

Email proof of your review to OutcastPressSubmissions@gmail.com & we'll mail you a free bookmark & stickers!

www.ingramcontent.com/pod-product-compliance
Lightning Source LLC
Chambersburg PA
CBHW020841260626
47169CB00003B/1076